Until Death

C.M. Serpell

About the Author

C.M. Serpell lives in the South West of England with a growing collection of four legged companions.

She spent most of her career working in a prison. Whilst there, she worked with men convicted of a wide range of offences. She worked in various roles from rehabilitation and substance misuse, to teaching business start-up and social enterprise. She has now hung up her keys and fulfilled a lifelong dream of becoming a published author.

This is a work of fiction. Names, characters, places, and incidents either are the product of the author's imagination or are used fictitiously. Any resemblance to actual persons, living or dead, events, or locales is entirely coincidental.

First paperback edition September 2023
ISBN 978-1-7393659-4-3 (paperback)

Contact:
www.cmserpellauthor.co.uk
Instagram: @cmserpellauthor
Facebook: C.M. Serpell Author

Dedication

For my friend that got away.

Contents

PART 2: OLIVA

PART 3: THERAPY

PART 1:
TILL DEATH

1
The Wedding

Catherine took a deep breath and linked her arm through Max's, looking up as the opening chords of Mendelson's Wedding March began. Her eyes were met with a sea of smiling faces, and she felt like she was floating up the aisle towards her future husband.

This was the moment she had dreamed of since she was a little girl. Her grandma had kept her mother's dress, and sometimes she would be allowed to take it out and look at it, twirling around the room and imagining how her mother looked when she married her father. As she got older, Catherine tried the dress on and stared at herself in the mirror. This was the dress that she would wear one day, the dress her mother would have been proud to see her wear. She would never be able to go dress shopping with her mother, but that didn't mean she couldn't wear a dress chosen by her. Her eyes filled at the memories, the mirror reflecting her emotion back at her. She took a deep breath to compose herself; the makeup artist had spent far too long for her to ruin it all now.

Catherine's parents died in a car accident when she was younger, and her grandparents had long since passed. She had no other family. Max, Patrick's younger brother, was giving her away. She liked Max; he was more down to earth than the rest of the family – the only one who hadn't followed the family footsteps into a career in law.

'Why would I want to spend my days with a load of stuffy old farts?' was his reasoning behind the break in tradition. He was a property developer, a career entertained by his parents as long as Patrick continued to shine in their spotlight of scrutiny.

As they reached the alter, Max winked at Catherine and gave her arm a squeeze before handing her over to her fiancé.

As Catherine looked to her future husband, his smile dazzled her. From the moment she first laid eyes on him, her insides would somersault each time he grinned at her. He had the kind of face that made you feel like you were the only one in the room. He was boyish yet distinguished all in one. She loved watching old films with her grandma as a child, and he reminded her of a young Robert Redford. He had a way about him that made others drop everything to please him, seeking the approval that would earn them a smile. The thought of being his wife, the one he chose when he could have anyone, caused her heart to throb.

'I give you this ring as a symbol of our love. All that I am, I give to you. All that I have, I share with you. I promise to love, cherish and worship you, in sickness and in health, till death us do part.' Patrick hesitated. Catherine followed his eyes and saw him frown at the antique diamond engagement ring she had forgotten to remove. She moved to take it off, but he didn't let go of her hand. The edges of the ring dug in as he held her hand tightly. 'With this ring, I thee wed,' he finished slipping the ring onto her finger. His frown was quickly replaced with one of his winning smiles, directed at the congregation.

Catherine resisted the urge to rub her fingers where the metal of the engagement ring dug in and turned to the vicar, ready to say her vows.

'I give you this ring as a symbol of our love. All that I am, I give to you. All that I have, I share with you. I promise to love, cherish and obey you, in sickness and in health, till death us do part.' Max passed her Patrick's ring, and she continued with her vows, slipping it onto his finger. 'With this ring, I thee wed.'

'I now pronounce you man and wife'.

At the first opportunity, Catherine moved her engagement ring to her right hand, leaving the platinum wedding band on its own. Patrick watched the manoeuvre.

'I'm sorry,' she said, 'I meant to move it before I left for the church, but then Max arrived…'

'It doesn't matter. I just wanted everything to be perfect and in keeping with tradition, but I know you're sometimes forgetful. Don't worry, I still love you.' He kissed her on the cheek, watching her neck turn pink as she blushed at his touch.

As the classic Bentley crawled along the sea front, Catherine saw people craning their necks to glimpse the newlyweds. She beamed with pride, squeezing her husbands's hand. Her eyes focused momentarily on the bandstand by the beach. They had agreed not to stop there for photos. Patrick said it was tacky. The drive to Wadhurst Castle was around 45 minutes, but it was important to her future parents-in-law that she and Patrick got married in the same Church they had, so she had agreed to the long commute. Patrick reasoned it would give them time alone in the car after the ceremony.

At the castle, the photographer whisked them away for their photos in the expansive grounds before rounding up family for some group shots. The weather was perfect, and Catherine didn't need the lightweight lace shrug she bought. The photographer captured the perfect couple, gazing into each other's eyes.

The engagement had been short, and Catherine wasn't able to meet all the guests before the wedding. She was introduced to many of them as they congratulated the newlyweds. She barely had a chance to speak with the few friends she invited. Patrick encouraged her to let go of her old lifestyle and friends from when she worked at the bar. He said they wouldn't fit in with her new lifestyle. She insisted that her friends were her friends no matter what and that she wouldn't ditch them just because she was married now. 'Besides, your money is yours, not mine'.

'My money is your money. I want you to have everything you deserve. After the wedding, we'll go shopping and get you a whole new wardrobe, everything you need to be the wife of a future Judge, because in a couple more years, that's what I'll be.' Patrick's face shone with enthusiasm.

Catherine's stomach fluttered with anxiety at the thought of fitting in with the beguiling other women in her husband's life. His secretary was the worst – didn't even attempt to conceal her crush on him. When she mentioned it, he had dismissed her concerns and wouldn't have a bad word said about the woman.

Patrick tapped his champagne flute with a knife, signalling for the room to fall quiet.

'Thank you all for coming today to see my beautiful wife make me the happiest man alive. I have watched everyone around me meet their spouse and settle down, having children, and couldn't wait for my time to come. I never thought that when I finally did meet the one, the story would start with, *she was working as a waitress in a cocktail bar*, but here we are.'

The guests laughed. Catherine bit her lip, feeling all eyes on her as the laughter rang in her ears. She hated it when he made that joke. Patrick turned to her.

'Catherine, thank you for agreeing to marry me, for making me happy, and for completing my life. You look outstanding. Your dress is perfect.' He turned to their guests, 'Can you believe she was going to wear some tatty old family dress? I said to her, you are going to be a Walker; take my credit card and get something befitting of the future Mrs Walker.' His quip was met with more laughter.

'Darling, I can't wait to start our life together. Who knows, maybe next time we see everyone there will be the pitter-patter of little feet on the way.' He winked at their guests. 'I ask you all to raise your glasses to my wife, Mrs Patrick Walker.' He pulled her to her feet and kissed her, to applause and raucous cheering.

With the wedding breakfast finished, the newlyweds took to the dancefloor for the first dance. Patrick whispered the words to their song in her ear as they moved in time with the music. His breath on her ear caused electric shivers down her spine, the words to Every Breath you Take, a further declaration of his love for her. As the guests filtered onto the dancefloor, Patrick's brother, Max, tapped Catherine's shoulder to cut in. Patrick stepped aside and pulled his mother from her seat to a smattering of applause. Myra beamed as her son's competent steps led her around the dance floor until the song ended. He left his mother at his father's side and re-claimed his bride with a theatrical twirl.

Later, as Patrick drank shots at the bar with his old school friends, Catherine finally sat down with her friends. She looked around before stretching her feet out under the table cloth and slipping off her heels.

'How was the food? Was everything okay?'

'Everything's been great, food was amazing. Could've done with bigger portions, though. I suppose that's always the way; the more it costs, the less you get!' Pia joked. Pia was Catherine's oldest friend. The only people in her life who knew her before her parents died were Pia and her family. They went to school together. After it happened, most of the other children didn't know what to do or say to the girl who had become an orphan, but Pia gave her a hug and invited her for tea as normal. 'Anyway, what happened to your mum's dress? For your whole life, you have said you wanted to wear it, to have her with you on the day.'

'Patrick said it was a silly idea. He was worried people would think we didn't have the money for a new one. I don't mind. I'm just lucky to have met someone who cares about me like he does. He just wants me to have the best.'

Her friend frowned and pulled her into a hug. 'As long as you're happy.'

Catherine swallowed, pushing aside thoughts of her parents. She allowed herself to be manoeuvred into some group photos before her new mother-in-law pulled her away to say goodbye to some guests. Catherine had never met them. She looked over at the bar for support – it didn't look as if Patrick would be in any fit state to support her with any relatives tonight.

2
Mrs Walker

Patrick pressed a button, and the electric gates to their sprawling property opened, allowing the taxi to take them to the door.

'I have to go into the office, so will you be okay if I take the cases in for you to unpack, then head straight off?'

'We've only just got back from our honeymoon. I thought we might have a little longer before you have to go back to work.'

'Come on, Catherine, if you want the nice house and the honeymoon in Fiji, someone has to earn the money to pay for it'. Patrick handed the taxi driver a £50 note and asked him to take the cases in while he rang his secretary to let her know he was on the way.

Catherine stood in the silent house, looking at the suitcases piled in the hallway. She wished she had asked the taxi driver to take them up to the landing, but it was too late now. Her phone buzzed with a message from Pia welcoming her home and suggesting lunch later in The Lanes. She looked at her watch and texted back, arranging to meet in an hour.

'Wow, Cat! Look at you,' Pia gave a low, appreciative whistle as her friend approached the table.

Catherine gave a mock bow and smiled. She knew the post-holiday glow suited her and had chosen a white sundress to complement her tan. She ordered a cocktail; why not? She was still in holiday mode and picked up a menu.

'Tell me everything.'

'Oh, Pia, it was just wonderful! We had our own private beach with walkie talkies to order anything we wanted. We had whatever dinner we wanted each night, cooked by a private chef. On our last night, they set up a table on the jetty so we could eat while the dolphins swam around. We went horse riding and scuba diving. It was magical. Can you believe they even did our laundry so we have come back with suitcases full of clean clothes?!'

'Did you meet any other people to hang out with?'

'There are only 14 couples on the island at a time, and I don't think it was full. We didn't see anyone else; it was just us.'

'For two whole weeks? I know you are married to the man, but just Patrick for two weeks sounds boring! Think of how much fun we always have in Kavos every year, meeting new people and dancing until sunrise.'

'I'm married now.' Catherine shrugged.

Pia looked chastised and took a sip of her cocktail. 'I take it we won't be having our girls' holiday this year then?'

'I'll have to ask Patrick.'

'Since when did you need to ask for permission to do things?' Pia snorted. 'Also, when am I going to finally get to see this mansion of yours?'

Catherine changed the subject. It was no secret that her best friend and her husband didn't get along, but they were the two people who meant more to her than anyone else. She had to find a way for them to get on. A few drinks later and Catherine checked her watch.

'Whoops, Patrick will be home soon.' They said their goodbyes, hugged, and Catherine flagged down a taxi.

Patrick was home when she arrived in the taxi. She paid and hurried in apologising and leaning in to kiss him on the cheek. He pulled back as fruity vodka fumes wafted around him.

'Are you drunk?'

'Just a few welcome home drinks with a friend. How was your day?'

'Fine. Go and sober yourself up, and put on something that shows a bit less skin. You aren't in a cocktail bar now, and my parents are coming over for dinner. Luckily for you, my secretary arranged dinner for us all tonight, knowing we wouldn't have a chance to get much in. It just needs heating up.'

Her shoulders slumped at his remarks. She wouldn't have ordered cocktails if she knew Dick and Myra were coming. She scurried upstairs to change and brush her teeth.

'Catherine, Darling, my favourite daughter-in-law. Shall we go and get on with dinner, leave the men to their discussions.' It wasn't a question. Catherine looked at Patrick with pleading eyes, but he nodded for her to follow his mother.

As they lit candles on the dining table and prepared drinks to have with dinner, Catherine listened to Myra wittering on about how Catherine was a Walker wife now, the expectations of her that came with this. She knew Myra had old fashioned values, but the way she was talking, you would think that she expected Catherine's sole purpose in life to be catering to Patrick's every whim. She was all for having dinner on the table and ironing a few shirts: she wasn't going to be working after all, but being expected to leave the room after dinner when the men were talking and other outdated actions such as this was preposterous.

'Myra, this isn't the 1950s. I do still have my own life, you know.'

'I'm only trying to help, dear. You need to know what it will be like being married to a Walker. Behind every successful man is his wife, supporting him, helping him to be the man of the house. Patrick is going to have to put a lot of hours in. There will be functions and dinners, and you will be expected to attend. He is on the path to becoming a Judge, and I won't have a cocktail waitress getting in the way of that.' Myra's lip curled as she said cocktail waitress.

Catherine recoiled, blinking back tears. Surely Patrick wouldn't let his mother speak to her like that. She would talk to him later and ask him to have a word with her.

'Welcome home. Here's to your future,' Dick raised his glass towards his son and daughter-in-law.

Patrick put his hand on Catherine's and smiled, reassuring her that everything would be okay.

'Jolly good food as well, well done, Catherine,' Dick quaffed, spurred on by a few glasses of champagne.

'Yes, you must share your secret,' Myra said sweetly, leaving Catherine wondering if her earlier brusqueness was all in her imagination.

'You will have to ask Elsie. She organised it.' Catherine gritted her teeth. They had discussed that Elsie organised dinner when they were in the kitchen together. Myra looked at Catherine, daring her to challenge her.

'Ah yes, of course. Don't worry. You will soon get on top of things. Such a lovely girl, Elsie. We have always liked her, haven't we, Dick?'

Patrick carefully hung his silk tie alongside the others in his wardrobe, then placed his socks, shirt and trousers in the laundry basket. He stood in his boxer shorts, brushing his teeth at the his and hers sinks in the en-suite when Catherine broached the subject of Myra. Patrick spat out his toothpaste and swilled out the sink slowly before turning and saying he couldn't believe how ungrateful she was being when all his mother wanted to do was help her fit in.

'Not everyone is going to welcome you with open arms. Let's face it, you are from a, shall we say, different background to most of the people in my world. People can be fickle. Mum just wants you to fit in and to make sure you don't feel you aren't worthy. She's only trying to help.'

'The only one who has ever made me feel unworthy is your mother.'

Patrick clenched his jaw and dried his mouth on a towel before padding into the bedroom. Catherine could see the subject was closed. As he took his pyjamas from the cupboard, she took in his rippling back muscles and stepped closer so she could wrap her arms around him. His body stiffened, but he turned and wrapped his arms around her. He kissed her on the head, then gently moved his kisses down her face until his lips reached hers. He picked her up effortlessly, and she instinctively wrapped her legs around his hips, their bodies, puzzle pieces fitting together as he carried her to the king-sized bed.

Afterwards, she lay in his arms. This is what she loved. When it was just them. No work, no secretary, no parents or old public-school friends. When it was just the two of them, nothing else mattered.

The first weeks of marriage passed slowly. It was not quite what she had expected.

Their short engagement had been a whirlwind of meals out, weekends away and Sunday mornings in bed with newspapers. It was like something from a film, and she had to pinch herself some days. When Catherine met Patrick, she was living in a shared house in Moulsecoombe. The area was okay; it was close to where she grew up, and she was working at a bar in London. The commute was long, but the tips made it worthwhile. The bar was in Kensington and popular with the after-work crowds who had plenty of time and money to spend on trendy cocktails and posh burgers. Patrick was at the bar celebrating winning a big case at work. He flirted with her all night and gave her his card before he left. She didn't call. She couldn't deny the attraction, but she knew his type – he would only be after one thing. Patrick returned a week later and requested that her manager send her to their table. His friends were loud, raucous, and she heard some of them making lewd comments about the other waitresses. It came with the job. She smiled as she brought them more drinks, making sure to keep just out of their reach, when possible. When she returned from her break, she saw Patrick talking to her manager again, and her heart sank. She wracked her brains, considering if she had got a drink wrong or spilled something. When she cautiously approached the table, he flashed her that winning smile and let her know that her manager had agreed she could have a glass of champagne with them. She didn't have a chance to object before one of the other waitresses appeared with a bottle of Moet in an ice bucket and a tray of glasses. Patrick moved aside in his booth, indicating for Catherine to join him. His thigh was warm against hers; her stomach was doing somersaults. He put one hand on her leg, causing her hairs to stand on end as he handed her a glass of champagne. Catherine remembered this moment forever; the moment she fell in love with Patrick. The rest of the evening had passed by in a blur; she had to return to work, but Patrick had asked for her phone number before he left. His friends were drunker than he was and asked if she had any friends she could put on Patrick's bill for them. She ignored them and their insinuation. She ignored her colleague, Ashleigh, hovering, clearly angling for an invite. Patrick gave his friends a warning glare before giving her a chaste peck on the cheek and leaving. She didn't expect to hear from him. What interest could he possibly have in a penniless orphan like Catherine?

Fast forward six months, and Catherine had given up her job and her room in the shared house and was Mrs Walker. The area where she now lived was a far cry from the student area of Moulescoombe. She now lived in a six-bedroomed property on a street off the affluent Dyke Road. There were electronic gates to enter the property. They had a housekeeper and a gardener - although she still couldn't bring herself to let someone else wash her underwear. They called her Mrs Walker, no matter how many times she insisted they called her Cat. The grounds of the house were a good size, given how centrally located they were, and they were lucky enough to have a swimming pool with a terrace. In 20 minutes, Catherine could walk to the seafront or to The Lanes for a spot of shopping.

Since the wedding, Catherine found herself drifting around the big house aimlessly. There was little to do - the housekeeper was efficient at her job, and the gardener ensured the garden never had a weed to be found. She perused the bookcase; the volumes of big, old, heavy books – statutes, the criminal law compendium, criminal procedure. They had the wonderful smell of leather-bound books, but the words meant nothing to her. In the shared house, the bookcase was filled with battered paperbacks that various people who had come and gone over the years had left behind. She missed the bright covers and unassuming fiction. She hadn't brought any books with her; they would look out of place in this house. Patrick bought her a Kindle as a wedding gift to replace the books she left behind. She hadn't wanted to appear ungrateful, but she was sure she had told him how much she loathed the idea of Kindles. He always wanted to have the latest gadget, and newest technology. They couldn't replace a real book. Perhaps she would walk into town and pick up something to read to pass the time.

The Lanes shopping centre was busy with the tail end of the tourist season. She pottered from shop to shop, running her fingers over the books, the pretty throws and the cushions. Trying on hats, sunglasses and colourful scarves. She had her pristine credit card in her purse, Mrs Walker. She hadn't used it yet, feeling more comfortable with her battered old debit card and the last of her own money. She eyed up the cashmere scarves, stroking the soft fabric. These were scarves befitting of Mrs Walker. The sales assistant rang one up, and she signed her new signature on the receipt. Spurred on, she went back to the bookshop and bought a pile of fresh new paperbacks, some sparkly earrings, and a little hanging ceramic ornament saying 'Hove, actually' to hang in the downstairs loo – an in-joke used by Hove residents, signalling they live in Hove, not in the noisier districts of Brighton. She selected a large bunch of lilies from the florist and checked her watch; almost time to start preparing dinner.

Myra gave Catherine a set of Mary Berry cookbooks as a wedding gift. Some of the pages were marked with post-its declaring them her son's favourites. Catherine rolled her eyes as she looked through the book, though she planned to cook one of the dishes for him tonight – Venison Wellington with caramelised onions and port jus. She opened a bottle of wine and snapped a quick selfie with the cookbook and the wine to send to Pia, *Wish me luck! #domesticgodess.*

'Something smells amazing,' Patrick declared. He handed his wife a bunch of red roses and kissed her.

'You're in a good mood.'

'That I am Mrs Walker, that I am. I got a big new case today, and if all goes to plan, this could be the one that gets me my Judgeship.'

'Does that mean I have to call you Your Honour?'. She smiled playfully as she took his coat from him.

'Only if you have been a bad girl.' Patrick gave her a cheeky slap on the bottom and pushed her backwards against the fridge, kissing her hungrily.

The kitchen timer went off, and she twisted away from him, having spent far too long cooking to let the meal be spoiled. She pulled out a chair and put a glass of Shiraz in Patrick's hand while she dished up.

'Not a bad first attempt.' Patrick leaned back in his chair.

Catherine looked down at her empty plate and then took a large gulp of wine. 'I'll get dessert.'

'Not too much. I don't want everyone teasing me about my fat wife.' He laughed and drained his glass. 'Any more Shiraz?'

Catherine topped up his glass, and her knife hovered over the cheesecake, unsure how much was too much, before carefully cutting herself a small slice. She pushed the cream in Patrick's direction.

'I have arranged to have some people from work for a dinner party in a few weeks. I know you aren't ready for cooking for others yet, so I'll book the caterers. Can you liaise with them to get it organised? Speak to Mum and she will help with menu options. Oh, and Elsie is going to help you pick out something to wear. It's important that we make a good impression for our first dinner party.'

'Of course. Though, no need for Elsie to help. I am capable of choosing my own clothes.'

'Well, it's all arranged now, so you may as well let her help. She is looking forward to getting to know you better, and you don't want to offend her.'

Catherine stacked the dishes in the dishwasher and pushed her uneaten cheesecake into the bin. Patrick told her to go to bed without him and disappeared into the study.

3
The Shopping Trip

'Hello? Hello? Catherine.'

Catherine froze, pulling her dressing gown around her. Who was that? Whoever it was, was in the house. She pulled the top of her dressing gown tighter and peered around the kitchen doorway into the hall to see Elsie with one foot on the stairs.

'What are you doing in the house?' she spluttered.

'Didn't Patrick tell you? I'm here to take you shopping.'

Catherine felt Elsie's eyes travel over her dressing gown before they rested on the large grandfather clock in the hall. It was 9 am. If she wanted to have a cup of tea in her pyjamas at 9 am, she jolly well would. Hell, if she wanted to stay in her pyjamas all day, she was perfectly entitled to. Why did she feel so inferior?

'I'll make a cup of coffee and give you some time to make yourself presentable.'

Catherine patted her hair down and looked toward the kitchen.

'Don't worry about me. I know where everything is. I helped organise it when Patrick bought the house.'

Catherine ran the shower and peered onto the landing to check Elsie hadn't followed her upstairs. She tapped a text to Patrick.

Elsie has a key?!

She's always had a key; easier for when I need her to drop off and pick up papers for work.

She can't just let herself in. I could have been naked!

The phone rang in her hand.

'Often walk around the house naked, do you?'

Catherine could hear Patrick smiling. 'Well, no, but I might'.

'I'll tell Elsie to knock in future in case the lady of the house is naked. I'm imagining you naked now. I can hear the shower running. Will you be thinking about me while rubbing soap over your body?'

She lay on the bed and allowed herself to imagine him in the room with her, idly running her hand up her thigh.

'What time will you be home tonight?' she asked huskily. In the corner of her eye, she noticed the door to the bedroom opening and saw Elsie appear. 'What the fuck!' she shouted. Her phone clattered to the floor as she grabbed for a towel.

'Just checking you're okay; you've been a while.' Elsie smirked. 'I'm ready to go when you are.'

Catherine showered quickly, scraping her hair into a mum bun and pulling on the first clothes she could find. She rushed down to find Elsie standing by the open front door, keys in hand. They travelled to the train station in silence.

'Where are we going?' She asked quietly as they parked at the station.

'Knightsbridge.' Elsie's voice was clipped. 'Patrick wants you in the very best.'

Catherine looked down at the jeans and Ugg boots she was wearing in anticipation of Brighton shops. She put her hand to her hair, patting down the wisps escaping from her messy bun. Despite the butterflies in her stomach, a slight giggle escaped as she remembered the scene from Pretty Woman where the staff in the posh shops refused to serve Julia Roberts.

Seated opposite each other on the train, Elsie pulled a Montblanc pen from her bag. 'A gift from Patrick when we won our first case together,' she said as Catherine looked. 'Right, I suggest we start in Harrods as it's an easy one stop shop, then anything else we need we can get afterwards. Patrick gave me his card, and we made a list of things you need.'

They spent a few hours in Harrods. Catherine was pushed and prodded into an assortment of dresses, skirt suits, hats, shoes. Even new underwear. Although the clothes were soft, luxurious, with undeniable quality, none of it was her. Catherine allowed herself to be dragged from shop to shop until Elsie declared they should take a break for coffee.

'Come on, Catherine, you could look a little interested! Most wives would be over the moon if their husband sent his assistant with a credit card to buy a whole new wardrobe.'

'I am. I'm sorry. I just don't see when I will need all of this.'

'There are so many events coming up; you will need lots for the Christmas season. Your job is to make Patrick look good, so he wants you to have all new things to do that.'

'I suppose that makes sense,' Catherine reluctantly agreed, 'you must let me treat you to something whilst we are out. Oh, and I'll pick up a little something for my husband.'

'Savile's isn't far if you want to get him something from there.'

Catherine blushed. 'I have something in mind. Is there anything you need to do and we could meet back here in an hour?'

After a long day, Catherine was finally home. She had a message from Patrick saying he would be back late again, so she went about putting away the shopping. Most of it was being delivered the next day, so there wasn't much. She ordered an

Indian takeaway and moved from room to room restlessly. The house was wonderful. It just wasn't to her taste. Patrick was older and happy to go with the traditional décor suggestions that his mother made, whereas Catherine grew up in a house filled with warmth, cushions, colour, fairy lights and candles. This house was immaculate, but its stark colours made it feel cold and not lived in. Catherine and Patrick were like chalk and cheese, but she knew no other man would make her feel the way he did. She felt safe. He gave her butterflies in her stomach just by looking at her.

The next afternoon, Catherine excitedly unwrapped parcel after parcel, putting the clothes away. Without the watchful eyes of Elsie and the shop assistants, the soft fabrics and beautiful cut and textures became more appealing. She held dress after dress up against herself, twirling around the room, as she had with her mother's wedding dress as a child. She pictured herself at large parties at country house estates, mingling with the other wives. Perhaps one day, nurturing a little bump.

The mechanism of the electric gates came to life as Catherine was stuffing the empty packaging in the bins, and Patrick's Jag silently crawled up the short drive. She hovered in the doorway, taking Patrick's coat as he held it out.

'Wine?' Catherine led them through to the kitchen where she had left a decanter of red by the Aga.

'I take it you got your deliveries?'

'I did. Thank you for looking after me.' She put her arms around her husband's neck and kissed him on the lips.

'A little birdie told me you didn't go to any jewellery shops yesterday…' Patrick put his hand in his pocket and produced a jewellery box. He slid the lid open as he held it towards her. Catherine squealed at the glittering diamond earrings, the light bouncing off the large angular surfaces.'

'I got you a little something, as well.' Catherine held Patrick's eye contact. 'I was going to wait until after dinner, but…' She stepped back, widening the space between them and slowly undid the buttons on her shirt, giving him a glimpse of the dusky pink silk of her bra. His eyes focused on her chest as she leaned back against the kitchen table, letting the thin fabric of her shirt fall open. As he stepped towards her, she undid the buttons on her Levi's, sliding down the zip to expose the lacy trim of the matching silk knickers. Unable to wait any longer, he grabbed her roughly and kissed her, pushing her back against the table, dinner forgotten.

4
The Dinner Party

The day of the dinner party came. Catherine had butterflies in her stomach all week. Her hairdresser came to the house in the afternoon and secured her hair in an elegant pleat, showing off her diamond earrings and delicate collarbones. Catherine carefully applied her makeup and was ready to step into her dress. Patrick wore a formal dinner suit with a burgundy bow tie to match her dress. She stifled a giggle at the formality of it all. 'If Pia could see me now!' She stepped into her cocktail dress and pulled the lace fabric up over her shoulders, turning her back to Patrick, who slowly pulled the zip up. She felt a shudder of excitement as his fingers brushed against her skin, causing her hairs to stand on end.

'Remind me who is coming tonight,' she asked, immediately glazing over when he reeled off a list of legal titles.

'I do hope you won't be too bored, but it really is important for us to make the right connections now to secure this Judgeship. As you know, my father is a Judge, and his father was a Judge. One day, our son will follow in the family footsteps and be the fourth in the line of Walkers who have presided over the courtroom.'

'Welcome, come in, come in, I'm Cat, let me take your coats'.

'Catherine.' Patrick corrected.

'Cat, as in a kitty cat. Well, I shall find that easy to remember. A cute little kitten such as yourself,' boomed Mr Justice Some-one-or-other, laughing boisterously. His wife plastered a smile on her face.

'It's Catherine,' Patrick reiterated. 'Catherine, Darling, could you ask the caterers to bring through some hors d'oeuvres whilst I pour our guests some drinks?'

'I say, caterers, is it? Kitty-Cat not like cooking then?'

'On the contrary, she is a marvellous cook, but I wanted to show her off and let someone else sort out the dining for tonight.' Patrick opened a globe-shaped drinks cabinet revealing a selection of spirits. 'What can I get you?' He poured generous measures for their guests and others as they arrived.

Catherine smiled, answered questions, and laughed at the jokes, but was pleased when the men took themselves off to Patrick's den for cigars. The other couples were much older than her, and Patrick even. The men were the type that would come into the bar she used to work in and behave appallingly towards the waitresses, when their wives were not in tow. The bar was often frequented by high class escorts, and staff were expected to turn the other way when money changed hands. She didn't mind as long as they kept their wondering hands off her. She had built a good relationship with some of the girls who came in, and they would sometimes have drinks after her shift. Catherine missed the comradery you got working in a bar.

'Catherine, what do you think?'

Her mind was brought back to the room. 'I'm so sorry, what's that?'

'Boarding school. Will you send your children to boarding school? After all, Patrick and his father both attended

Fitzwilliam's, didn't they? I imagine you will want to keep up the tradition?'

'God, no!' Catherine blurted out. 'I mean, I shouldn't think so. I went to a state school, and it was perfectly fine. I can't imagine why people have children and then send them away for someone else to raise.'

Her companion, who asked the question, sniffed and looked around. 'Well, state school hardly got you far in life, did it? Marrying Patrick has done more for you than state school ever did. Surely, you want more for your children?'

'Well, that's a discussion for my husband and I to have. I'm not pregnant yet, so we have plenty of time to decide. Anyone for another drink?' Catherine's tone was bright as she leapt to her feet overzealously.

'I doubt you would get a place now anyway; the wait list is years long.'

Catherine wished Patrick was by her side to help her navigate these women. She was used to the men, but the women were a whole different breed. She was pleased to discover the kitchen was pristine. The caterers had washed and put away everything; the only sign that anyone had been there was the leftovers in the fridge. Patrick called taxis for their guests around midnight, and she was pleased to have him to herself.

Catherine sat at the dressing table, carefully placing her earrings in a ceramic jewellery dish and removing the hair pins woven tightly beneath the hairspray, holding her style in place. Patrick removed his bow tie and loosened his shirt, and she was reminded of watching her parents one time when they got back from a party. They were so happy. She remembered them laughing together, her mother's eyes shining. They always shone when she looked at her father. Her mother wore a different perfume when she went out in the evening, and Catherine thought she always smelled so glamorous – as if she was about to walk onto a movie set.

'You're daydreaming again'.

'Just remembering Mum and Dad. I wish you could've met them.

Patrick squeezed her hand as she looked up at him, her eyes misty. He downed his nightcap and kissed her upturned cheek where she sat looking at the photo of her parents she kept in the drawer of the dressing table.

Catherine glanced at the clock as she stretched out lazily in bed, 8 am. Patrick promised he wouldn't be working this weekend, and they were going to spend it together. She frowned as she rolled over and felt the cold mattress beside her. The house was silent. She slipped on her slippers and wandered onto the landing in search of her husband. The strong aroma of coffee drifted up the stairs, and she followed the scent down to the kitchen to pour herself a cup. His office door was closed. He didn't hear her push it open, and she leaned against the door frame, gazing at the back of his head, a slice of morning sunshine highlighting the grey speckles in his hair. The wireless headset and low murmur indicated he was on the phone, but she couldn't work out what he was saying. Whatever it was, she could tell from his rigid posture and the throbbing vein in the side of his neck that he wasn't happy. There was a soft clicking as he fidgeted with the stapler in his hand. Without warning, his chair spun around, and she leapt back as he threw the stapler across the room, leaving a dent in the door frame as it fell to the floor. Patrick started at the sight of his wife, knocking dark coffee over his desk.

'Now look what you've done. What the hell do you think you are doing? Creeping around like this? Listening to my calls?' He roared, as his red face contorted into a rage she hadn't seen before.

Catherine shrank back, away from the open doorway, backing into the hallway. She ran up the stairs to their en-suite and sat on the toilet, staring at the locked door. Her heart raced, and tears burned the inside of her eyelids, threatening to escape. She took a couple of slow, shaky breaths and waited for her heart rate to slow. She put the shower running and left her dressing gown on the chair, feeling her breathing slowly return to normal as the hot water washed over her. When she unlocked the door, Patrick was putting his trainers on.

'I'm going to the gym. Then I need to go into the office.'

'I thought we were going to spend the day together.'

'That was before I had a witness disappear. I need to go for a run to clear my head and then do some damage control before I have to stand in court on Monday looking incompetent. I already look stupid enough to my superiors with that stunt you pulled last night.' Patrick's tone changed. 'I'm Cat. Kitty-Cat. You were all over him.'

Catherine didn't have a chance to reply before he stormed out of the room. She stared at the open door, tears filling her eyes again as her breath caught in her throat. She looked around, and her eyes rested on her phone. She hovered her finger over Pia's name but stopped herself. She caught a glimpse of her tear-stained face in the mirror and looked down at her shaking hand. Had she been flirting with the Judge last night? She thought back, analysing every word, every action.

5
I'm Sorry

Patrick arrived home from work brandishing two dozen red roses. Catherine hesitated, her face still puffy from crying.

'I'm sorry about earlier. This case is stressing me out, and then seeing you creeping around after I had to watch you flirting last night… I over-reacted. You know I love you.'

She took the flowers, breathing a sigh of relief and let Patrick put his strong arms around her. Everything was okay when his arms were around her. She was safe.

Saturday night and Sunday were like the early days of their relationship. They enjoyed a meal at The Grand, watching the sunset until it was replaced by moonlight reflecting off the water. The bright lights of the pier in the distance had a mesmerising effect – the whirling and spinning of the big wheel and rides, the sound not reaching them in the ambient atmosphere of the restaurant. After dinner, Patrick playfully declared he would win her a teddy bear on the pier. They held hands like teenagers, ate candy floss, and Patrick put a plastic ring from the grabber machine on her finger.

On Sunday, Catherine was woken by Patrick bustling into the bedroom, whistling and holding a breakfast tray.

6
Pia's Visit

'It's taken way too long for you to invite me to the Walker Mansion.' Pia dropped her bag on the floor, then immediately picked it up again, looking around.

Catherine led her from room to room, knowing her friend well enough to know she was expecting the full tour. They moved around the house, Catherine hovering in the doorways whilst Pia tried each sofa, watched the electric blinds open and close as she pressed the remote control, and filled the shower with music using the state-of-the-art sound system. She surveyed the rows of matching suits in Patrick's wardrobe until Catherine firmly pushed the doors closed.

'Come on, let's go for a swim.' Catherine led Pia downstairs to the kitchen, where she mixed fruit juice in a jug and added a generous slosh of vodka. The pool was surrounded by a terrace that connected it to the house. Beyond and to the side was the well-manicured lawn and plants. The pool house provided towels and swimwear, with a bathroom and an area to change. Catherine threw a couple of towels at Pia and spread her own on the sunlounger beside her friend. The late summer sun provided them with the perfect day to sit by the pool, watching its ripples shimmer in the sunlight. Catherine took her Kindle from her tote and wedged a baseball cap on her head, giving an exaggerated smile to Pia. They bought matching knock-off Fendi ones on holiday a few years ago, and they had become their poolside tradition. Pia reciprocated by donning her matching hat and rummaging in her bag for a book.

'Shoot, forgot my book. Where do you keep yours? I didn't spot any on the mansion tour? Do you have to keep the chick-lit hidden away?!'

'I left all my books at the old house. Patrick bought me a Kindle instead.' Pia looked at her, opening her mouth to speak, then immediately closing it again.

'I know, I know. I've always hated the idea of them, but it was a gift, and I didn't want to offend him.'

'God forbid, His Lordship consider your feelings – you have always ranted about how nothing replaces a real book. In fact, I distinctly remember you once declaring you would rather throw yourself to the rocks at Beachy Head than get a Kindle.'

At Catherine's glare, Pia held her hands up, palms facing her in mock surrender as Catherine hoisted herself up from the sun lounger and disappeared into the pool house. She returned with a grin, brandishing a brightly coloured paperback.

'I keep a secret stash, don't tell,' she said, mischievously, smelling the book's pages before throwing it towards Pia, 'nothing beats the smell of a real book'.

'Why, Mrs Walker! What would your husband say?' Pia trilled in a mock southern drawl.

The pool heater kept the water at a nice temperature, and they enjoyed an afternoon of swimming, reading and chatting.

At some point in the afternoon, the gardener arrived and gave the plants a much-needed drink when Pia, spurred on by the vodka cocktails, decided it would be a good idea to commandeer his hose pipe. Catherine was snoring gently; her baseball cap pulled over her face when her friend approached stealthily, before pressing the trigger on the spray, covering Catherine's body with a generous squirt of cold water.

Squealing, Catherine was up quicker than Pia anticipated, and Pia found herself on the receiving end of an unceremonious shove, ending with a splash. Catherine grinned and held her nose as she plopped into the pool beside her friend. Surfacing and swimming to the edge, Pia groaned as she saw her clothes were now sitting in a puddle of water.

'Throw them on the aga - they'll dry much quicker than they will out here'.

Pia was in the kitchen in her bikini, draping her denim shorts on the aga when the front door slammed. The kitchen doorway framed Patrick's bulk. He stared at her, wordlessly. She rubbed her arms, suddenly cold, her skin prickled with goosebumps. If he wasn't her best friend's husband, she would think he had been looking at her bum.

She moved to the door, shouting. 'Ca-at, Patrick's home.' Patrick winced. She gave him a toothy smile and headed for the pool.

He watched her stride across the patio to where Catherine was sprawled on a sun-lounger. He hadn't expected Pia to have that figure under her disconcerting attitude. She said something to the gardener as she passed him, throwing her head back and laughing at his response. Patrick glanced back at Catherine in her bikini and then the gardener. He gripped the edge of the work surface, his jaw clenched. Whatever Pia said when she approached Catherine caused her to look towards the window. Patrick raised his hand in greeting. With a sigh, he popped the cap off a beer bottle, heading out to the pool.

'Good day, ladies?'

'Yes! So lovely to have a sunny day to enjoy the pool. And Pia's finally seen the house. How was work?' As Catherine stood to give Patrick a kiss, she followed the direction of his eyes to the gardener. She pulled a kaftan on and resumed her position on the lounger.

'You know I can't talk about the case. I'm glad you've had a nice day, though. What's the plan for dinner?'

'Yeh, Cat, I'm getting kinda hungry now as well.'

'Catherine', Patrick muttered. He took a deep breath, followed by a swig of his beer. 'You must join us for dinner, Pia. *Catherine* and I would love to have you,' he said pointedly. 'Unless you have other plans? We wouldn't want to keep you if you have somewhere to be?'

The dishes clinked and clattered as Catherine cleared the table and filled the dishwasher. They had ordered Indian, and Pia had just wobbled off to the taxi Patrick called for her. As she cleared the kitchen, Patrick was silent, both hands around his beer bottle, his brow furrowed.

'Looks like you, Pia and the gardener had a nice day today.' His tone was low and level.

'Yeah, it was nice to just hang out.'

'With the gardener.'

Catherine jumped as Patrick's beer bottle whistled past her and hit the kitchen door. The remaining beer fizzed and seeped out of the bottleneck onto the floor where the now-chipped bottle landed.

'What are you getting at?'

'It's embarrassing, Catherine. My wife and her friend, cavorting in the garden, wearing practically nothing, flirting with the gardener. The pair of you were all over him'.

Catherine's eyes darted around the room. She stuttered. 'You know I would never look at another man. You are everything to me.'

'Prove it.'

'Wha- what?'

'Prove it,' Patrick repeated, grabbing her and pulling her towards him.

'I'm tired. I'm not in the mood tonight.' She kissed him on the lips and twisted away.

Patrick's grip tightened. He forced his tongue into her mouth, kissing her hard, sliding his hand up her top.

'Patrick. I'm not in the mood,' she repeated.

He pushed her away from him. 'Too busy thinking about the gardener? If that's the kind of man you want, you know where the door is. See how you like slumming it after this lifestyle - I give you everything you could ever want.'

Catherine's lips trembled. Tears teetered in her eyes, threatening to spill down her cheeks. Her breath caught in her throat. Her heart missed a beat, aching at the thought of losing him. A sob escaped from her lips as Patrick turned away from her.

'Wait.' She moved towards him, reaching her hand out to his waist.

Patrick's back stiffened at her touch. 'I thought you weren't interested.' He stepped towards the door, moving away from her. Her hand fell from his waist, hanging at her side.

Catherine followed, squeezing her arms around him until he turned to face her. She looked up at him, her cheeks wet from the silent tears flowing down them. She held his eye contact. Patrick brushed her tears away with his thumb and kissed her on the forehead. She angled her face towards him, beginning to unbutton his shirt.

Catherine lay alone in their bed, her eyes swollen and sore from her earlier tears. She was sore between her legs. Patrick had been rough, animalistic even. He slapped her thigh and said he didn't realise she had it in her – she hadn't; it was all him. Afterwards, he disappeared into his study.

Hours later, she woke as he crawled into bed and wrapped his arms around her, kissing her neck and whispering how much he loved her.

7
Dinner with Mr & Mrs Walker, Sr.

Walker family tradition dictated that Patrick and Catherine attend a roast dinner on the last Sunday of the month with Patrick's parents. Each month, Catherine carefully chose a different bunch of flowers from the local florist, ensuring the perfect seasonal mix in shades that would complement their home. She took care to ensure her makeup was flawless, her dress demure, and her jewellery classic yet stylish. She surveyed herself in the full-length mirror, frowning at her stomach. She pulled at her dress in an attempt to stop the fabric clinging to her swollen abdomen; her body reminding them that her period was due. Catherine wasn't ready to start trying for a baby, but Patrick was keen for her to produce him a son and heir as soon as possible.

'Just think, it won't be long before there is a little baby Walker in there,' he said as he saw her pulling at her dress. Patrick ran his hands tenderly over her stomach. 'Do you think we have time to try before we leave?'

Catherine sighed and said nothing. She glanced at her makeup bag where she kept her contractive pill, straightened her dress and spritzed her decolletage with perfume. She gave him a firm kiss and nodded toward the door.

The table in the formal dining room was laid with multiple sets of cutlery, serviettes and an array of different glasses and side plates. Catherine smiled at the effort her mother-in-law went to each month. She held up the flowers and said she would find a vase if Myra directed her to the right cupboard before arranging them neatly in the crystal vessel. Max arrived as Catherine finished and swept his mother and then Catherine into hugs, planting flamboyant kisses on their cheeks. Patrick and his father were in the study discussing a case. Max stayed to help in the kitchen.

Patrick poked his head in as Catherine was bent over double, tears streaming down her cheeks with laughter. Max leaned back against the sink laughing, and Myra's eyes twinkled as she set the roasted meats on the side to rest.

'Looks like everyone is having a party without us in here.' He shouted for Dick, letting him know dinner was almost ready. 'What's the joke?'

'The moment has passed, brother dearest; the moment has passed'. Dick gave Patrick a jovial slap on the shoulder and picked up some dishes of vegetables to carry through to the dining room.

Patrick's eyebrows narrowed. He looked from Catherine to Max and back again. The muscles in his jaw twitched as he clenched his teeth. He reached behind Catherine and picked up the carving knife to start cutting the meat.

'Leave that. You know your father likes to carve the meat.' Myra pulled the knife from Patrick's hand and shooed them all out of the kitchen with instructions to find a seat at the table.

Max pulled out a chair beside Catherine, looking at his brother, daring him to say something. Catherine gave Patrick a pleading look as he sat opposite her.

'Don't get too comfortable by my wife's side, Max. I'll be the one taking her home.'

Myra huffed. Catherine was told the story of Sarah Jane – a girl who both brothers had a crush on during their teenage years.

'Patrick never got over the fact that she preferred the better-looking brother.' Max's eyes twinkled with good humour.

Catherine studied the brothers. They both had dark features with similarly shaped noses and mouths, but where Max's eyes sparkled with light, Patrick's were dark like bottomless pools. Max was softer facially, and his smile revealed dimples, whereas Patrick's smile deepened his chiselled features. Patrick's confident masculinity made Catherine's insides fizz with excitement. It was what drew her to him, like a drug. Tonight, her stomach fluttered. There was a tension in the air that she couldn't read.

There was chat about Patrick's current case - he was defending a man who had attempted to kill his wife by running her over. Patrick voiced his frustration with how the wife was managing to appear sympathetic to the jury. Catherine leaned back in her chair and breathed out upon finally gleaning some details of the case causing his fluctuating moods.

'The woman was cheating on him, made a fool of him, and he is the one standing trial,' Patrick explained. His jaw twitched as he spoke. 'She has admitted the affair. What happened to the sanctity of marriage?' He reached across the table and squeezed his wife's hand.

'It's hardly an excuse to run her over, though!'

'Clearly, our marriage vows mean a lot to you,' Patrick sarcastically retorted to his wife.

'No. You know that's not what I'm saying, but you can't just try and kill someone because they cheated on you.'

'Patrick will always be a crusader for the old boy's club, same as Dad. What is it the marriage vows say? Love, honour and *obey*?' Max stressed the word obey.

Catherine's eyes darted around the table, willing Myra to step in. Instead, Dick joined the debate, acting as a judge between his sons. Eventually, Myra put an end to it when she stood and declared they were to change the subject by the time she and Catherine brought dessert out. Chastised, Max made a joke about the case being dismissed. Patrick laughed, and they apologised for getting carried away. Myra winked at Catherine and instructed the men to clear the table whilst they prepared dessert.

Patrick was silent on the way home.

Catherine began getting ready for bed whilst he was in the bathroom. She heard the shower running and took the opportunity to change into one of her new lingerie sets, positioning herself on the bed for when he came out of the bathroom. As the door opened, steam billowed into the room, and he looked at her, a white towel draped loosely around his hips. Her eves roved salaciously over his damp body, and she quivered, looking at him expectantly.

'What the hell are you wearing? You look like a prostitute,' he laughed as he looked at her. She watched as he turned, his toned back rippling as he pulled on pyjama bottoms. He strode across the room and pulled at the cover to get underneath, immediately rolling away from her and turning his bedside light off.

Stumbling to the bathroom, Catherine choked back the urge to cry. She pulled off the bra and French knickers, throwing them into the bin. Looking around for something to cover her body, her eyes rested on Patrick's dressing down. She wrapped herself up and crept back to the bed, crawling under the cover, careful not to disturb him. Not for the first time, she found herself lying in bed, curled into the foetal position, staring at the same spot on the wall. Her chest tight as though there wasn't enough air in the room.

8
Law Society Christmas Gala

Elsie and Patrick were in the study, working on a case. Elsie's laughter carried through to the hallway, and Catherine felt a pang of jealousy in her stomach. If Patrick was interested, he would have been with her years ago, she rationalised. She looked at her husband's coat draped over the bannister, and picked it up to hang it. Her hand drifted to the pocket, stopping as her fingers began to ease their way in. She glanced at the closed study door and shook her head, hanging the coat up in the cupboard. Of course, there was nothing going on.

Patrick was working late a lot, and Elsie was at the house more than usual. She knew they had a few big cases on, as well as the Sussex Law Society Christmas Gala tomorrow night. Catherine arranged a tray with coffee and biscuits and knocked on the door. Patrick laughed as he told her to enter, saying she didn't need to knock in their house. He rolled his eyes at Elsie, laughing again. Catherine's skin prickled, and she left the room, closing the door.

The Sussex Law Society Christmas Gala was being held at Wadhurst Manor. Catherine looked forward to returning to where she and Patrick had been married. It had only been a few months, but things had been fraught lately, and she was hoping that the memories of their wedding would rekindle the magic of their relationship before the wedding. They booked a room and arrived early to get ready. Catherine had booked the hotel hair stylist and wore a strapless ballgown. Patrick's dark eyes lit up as he looked at her. The dress accentuated her delicate bone structure. Her hair was up, with curly tendrils hanging down. Patrick brushed them to the side and kissed the nape of her neck. She shivered as his kisses moved around to her collarbone. This was her Patrick, the Patrick she loved. This man was caring, gentle and tender. He held out his arm, and she took it, allowing him to escort her from the room. They swept down the grand staircase and followed the signs for the room the party was in. There was a bar at the side of the large ballroom, and a stage had been set up at the edge of the dance floor. The party was to begin with a ceremony celebrating the successes over the year and giving out individual and company awards. Patrick offered to get drinks whilst Catherine found their table. She nodded to a few people she recognised from the wedding as she made her way around the room, smiling. She glowed as she found their table, waving her hand in greeting at Patrick's colleagues already seated.

One of the women she recognised from the wedding rose to hug her in greeting. Catherine hesitated, the woman's name on the tip of her tongue. She racked her brain, cycling through names and place settings from the wedding. Luckily, Patrick appeared with their drinks, greeting Diane and her partner, Bill. Catherine sat. She and Bill made eye contact as Patrick and Diane talked shop until Diane saw their faces and apologised, changing the subject.

'Anyway, enough shop talk for now. There will be enough of that when the ceremony starts. Tell us how you have been since the wedding. How is married life treating you?'

'I couldn't be happier,' Catherine gazed at her husband. 'The swimming pool helps, of course!' They all laughed, and Patrick joked that it was just a ploy to try and get her in her bikini as often as possible.

'And what about the pitter-patter of tiny feet? I know I shouldn't ask, but Patrick did say at the wedding that you both wanted to start a family as soon as possible. Bill and I have three – thank goodness we also have an au pair!'

Catherine opened her mouth to speak, but Patrick answered, saying he was sure that it will happen when the time is right. She grimaced as she thought of her contraceptive pills in her bag up in the room.

'We really should start thinking about it a bit more, darling,' Patrick was saying. 'I am sure there are all sorts of things we should be thinking about, folic acid, cutting out alcohol and caffeine etc.'

'I can recommend an excellent fertility specialist we saw before our third. She will help with all of that and guide you through what you can and can't eat. She introduced me to hypnobirthing as well – I can give you the details of our instructor for that as well. She was wonderful.' Dianne handed her phone to Catherine, saying to put her number in and they would set a lunch date.

Catherine took a few big gulps of her wine, making a mental note to Google hypnobirthing later.

'Kate Middleton had a hypnobaby, you know. It's all the rage.' Dianne was still talking.

Patrick nudged his wife, who nodded and smiled at the right intervals.

Operatic music signalled the beginning of the Awards Ceremony. Strobe lights darted around the room as people hurried back to their seats, glasses in hand. The compere read out award winners and prizes, and people made their way to the stage - glamourous dresses rustled through the tables, the spotlights picking out diamonds, sending the light bouncing in all directions. The men confidently strode to the stage, leaving a trail of testosterone. Lawyers chortled at in-jokes, and Catherine shared an amused grin with Bill. Comrades in this world, within which they were on the periphery. Dianne won an award for a sustainability project she had implemented, and they raised a glass on their table. It was soon the turn of the barristers. Catherine put her arm through Patrick's as they announced the nominees for Sussex Barrister of the Year. She beamed as the tables around them turned their heads when his name was announced as a nominee and tightened her grip on his arm, hardly daring to breathe as the compere opened the envelope.

'And the winner of Sussex Law Society's Barrister of the Year is…'

Catherine held her breath.

'Patrick Walker.'

Catherine released her hold on Patrick's arm. She turned to congratulate him, but he was already halfway out of his seat. A round of applause propelled him towards the stage, and he confidently stepped up and approached the microphone. The compere hesitated for a moment before joking to the audience that it looked like Patrick had something to say. The room fell silent. He took the microphone, and Catherine noticed people sitting up in their seats, stopping their hushed conversations. She imagined him in a courtroom, power emanating from his presence. She listened as Patrick thanked the event organisers and went on to accept his award. He shook hands with the compere and stepped down from the stage, stopping to chat or accept congratulations as he made his way across the room. At some point, staff put extra bottles of wine on the tables, and they listened politely to the remaining awards. Catherine was pleased when the final round of applause filled the room. Music started playing, and people rose from their seats in search of drinks and socialising. A few early birds made their way to the dance floor. She had a warm glow inside, and her cheeks felt warm and rosy. Patrick made a beeline for the bar. Catherine stood, wobbling slightly, her glass spilling its remaining contents across the table.

'Easy now. Come on, let's get you some fresh air.' Bill jumped out of his seat and steadied her. She leaned into his supportive arm around her waist and let him guide her to the French windows leading to the terrace. He lowered her to a bench and went to fetch a glass of water.

'There you are!' Patrick exclaimed. Dianne said you caused a bit of a scene.

'Hardly! I just needed a bit of fresh air. I am feeling much better now, so let's head back in'.

Bill returned with a glass of water, and Catherine took some grateful gulps, condensation on the edge of the water glass dripping onto her dress. Patrick looked down at her and rolled his eyes at Bill, giving him a pat on the shoulder. Bill accepted his dismissal and left them on the terrace.

'Look at the state of you. Making a drunken scene, spilling drinks and now spilling water all over yourself. I think it's best you sleep it off.' Patrick hissed.

'I'm fine. Don't be so over dramatic. I'm looking forward to having a dance.'

Patrick's eyes flashed. 'Dramatic?' He spoke in a low voice, his teeth clenched. 'You - are an embarrassment. First the gardener, then my brother, and tonight you have been all over Bill. Don't think I haven't noticed the two of you exchanging looks all evening, and then I hear you are getting cosy on the terrace.'

'We weren't getting cosy. He helped me out for some fresh air when I fell.'

'So, which is it? You are drunk enough to be falling over, and Bill had to help you stand up, or you aren't drunk, and you just chose to come out to the terrace with a man who isn't your husband? Someone else's husband, in fact, someone who has been very nice tonight offering to help you with your fertility issues.'

Catherine frowned as she leapt to her feet. 'MY fertility? There are no issues with my fertility. I'm not pregnant because I'm on the pill. We never discussed trying for a baby this soon, YOU decided.' She spun on her heel, heading in the direction of the French windows. Patrick grabbed her arm, and she shook it off. 'Don't touch me.'

'You're my wife. I will bloody well touch you whenever I want.'

'You aren't the hot shot lawyer in the courtroom now, Patrick. You can't order me around like all your minions.'

There was a sharp crack as his palm made contact with Catherine's cheek. She stepped back, stumbling on the uneven terrace. She couldn't breathe, as if the air had been knocked out of her. Her ankle twisted, and the floor rushed towards her. The terrace was cold beneath her, and her ankle throbbed as she raised her hand to her stinging cheek.

'There you are!' Dianne burst through the doors. 'Oh!'

Patrick bent down to help Catherine to her feet.

'I was just coming to get you for a dance.'

'I don't think she will be dancing this evening, Dianne. She has had a bit too much to drink and fallen over. I'm going to take her up to her room. Could you give my apologies to anyone who asks? I will be back down shortly.'

Dianne nodded sympathetically and offered to fetch Catherine's shawl and bag.

Catherine said nothing, her head turned away from Dianne, her wayward hair hung over her burning face. She squeezed her eyes closed and leaned into Patrick's body.

Catherine woke as Patrick closed the door. She looked at the clock. She had slept in. Her mouth was dry, and her head hurt. She put her hand to her cheek and winced. Patrick held a tray with a pot of coffee, cups and a selection of pastries.

'I didn't want to wake you, so brought you some breakfast. I ate downstairs with the others.' Many of the other partygoers stayed at the hotel, and their party had their own area in the breakfast room. Patrick explained he told the others she was a bit hungover and was having a lie in.

Catherine's head throbbed as she pulled herself up to lean against the headrest. Patrick looked with concern, tenderly pulling the duvet up around her. She flinched as he put his hand to her bruised cheek.

'It might be best to stay off the drink for a while - we can't have you getting in that state again.'

Catherine said nothing. She closed her eyes, hoping everything would be back to normal when she opened them. When she re-opened them, she still saw Patrick's face looking at her, etched with concern. She needed to clear her head. She took a few big gulps of coffee, the hot liquid burning slightly as it ran down her throat. She drank it all and eased her bare legs over the edge of the bed, taking a moment to steady herself as she stood. She winced as she put weight on her ankle and took a deep breath before hobbling to the bathroom.

'I need to shower.'

Closing the door, Catherine looked in the mirror. Her eye makeup was smudged underneath her puffy eyes. There was a purple bruise on her cheekbone with a small rust-coloured mark where her cheek split. Her ankle was visibly swollen and coloured in shades of purple to match her cheek. Her cold fingertips felt nice on her swollen cheek as she gently touched her skin. Hobbling into the shower, she let the water run over her skin, trying desperately to wash last night away. The water was as hot as it could be without scalding her. She gingerly dabbed the towel over her face, trying to remove the traces of last night's makeup without setting off the pain in her cheek again. It looked worse after a shower. Catherine's makeup bag wasn't by her washbag. She looked around. It was there last night when she did her makeup. The cupboard under the sink was empty. Then she spotted it on the window ledge. Carefully applying foundation, she did her best to cover the bruise, drying her hair and leaving it loose around her face. Teeth brushed and starting to feel more alive, Catherine looked in her makeup bag for the paracetamol she kept there with her contraceptive pill. Her little pill pack was missing. She emptied the makeup bag, spreading its contents over the countertop, frowning. She never took them out of her makeup bag. They were there last night, she was certain.

Patrick pushed the bathroom door open.

'Are you nearly finished? I thought we could spend the day together. I've been neglecting you; I know that. I was going to suggest London for lunch and shopping, but then I saw your ankle when you got up.' Patrick looked at her bruised face. 'Why don't we snuggle down at home and have a film afternoon? You are lucky you didn't do yourself more damage with that fall. Those bruises look sore.'

9
Lunch with Dianne

A few days after the Gala, Catherine's phone chirped with a text message from an unknown number. She opened the text and saw it was from Dianne, asking if she was free for lunch one day. Catherine touched her face. Her cheekbone had developed from purple colouring to a faded yellow. She hadn't been out since the Gala. Patrick asked who the text was from, and Catherine hesitated before telling him. Neither of them had mentioned children since the Gala.

'Patrick…'

Patrick held his palm up. 'You should go. Dianne is a good person, and you could do with more people like her in your life. Make sure she gives you the details of the fertility specialist, and we can get booked in.' He leant down to where Catherine sat on the sofa with her legs curled beneath her and kissed her on the top of her head. 'You owe me after lying about the pill.'

'Patrick…'

'No. The matter is not open for discussion. You said you wanted children, and I want a son and heir. Or was that just a ploy to get me to marry you? Are you just in it for the money?'

'How can you say that?! I do want children. You know I do. I just wanted to enjoy some time together before we have a baby.'

'Is it me? Don't you want to be with me? Is that why you insist on looking at other men? Perhaps you would rather have a child with my brother? You seem to laugh a lot more with him than me these days.'

'Don't be ridiculous. You know I want to have a baby with you.'

'Oh, so I am ridiculous now.'

'That's not what I'm saying, and you know it.'

'Are we having a baby or not?' His question hung in the air.

Catherine sighed and nodded. Patrick scooped her up off the sofa, showering her with kisses. His face lit up. Ironically, after their conversation, he looked more like Max when he was happy like this. The depths of his eyes sparkled, and his face exuded a rare show of emotion. She laughed at his enthusiasm. She never had found her pills anyway. Patrick looked at her, his eyebrows raised suggestively, and she kissed him passionately.

They lay entwined together in the bedroom. Patrick insisted on putting a pillow under Catherine's hips and offered to fetch them both a drink. He returned with cold cans of fizzy drinks and Catherine's phone, reminding her to reply to Dianne.

'Enjoy the fizzy drink while you can. We need to look at changing your diet to make sure we have the best chance of getting pregnant. No more sitting around eating Cheesecake with Pia. Yes,' Patrick looked at Catherine, 'I saw the empty box in the recycling. It won't do you any harm to lose a few pounds anyway.'

Catherine ran her hand over her naked stomach. Her skin was taught, and she raised her leg in the air, flexing and pointing her toes, looking at the muscle definition in her thighs and calves. Her ankle still throbbed; she would need to take it easy for a while. Whenever the weather allowed, she swam outside, and other days, she either used the gym in the house or attended yoga classes. She always tried to stay in good shape. Patrick reminded her about the block of sessions with a personal trainer he had got her that she hadn't yet gotten around to booking.

Catherine arranged to meet Dianne the next day at a café near the law offices where she worked. She stopped at an off-licence on the way and purchased a bottle of local flavoured gin and a gift bag to apologise for the scene she had caused at the Gala. She arrived first and ordered a strong coffee. If Patrick had his way, she would have already given up the coffee. Dianne arrived as Catherine was perusing the menu. They exchanged pleasantries, and Catherine gave Dianne the bottle of gin with a sheepish grin.

'Don't be daft; there was no need, but thank you. We've all been there! Although you really did a number on yourself… goodness knows how you managed to get that nasty cut on your face, you looked more like you had been punched than fallen.' Dianne laughed as Catherine looked down, her hand subconsciously touching her face.

They ordered food and talk quickly turned to children. Catherine found herself telling Dianne about her hesitancy to have children so soon. Dianne sensed there was more to it and tucked into her Quinoa Salad, giving little more than the odd word of acknowledgement as Catherine shared her anxieties about Patrick's moods. Dianne was well versed in the testosterone-fuelled world of law and gave a sympathetic nod of acknowledgement in response to Catherine's words. Catherine's eyes glistened with tears. Dianne's filled with concern.

'It's just sometimes he can be so… ignore me, I'm just being silly.'

Dianne handed her a napkin and reassured her that everything would be back to normal once the case he was working on was out of the way.

'It's clear how much he adores you. He would hate to think you were upset. He broke a lot of hearts when he chose you. You should be flattered that you married the most eligible bachelor in chambers.' Dianne smiled at Catherine and indicated for the waiter to bring them dessert menus.

Catherine left the lunch date with contact details for a variety of fertility and pre-natal specialists, and the agreement that they would meet again soon. She also learned that Patrick had already reserved a place at Fitzwilliams, the boarding school. She hadn't reacted when Dianne mentioned it, assuming she already knew. Catherine sat quietly in the taxi on the way home, staring out of the window. As they drove along the sea front, she was reminded of an evening when they first began dating. They drank cocktails at one of the beach side bars, watching the early evening sun reflecting off the water. They spoke about their hopes for the future – this was the first time they discussed marriage and children. The topics were shied away from in the early stages of many relationships, whilst both people quietly hoped the other wanted the same. Catherine and Patrick realised straight away that they both wanted the same things: marriage and children. Catherine was happy to be a stay-at-home wife and mother, raising their children while Patrick climbed the career ladder. They were the perfect match. She hadn't explicitly said she didn't want her children going to boarding school, but then again, Patrick hadn't asked.

10
Pia's Birthday

Christmas was fast approaching. The shops were filled with festive décor and enticing displays. Catherine loved Christmas. It reminded her of her childhood, when her parents were alive. They would take her to see Santa and to the fairground that came to town in December. This time of year made her wistful, thinking of things she would do with her own children one day. It would be lovely to have a baby around next year. Catherine was pulled from her reverie by Patrick calling her name. She looked at the clock. Pia would be here soon for pre-drinks, then they were going into Brighton for Pia's birthday. They hadn't been out properly since the wedding, and Catherine's stomach fluttered with excitement. She rummaged through her clothes, pulling out skirts, dresses, jackets, heels and small glittery handbags. Her 'going out' clothes hadn't been sorted properly since she moved. Her eyes honed in on her favourite red dress peeking out of the pile. She pulled it on. The figure-flattering midi dress hugged her curves in all the right places. The off-the-shoulder straps showcased her cleavage. Catherine frowned as she noticed her visible knicker line, reaching under the dress to pull them off. She swept her eyes back over the dress and selected a pair of New Look heels. A large pair of hoop earrings and a sparkly gold clutch bag completed her outfit. Catherine's hair was curled, and she applied her favourite Mac Ruby Woo lipstick before looking in the mirror again. A quick look at her phone told her Pia was on the way. Catherine expertly navigated the stairs, used to heels from the club she worked in, and tapped on Patrick's office door, huskily announcing herself. She pushed the door open and struck a sultry pose in front of his desk. He said nothing, but his eyes flashed. Her smile faltered, and she rubbed her lips together, looking at the desk, the floor, anywhere but Patrick. The room felt cold, but she couldn't work out what was wrong. The silence stretched out endlessly. Eventually, Patrick let out a bellowing laugh. Catherine looked at him. She smiled back at him, not sure what the joke was.

'You had me going for a minute there. I thought you were actually going to wear that.'

'What do you mean?'

'You look like a cheap tart. This is a joke, right?'

'No.' Catherine raised her chin and made eye contact with Patrick. 'This is what I'm wearing. I love this dress, and if you don't like it, tough, you aren't coming out with us anyway, so you don't have to look at it.'

His demeanour changed. The smile disappeared in an instant. His jaw clenched, and Catherine noticed his hands curled into fists as he handed her a tissue and told her to wipe the slutty lipstick off when she went upstairs to change.

'I'm not changing.'

'You are. My. Wife. You will not go out looking like that.' Patrick's voice was low, his speech slow. 'Can you imagine if anyone I knew saw you? I'd be a laughing stock. Get upstairs and change.' He slammed his fist on the desk, causing Catherine to jump. 'NOW,' he roared.

The doorbell chimed, and her eyes widened. She looked from Patrick to the door and back. He said he would let her friend in while Catherine made herself presentable. As Patrick left the room, her body sagged against the nearest wall, her heart racing. She heard Pia and Patrick making polite conversation in the hall and waited until the sound faded as they moved to the kitchen, signalling the all-clear for her to stumble up the stairs in her heels.

Catherine shut the bedroom door, and tears ran down her cheeks. She looked in the mirror, clutching the scrunched-up tissue Patrick had given her. Her tears ran her mascara down her cheeks, leaving dark black trails. She wiped her cheeks with her palms, smudging the make-up sideways. Throwing the tissue in the sink, she poured makeup remover onto a cotton pad and wiped her face until all traces of her makeup were gone. She pulled at her dress, hearing one of the seams creak as she stretched it too far. She glimpsed herself in the full-length mirror, standing in just a bra and heels, her face swollen and red. She choked back a sob and pulled open the drawer containing her going-out clothes, looking for something that wasn't too creased. Her eyes settled on a blue skater dress. She pulled it over her head and looked down at her chest. She pulled it off and tried another dress. This one was similar. Eventually, Catherine pulled on a pair of skinny jeans, block heels and a white vest top with a loose white shirt over the top.

Pia pushed the door open, clutching two glasses of white.

'What's taking so long? Let's get drunk!' Pia handed a glass to Catherine and took a large slurp of her own. 'Where's your sexy red dress?' Catherine snatched it up from the floor, saying it had a hole in it and launching it toward the bin.

Pia picked up the blue dress.

'Too small.' Catherine snatched it away and put it back in the drawer. 'I just need to put some makeup on, and I'm ready.'

'You are NOT wearing that,' Pia said.

'Oh for god's sake, not another person telling me what I can and can't wear. I'm not changing again. I'll meet you downstairs, go pour some more drinks.' She picked up her makeup bag and stomped into the bathroom, shutting the door firmly behind her.

Pia and Patrick were stood glaring at each other when Catherine stepped into the kitchen. She looked between them, put her now empty wine glass in the dishwasher and drained the cocktail Pia had made for her.

'I wanted her to wear her lucky red dress, show off that sexy body of hers, don't you agree, Patrick?'

'She can wear what she wants. It's her body.' Patrick put his whiskey glass on the counter top and strode from the room, glaring at his wife as he passed her.

'What the fuck is his problem? And what did you mean when you said not another person telling you what to wear?' Pia asked as soon as they were seated in a booth in the bar.

'Nothing. He has a stressful job, and he can just be a bit… abrupt sometimes. He doesn't mean it; I know he loves me.'

'So, he is telling you what you can and can't wear now?!'

'He just wants me to look my best.'

'Your best is that fabulous red dress. Tits up here,' Pia held her hand up to just below her chin, 'and legs that make every man want to see how long they go on for.'

'Maybe I don't want other men looking at me.'

'Can you hear yourself, Cat? It's like I don't know who you are anymore. Next thing, you will be telling me he caused that bruise on your face last week.'

Catherine looked down, chewing her lower lip. She looked at her nails, picking at the loose edge of her nail varnish. Pia watched her, feeling the fight drain from her body, resisting the urge to put her arms around her friend.

'I'm sorry, babe. Let's just have a good time.' Pia squeezed Catherine's forearm and waved to the girl at the next table carrying trays of shot glasses.

The taxi dropped Catherine off first. She handed a couple of notes to the driver to cover the cost, waving away Pia's objections, her diamond ring catching the light from the street lamp. Pia was trying to get Catherine to come back to hers, when Patrick appeared.

'What's all the commotion? You will wake the whole street up.'

'Nothing, Patrick. We were just saying goodbye.' Catherine glared at Pia and gave her husband a kiss on the cheek.

He recoiled. 'You stink like a homeless drunk.'

As the taxi drove away, Pia watched Catherine totter towards the house, Patrick an arms-length away from her.

11
Christmas Dinner

Catherine opened her eyes on Christmas morning and smiled at her husband. He was watching her with a sleepy grin. This would be their first Christmas together – last year, they had only been dating for a few months. Patrick invited her to spend the day with him, but she had spent it with Pia's family. They welcomed her into their family, and she had always spent Christmas with them since her grandma died. Pia's parent's household was always lively at Christmas. Her grandparents would stay overnight, and her brother and his wife would arrive in the morning with their two children. This year, she dropped a bag of presents off on Christmas Eve with promises that she would go for dinner after Christmas. She choked back tears at the thought of not seeing them on Christmas Day, but Patrick was her family now. He was her future.

Patrick put his hand on her hip and suggestively ran his fingertips up her waist and across her back, his fingers finding her hair and pulling her in for a kiss. She leaned in, her skin tingling with goosebumps. Patrick ran his hands over her body, his kisses becoming more urgent. Catherine was lost in the moment as they moved together, husband and wife in perfect sync.

Afterwards, Catherine lay smiling and sated while Patrick slowly trailed his fingers around her stomach.

'Just think, this time next year, there might be three of us.' She put her hand on her stomach and leaned in to kiss Patrick, pulling him close.

The jovial atmosphere continued as they prepared breakfast. Catherine teasing Patrick for not knowing where anything was in the kitchen. They worked together to prepare salmon on toast with poached egg, and Patrick poured bucks fizz as Catherine carried the plates to the table.

He placed a glass in front of her as she sat down and remained standing as he held his glass in the air. 'A toast. To many things. To our first Christmas with you as my wife. To what might be our last Christmas before the pitter-patter of little Master Walker's feet. To happily ever after, till death us do part.'

Catherine raised her glass and laughed. 'What if Master Walker is a Miss?'

'Then I shall buy her a pony!' Patrick waved his glass theatrically.

Catherine smiled at the thought of Patrick playing with Barbies and My Little Pony. Her thoughts turned to his reaction to toys everywhere, and her smile faded. Patrick noticed the dip in mood and raised his eyebrows in concern. She pushed her thoughts aside and said she was just excited and hoped she could be as good a mum as hers was.

Patrick raised his glass again. 'Another toast. To Catherine Walker, a fine wife who will be an even finer mother to Master OR Miss Walker. You will do Miriam proud.'

Catherine blinked back tears at the mention of her mother and squeezed Patrick's hand.

Myra was the perfect host, beaming at Catherine and Patrick as she took their coats. She told them to go on through to the

Drawing Room where the fire was lit. Max stood to greet them, kissing Catherine on the cheek and slapping Patrick's shoulder. Catherine looked sideways at her husband, her arm hung at her side, and she brushed his fingers with hers. Max patted the sofa beside him. She glanced at her husband again, and sat on the sofa opposite Max.

Christmas Dinner was exquisite; Catherine had expected nothing less. Myra had been preparing this for months, beginning by baking her Christmas cakes in September and regularly 'feeding' them brandy as they matured. They all agreed to wait until after dinner to exchange gifts, including Patrick and Catherine's gifts to each other. Catherine gifted Patrick a monogrammed leather holdall with a matching tan wallet. They all laughed when she presented him with cufflinks sporting the words Guilty and Not Guilty. Catherine opened two cashmere polo necks. Not something she would usually wear, but the fabric was beautiful. Patrick also handed her three mint green boxes from Tiffany. The first contained a charm bracelet. The second a charm in the shape of an old-fashioned key with a note from Patrick professing that she was the key to his happiness, and the third was another charm in the shape of a tiny baby rattle.

Max gifted them all books, Catherine opened a book on how to be the perfect wife, and Patrick received a law-themed joke book. He presented Dick and Myra with the latest releases from their favourite authors. Putting the books aside, Catherine asked Patrick to put the bracelet on her wrist, holding it out for them all to see the charms dancing as she shook her wrist. She pulled out her phone and snapped a photo to send to Pia.

'Something you kids want to tell us?' Dick asked.

Myra leaned forward in her seat, her face giving away her unbridled excitement. 'Yes, do we need to get that place at Fitzwilliam's brought forward?'

Catherine's smile dropped as Patrick told his parents that they weren't pregnant yet, but hopefully, it wouldn't be too long. He put his arm around her and pulled her close.

Catherine pulled away. 'We haven't actually discussed Fitzwilliam's yet.'

The mood in the room shifted. Patrick tensed, and Catherine saw Myra's smile falter briefly. Dick was the first to fill the silence, pointing out that Fitzwilliam's was a tradition for Walker boys.

'It's just that I want to be more of a hands-on mum. And anyway, we might have a girl!'

Myra pursed her lips into a thin line. She brushed imaginary crumbs from her dress and stood, offering more drinks. Her fixed smile returned, her tone light, although slightly too high.

'Myra, I didn't mean…'

Patrick glared at his wife before she could finish, telling her she had already said enough.

Max stood and began prodding the fire with the poker. He ended the conversation firmly and diplomatically by saying any child would be lucky to have them as parents, whatever school they went to. He then instructed Patrick to get more logs and offered to help Myra with the drinks. Catherine could've hugged him. Not used to the courtroom, Max didn't have the same propensity for drama that Patrick and his father did. He liked to fill silences and diffuse any awkwardness, whereas Patrick and Dick used silence as their weapon and awkwardness as a tool for destruction.

Catherine looked at Patrick. He started to reply to Max, then thought better of it and picked up the nearly empty log basket, stomping from the room. Max winked at Catherine as he followed his mother toward the kitchen.

Myra had made up the guest room for Catherine and Patrick so they didn't have to travel back on Christmas evening. Catherine thanked her mother-in-law for a wonderful day, giving her a hug before following Patrick up to bed. He stood with his back to the bedroom door, getting undressed as she opened it, and she crept up behind him, slipping her arms around his muscular torso.

'Not now'. Patrick's voice was gruff, his body tense.

Catherine kept her arms around him and turned her head so her cheek rested on his back. She breathed in the scent of his aftershave, the familiarity comforting. Patrick jerked his body, loosening her hold and causing her to take a step back.

'After what you said to my mother, I don't know how you can think I want you anywhere near me. Perhaps you enjoy embarrassing me?'

She stepped towards him and put her palms on his back. She started to speak but couldn't get her words out as she felt Patrick's elbow connect with her stomach. She doubled over, gasping, her arm feeling for something to hold onto as she struggled for air. Her hand found the smooth wood of the post at the end of the bed and clutched onto it as her body struggled for air with raspy breaths. She opened her eyes, and the room was hazy, black dots obscuring her vision. Slowly sinking onto the bed, her attempts to pull air into her lungs slowed, losing their urgency as her breathing returned to normal. Her stomach and ribs were hot, like a fire was burning under her skin. Carefully exploring them with her hand, her cold fingertips offered a light relief through her dress. A look of confusion crossed Catherine's face. She looked around the room for Patrick; the door to the en-suite was closed. She reached for her phone, then stopped, instead carefully standing and peeling off her clothes, wincing with every movement. Gingerly, she pulled back the bedcover and sank into the mattress, closing her eyes and willing sleep to overcome her. Her jumbled thoughts were interrupted by Patrick whistling in the shower. A single tear slid down her cheek as she recognised their wedding song.

12
I'm Sorry

Catherine lay motionless in the bed. The memories of last night flooded her mind – it was easier to squeeze her eyes shut and pretend it hadn't happened than risk moving and having to face up to reality. As she breathed in, her ribs ached with pressure. Slowly, she uncurled her legs from the foetal position; as she did so, a sharp pain shot across her ribs and abdomen. She pulled herself up to sitting and heard a sob escape from her mouth. She cautiously made her way to the chaise longue where her overnight bag sat, pulling out the clothes she had selected for today's traditional brunch at the Country Club. Spasms of pain flew across her body as she attempted to put tights on. Catherine pulled on her skirt and one of the new cashmere tops Patrick had bought her for Christmas and gave in to the pain, leaving her legs bare. She froze as she heard footsteps on the stairs, her senses heightened.

Patrick pushed the door open and put a cup of coffee on the dressing table. He kissed Catherine on the cheek, either not noticing or not caring that she turned her head away from him.

'I've told Mum and Dad that you are suffering with a hangover, so they have gone on to the club for the brunch. I said I would drop you home, then meet them there.' Patrick suggested she cancel her visit to Pia's this evening and said he would be home as soon as he could get away.

Later, Catherine's heart sank as the electric gates whirred open, the gentle pur of Patrick's approaching Jaguar given away by the crunch of tyres on the gravel drive. She pulled the blanket up over her on the sofa, closing her eyes. She kept her eyes closed, and her heart raced as she sensed Patrick creeping into the room. She felt his breath on her cheek as he leaned in to kiss her. Her heart continued to pound as she focused on keeping her breathing steady. Patrick tucked the blanket around her, and she fought back a squeal of pain. His footsteps retreated, and the room became dark as the door clicked shut. She lay still as she listened to him moving around the house.

When the door clicked open again, Patrick called her name until she was forced to open her eyes, feigning sleepiness.

'Come with me.'

Her eyes sought out his, questioning, fearful. He took her hand and kissed it.

'I love you. I'm so sorry for being an arse. Please let me make it up to you.'

Catherine let herself be led upstairs and into the bathroom. The mirror was misted with steam from the hot bathwater, and petals were strewn around the bath and sat atop the foam from the bubble bath. Candles filled every surface, flickering and dancing in the dimly lit room. Her Kindle was beside the bath with a glass of wine. Catherine stood still, staring at the bath. She pulled the cord of her dressing gown tighter around her, willing Patrick to leave the room.

'Let me help you,' he said gently, moving her hands from the cord, letting them hang limply at her side. He carefully undid the cord and pushed the dressing gown over her shoulders, letting it slip to the floor. Catherine let him undress her and help her into the bath. She watched as he looked at her bruised body. Neither of them said anything. The hot water stung as she immersed her body, the bruises absorbing the heat, causing them to throb. Tears stung her eyes. Patrick pressed play on the bathroom sound system, and the automated voice told her that he had selected their wedding playlist.

'I'll leave you to relax. I love you.'

Catherine lay in the bath, staring at the bubbles as they slowly evaporated. The water cooled, and the rose petals clung limply to the edge of the bath, but she couldn't bring herself to move. She was shivering when Patrick returned, still staring at the depleted bubbles and soggy petals. He pulled the plug and helped her out of the water, draping a towel over her shoulders. With another towel, he gently patted her torso dry and pulled a tube of arnica from his pocket. She gave a sharp intake of breath as he delicately applied the cold cream to her angry purple bruises. Patrick pulled her into a hug. The plug gurgled as the last of the water drained from the bath.

'You do forgive me, don't you? I couldn't live without you.'

Their eyes met. He ran his knuckle down her cheek, his palm resting on the base of her neck before he trailed a fingertip playfully across her collarbone. He looked at her questioningly. Catherine's body betrayed her, responding to his touch. Her lips parted, and her nipples stood to attention. He continued to trail his finger down her chest as she quivered. She let out an almost imperceptible moan and leaned towards him. In one swift movement, he took a step back, pulling her dressing gown from the back of the door and wrapping it around her.

'There will be time for that later. I have a surprise for you downstairs.'

Catherine followed Patrick to the dining room. More candles and rose petals adorned the table, shadows bouncing off the polished silverware. The heavy wooden chair was too far from the table, and she winced as she was forced to lean forward for her wine. This second glass began to dull the aches, and her cheeks warmed, glowing a rosy pink as the wine coursed through her body. Patrick put a bottle of red wine on the table, and the intense fruity aroma hit her senses, causing her stomach to rumble.

'Don't worry, steak is on the way!'

After dinner, Patrick handed the remote to Catherine with the instruction that she could choose whatever cheesy chick-flick she wanted and the promise that he would not grumble or comment throughout. She leaned her head on his shoulder and closed her eyes as festive music filled the room – she couldn't resist a Christmas film.

'Before you go to sleep, I have one last surprise to tell you about. I have booked us a mini break for New Year at a spa hotel.'

Catherine smiled and sighed, squeezing Patrick's hand. Her body sank against his, her tired brain scrambled to put her thoughts in order… they already had plans for New Year's Eve, didn't they?

As she succumbed to sleep, Catherine asked, 'Pia?'

'I'm sure she won't mind; we can have her for dinner anytime. She wouldn't begrudge you a night away with your husband.'

13
The Savoy

'What are your plans today?' Patrick smeared marmalade on his toast and gulped down the last of his coffee.

'Not much. Might do a food shop, and I'll probably just have a lazy day around the house.'

'Order the food online; no need to go out running around the shops when you can pay someone else to do it for you. While you are at it, why don't you treat yourself to some more new clothes? The tops I got you for Christmas look great. It will give you a chance to have a sort out and get rid of some of the old stuff you have around – those dresses you had when you went out with Pia can all go to charity. I am not sure if they are good enough for that even, but I suppose beggars can't be choosers!'

Catherine mumbled in agreement. She poured coffee into Patrick's reusable coffee cup and handed it to him in return for a kiss on the head.

'I mean it. Stay home and get cosy. Do all your shopping online, and I'll see you tonight. I might be late, so don't wait up.'

Catherine waited until the slam of the car door, followed by the mechanical grind of the gates, before running upstairs to text Pia, *Fancy heading into London for some shopping? Lunch on me to make up for cancelling our New Year plans xx.* Pia worked as a self-employed editor, so had the luxury of working hours that suited her. Catherine's phone chimed with a reply almost immediately, *Make it somewhere fancy, Patrick can pay ;) Hove station in an hour?* Catherine hadn't seen Pia since dropping the Christmas presents off on Christmas Eve – her ribs were still sore; the bruising had only just lost its ominous purple colouring. She pulled a slip on under her winter dress. She had never worn a slip before and giggled with Pia when she told her Patrick's mother had bought them for her, but it provided an extra layer to cover the yellowing marks on her torso.

Pia was early and bounded up to Catherine, embracing her in a warm hug. Catherine winced, turning her head away from her friend. They boarded the train, and Pia produced two cans of Gin and Tonic from her handbag, winking as the ring pull cracked. Pia asked to hear about the Walker Family Christmas, telling Catherine how much she had been missed at Pia's. Slurping her Gin and Tonic, Catherine reported that there was not much to tell and demanded to hear Pia's family news. They caught up and, spurred on by Gin, decided to have lunch at The Savoy.

The January Sales were still on, so they got the tube to Oxford Street. Pia bounced from sparkly dress to sequinned top, to neon bodycon. She favoured statement items that complimented her dark skin. They filled their baskets and took up residence in the spacious disabled changing room.

'The fuck is this shit?' Pia curled her lip in amused displeasure as she surveyed the contents of Catherine's basket. She pulled out a cotton polo neck, followed by a floor-length grey skirt. She held a fluffy polo neck up by her thumb and forefinger, dropping it beside the basket and continued to rummage, finding more of the same. 'Are you joining a convent? Have you suddenly turned 60?' Pia snorted, then snorted again at her own snort. Catherine stuffed the clothes back in the basket as Pia stripped to her underwear and wiggled into a rainbow sequinned mini dress.

'Would you?' She wiggled her eyebrows suggestively at Catherine, who was carefully trying on one of the offending polo necks. Her eyebrows stopped mid-waggle. 'Babe, are you okay? You look a bit green.'

The lights in the changing room danced like stars in front of Catherine's eyes. Her heart began to race, and there was a thud as she fell against the wall. Pia's warm arms were immediately supporting her friend and lowering her to the floor. Her skin was cool to touch, and Pia vigorously rubbed her arms. Pia gently guided Catherine to put her head between her legs, encouraging her to take deep breaths, breathing in time with her. The stars began to subside, and Catherine slowly pushed herself to standing, aware of Pia's eyes upon her.

'I'm fine. Don't know what came over me. Probably just the heat in here, and this thick top didn't help.' She indicated the polo neck, pulled off and discarded. 'Sorry'. She laughed lightly.

'You're not pregnant, are you?'

'Patrick wishes!' Catherine heard herself laugh and shrugged. 'Come on, let's pay for this lot and go get a drink. We can try it on at home.' After drinks, desserts and more shopping, Catherine invited Pia back to the house for dinner.

Laden with bags, memories of Catherine's earlier dizzy spell forgotten, Catherine and Pia linked arms and walked from the station to the house. Their breath billowed in front of them in the cool evening air, their cheeks flushed. Catherine hesitated as they pushed open the side gate to reveal Patrick's car in the drive. She fumbled for her phone in her bag and illuminated the screen, seeing no messages or missed calls.

'I thought Patrick was working late tonight?'

'So did I.' Catherine frowned. 'Can we rain check?'

Catherine tentatively stepped over the threshold, dropping her bags on the floor. Her voice echoed in the silence as she called her husband's name. Her head tilted to one side, straining for clues as to his whereabouts. The house remained silent except for the grumble of her stomach. Every sound was amplified as the darkness outside the windows crept into the house. Catherine shivered and moved from room to room, pulling the curtains. Patrick's study was empty, an empty coffee cup the only sign he had been home. Catherine's stomach grumbled again, reminding her she hadn't eaten since the desserts they had enjoyed earlier in the day. The under-counter lights bathed the kitchen in an eerie glow, the light hum of the fridge breaking the silence.

'Where have you been?' Patrick's voice was low, monotone.

Catherine's heartbeat skyrocketed as she clutched her hand to her chest. She laughed, then let out a deep breath. 'You scared the life out of me!'

'Where. Have. You. Been?'

'You said you would be home late, so I went into London with Pia.'

'Why would you be at The Savoy with Pia? Who were you really with?'

Catherine stumbled over her words, explaining that she took Pia for lunch to apologise for cancelling their New Year's Eve plans.

'Why do you need to apologise for spending time with your husband?'

'We were shopping, you said to get some new clothes. I didn't think I needed to ask your permission to go out.' Catherine looked at him, her eyes making contact with his, her chin raised.

Catherine followed Patrick into the hallway, where he picked up the bags, emptying them and sifting through the contents. He sneered, holding up a New Look bag. Pia's sequinned dress fell to the floor, and he seized it.

'I-It's Pia's. It must have got mixed up with my bags.'

'I can see it's not yours. I don't think the fabric would take the strain of your backside.'

'Fuck you, Patrick. How do you know we were at The Savoy anyway?'

Patrick laughed. 'Your bank statement, Darling Wife. You don't think I let you loose with my money without keeping an eye on what you spend it on, do you? I'll ask you again. Who were you with at The Savoy?'

'I don't have to answer these questions, Patrick. I'm tired. It's been a long day. I'm going to bed.' She clutched the bannister as the lights span in front of her eyes, Patrick's voice becoming a distant underwater noise. She took a couple of deep breaths, steadying herself, and forced one foot in front of the other.

'Don't you walk away from me!' Patrick roared, closing the distance between them in two large strides. His hand closed around her upper arm, a vice-like grip pulling her back towards him. Catherine felt the stars turn to darkness as her body crumpled into Patrick.

When Catherine woke, she was lying on her back in bed, her hands at her side, the duvet pulled up around her. Patrick watched her from the chair beside the bed, his expression unreadable, a crystal tumbler with what looked like whiskey in his hand.

'You fainted. I assume you haven't eaten dinner? This is why I like to know where you are, so I can take care of you, make sure you are safe and looking after yourself. Pia is clearly a bad influence.'

An icy feeling of dread crawled through Catherine's veins. She couldn't be? Her hand moved to her abdomen instinctively. She swallowed, her tongue sticking in her mouth.

'I'm fine. I'm just hungry.' Catherine smiled at Patrick, willing him to believe her.

Catherine stayed in bed when Patrick left for work. He brought her a camomile tea in bed and told her to stay there for the morning and get some rest. Catherine hated camomile tea. He suggested she stay home today. It wasn't a suggestion. After he left the room, she listened. The familiar cues, the slam of the car door, the crunch of tyres on gravel and the mechanical whir of the gates opening and then closing. Letting out a breath, Catherine sank back into the pillows. Could she risk going out to get a pregnancy test?

The tea swirled around in the bathroom sink, round and round in circles, until it was gone, mesmerising Catherine. As she turned on the hot tap, a sharp pain pierced through her stomach. This was different to the tenderness she was still experiencing in her ribs. The pain threatened to tear her stomach in half, and she doubled over in agony, crying out. Trying to pull herself to standing caused the pain to worsen, the black spots starting to appear in front of Catherine's eyes again. She dropped to the floor and crawled through to the bedroom, her hands and knees sinking into the deep pile of the carpet until she was near her phone. It was just out of reach. She used the voice activation setting to call Patrick. The dial tone rang and rang. She tried again, tears of pain and frustration burning her eyes.

'Call Pia'. Pia's cheery hello cut off the dial tone in two rings.

'I need you.'

Catherine curled into the foetal position, the line still open with Pia's voice in the distance shouting that she was on the way.

Catherine blinked in the harsh hospital light. Pia's hand rested on her forearm. The steady beep of the monitors created a sense of calm in the unfamiliar room. She begged Pia to try contacting Patrick again. The call was immediately routed to his voicemail, his smooth tones suggesting the caller leave a message. Catherine leaned back in the bed, the pain now subsiding.

A gentle knock at the door announced the return of the doctor. The corners of her eyes crinkled with a smile as she glanced down at her notes.

'Sorry for the wait. We were waiting for a few test results to come back. The good news is we know what caused the pain. When was your last period?'

Catherine blinked rapidly, sagging back into the bed. She frowned.

'I'm pregnant, aren't I?'

The doctor smiled at her and said they wanted to take her for an ultrasound to get more of a picture of how far along she was and to check everything was okay. She patted Catherine's shin and said she would be back after the ultra-sound to talk more about the next steps, but at this stage, there is nothing to worry about. Some babies like to surprise their mums with a growth spurt that can be painful. She lowered her tone, 'Trapped wind can also be a painful side effect of pregnancy, and it was probably a bit of this as well'. She winked and left Pia and Catherine in silence.

'All ready to meet your little 'un?' The nurse wheeled an ultrasound machine into the small room. Catherine nodded and squeezed Pia's hand. The nurse asked her to pull her top up so she could apply the ultrasound gel. As Catherine did so, she saw Pia's eyes move to the faint yellow bruising. She turned her head away, her eyes glassy. Pia said nothing, her lips pursed, and her

eyes remained focused on the bruises. As the nurse turned from her machine, Catherine noted an almost imperceptible flicker in the nurse's eyes as she looked at her stomach.

Catherine looked between the nurse and Pia, letting out a forced laugh. 'That'll teach me to learn my limits, won't it? Perhaps I should stay off the drink.' Her hand flew to her mouth. 'Oh no. I've been drinking. The baby…'

The nurse gave Catherine's hand a squeeze and said, more often than not, there would be little to no effect on the baby, but if she was still worried, they could run a few more tests later. Catherine nodded and gasped as the cold gel hit her stomach. The nurse ran the monitor over her stomach until she found what she was looking for and nodded towards the screen. Catherine let out a breath, and a smile slowly spread across her face. She glanced at Pia's expressionless face, filling the silence with babbled sentences about how everything would be great with a baby around.

'It's early days, but baby looks fine, a strong heartbeat, and I would say you are around three months along.' She handed Catherine a tissue and looked at Catherine's left hand. 'Is Dad on the scene? Are you safe?' The nurse was direct, but her tone was not unkind. Catherine spluttered as she tried to answer, rubbing her hands on her trousers. The nurse asked about the bruises on her ribs.

'Why? I thought you said the baby is okay? I told you; I fell over after a few drinks.'

Pia squeezed Catherine's hand, her eyes glistening as she asked if Patrick did this.

'I don't have to listen to this.' Catherine finished wiping the gel from her stomach and pulled her top down. 'Patrick is my husband. He loves me. Pia, thank you for bringing me here, but I'm fine now. I'll get a taxi home.'

'Don't be ridiculous. The doctor wanted to speak to you again anyway.'

Catherine looked at the door. She twisted her rings around on her finger and glared at her friend. The room was silent until the doctor returned with a follow up appointment and some advice on fainting and low blood pressure. Stuffing the leaflet in her bag, Catherine stomped out of the room. Pia scurried behind her until they reached the empty taxi rank at the side of the hospital where Catherine was forced to accept a lift home. They travelled in silence. Pia jumped as the door slammed shut, and Catherine retreated into the house.

14
Valentine's Day

The enormous bouquet entered the room before Patrick, and he poked his head around them, grinning. He set them on the dressing table.

'Happy First Valentine's Day, Mrs Walker.'

Patrick pulled Catherine from the bed and coaxed her to the kitchen for breakfast. Catherine looked at the table, noting that it was filled with everything the baby book suggested for breakfast. She slid a piece of toast from underneath the poached egg and avocado and nibbled at it, pushing the plate away.

'You need to eat more than that. Got to keep your strength up now you are eating for two.'

Patrick pushed the plate back towards Catherine, the draft wafting the eggy smell towards her nostrils. Nausea stirred in her stomach. She only just made it to the downstairs bathroom before the sparse contents of her stomach splattered into the toilet bowl. Her eyes watered as her stomach contracted again with nothing to show for its efforts. Breakfast was cold when Catherine returned to the table with a sheepish wave.

'Looks like Baby Walker isn't in the mood for breakfast.'

'I spent ages getting all this ready.' Patrick gestured to the table.

'I know, and we love you for it.'

Patrick wrapped his arms around Catherine, leaning towards her, then recoiled as the stomach bile and regurgitated food on her breath assaulted him.

'For God's sake, Catherine, didn't you bother to clean your teeth after being sick? I may as well clean up here if you don't want any of it. You go, clean yourself up. Just because you are pregnant doesn't mean you should let yourself go.' He turned his back to her, the dishes clinking as he rammed them into the dishwasher.

Catherine's toothbrush plopped back into the holder as Patrick's arms snaked around her waist. One at a time, she removed his hands, turning and softly kissing his cheek.

'You're never in the mood since we found out about the baby!'

'And you are always in the mood!'

'You make me out to be some sort of sexual deviant. I don't see anything wrong with a man wanting to have sex with his wife. I'm going to work.'

'I thought you took the day off.' Catherine's words met an empty space as Patrick strode to the bedroom door.

Later that evening, Catherine's skin prickled and her ears strained to hear what had woken her up. The moonlight cast a shadow across the bedroom, creating shadows in the silence. A crash downstairs. Cupboards banging in the kitchen. She trembled, looking at the empty spot beside her. Reaching for her phone, Catherine's hands shook as the names in her address book scrolled across the screen. She scrolled too far, Patrick's name disappearing and her finger hovering over Pia. Time stood still as she looked at her name. They hadn't spoken since the day at the hospital. She hadn't replied to Pia's texts. Another noise. It sounded like someone was on the stairs. Her fingers found their purpose, and she scrolled back to Patrick's name in her phone book. She hit call and immediately heard his phone ringing outside the bedroom door. She hung up and flopped back onto the bed, letting out a huge breath. She put her hand to her chest, releasing a shaky laugh.

'Hello Lover.'

The bedroom door swung open, hitting the wall with a thud, and Patrick leaned against the door frame. The landing light behind him illuminated his shape, giving him the appearance of being larger than he was.

Patrick stumbled towards the bed. The strong fumes of alcohol surrounded him.

'Come here, Wife'.

He fell onto the bed, grabbing Catherine's breast roughly. She cried out at his heavy-handed touch, inching away from him.

'Where have you been?'

'Where have I been? Out with people who know how to have fun, that's where I've been. Not that I have to answer to you.' He bopped her on the nose with his forefinger, then grabbed her wrist, closing the gap between them.

'You're hurting me.'

'You're hurting me.' Patrick copied in a high-pitched tone. 'You know you want it.' His grip on her wrist tightened. Catherine's t-shirt had ridden up where he pulled her across the bed, exposing her stomach. His eyes fixed on it, then scanned her body. He released his grip.

'Like I'd want to have sex with you anyway. Pregnancy is making you fat. Fat is not attractive, Catherine.' He rolled away.

She breathed out, rubbing her wrist and inched towards the edge of her side of the bed, easing the cover back over her shaking body. Her phone lit up on the bedside table. Glancing over her shoulder at her husband's body, she picked it up and opened a text from Pia, *I miss you.* Tears ran down Catherine's face, and she fell asleep clutching her phone.

15
The Club

Catherine stared out the train window, the world passing by in a blur of colour. She closed her eyes briefly, leaning her head back. When she opened them and looked around, she saw two friends moving through the carriage, laughing like co-conspirators. She unlocked her phone, and her finger hovered over Pia's name. It clicked as she locked the keypad and stuffed it in her bag.

The rails screamed as the train eased into the station. Catherine hung back whilst the other passengers jostled their way onto the platform, a hand subconsciously on her stomach. As the crowd began to thin, she followed the surge along the platform, onto the street and down the steps into the underground. The connection sent her body into autopilot, changing once, and then the conductor announced their arrival at Kensington Station. The crisp air hit Catherine's skin as she meandered up the steps, leaving the contrasting stale air of the underground below. The familiarity of her old work neighbourhood led her to stroll to the old bar, where she was greeted with hugs and demands for updates. She was twirled around for inspection, her new look appraised and met with approval as they told the new girls of Catherine's real-life rags to riches tale.

Catherine reluctantly regaled her former colleagues with stories of the wedding and honeymoon. They listened enraptured as she described the embellished lifestyle they wanted to hear about. She ordered lunch to eat at the bar, smiling as the conversation turned to her friends, and she caught up on their lives. It was their turn to captivate her with tales of dating mishaps and unruly customers. Her eyes sparkled as she laughed, a real belly laugh that came from being completely at ease. She cooed over photos of rapidly growing children, her cheeks rosy and a warm glow inside her, keeping her secret safe.

The bar began to fill up, and Catherine pushed her plate aside, rummaging in her bag for her purse. She left a generous tip and excused herself to use the bathroom.

The creaky hinge on the bathroom door announced the arrival of other people. Catherine reached for the lock on her stall door, stopping as she heard her name.

'She thinks she is so much better than us, coming back here to rub our noses in how rich she is now.'

'Don't be a bitch, Ashleigh. It's nice to see how well she is doing. She found her Prince Charming. I'd be lying if I said I wasn't a bit jealous.'

'Yeh, well, it could have been any one of us. I wonder if her precious husband told her that he spent the night with me before he started sniffing around her. He is nothing but my sloppy seconds.' Ashleigh laughed, cruelly.

'You had your chance, and you blew it. You can't blame her for taking it. Did she even know you liked him?'

'That's not the point. I bet I could still have him if I wanted to.'

Catherine remained frozen as they flushed and exited the stalls, not noticing that one was occupied. Her head pulsed with the rush of blood. She felt sure they would hear her heart pounding. She listened as their footsteps preceded the creak of the door, letting out a breath as it banged shut.

Her bag and coat were at the bar where she had left them, and she grabbed them, muttering to the new girl, whose name she didn't know, that she wasn't feeling well and could she say goodbye to the others. She walked briskly back to the station, descending the steps and slipping through the doors onto the waiting train.

Catherine's heart was still racing as she closed the front door, shutting herself away from the world. She ran up the stairs and turned the bath taps, pouring Epsom salts under the running water. Her thoughts raced around her head, and she scrambled to make sense of them. As the bath filled, she stripped off her clothes and slowly sank into the warm water. The warmth seeped over her body, bit by bit, and slowly eased her heart rate. She took a few deep breaths and closed her eyes, focusing on her breathing, following the pattern of the hypnobirthing video she watched online. Her lips moved imperceptibly as she repeated the affirmations: *I am confident and in control. I am in control of my body, my mind, and my emotions.*

~

Catherine laid the plates of Spaghetti Bolognese on the table, taking her seat opposite Patrick. She twirled her fork in the steaming mound of pasta, looking to Patrick as he took his first mouthful. As he smiled at her and groaned, she began her own meal. The bath helped to wash away her earlier feelings, and she gave him a relaxed smile.

'What did you get up to today?'

Catherine paused. She glanced at Patrick, feeling his eyes watching her, and then down at her plate. 'Not a lot'.

'You can't have done nothing all day. What's the secret?' He gave a forced laugh.

'I went into London to get some bits for the baby but couldn't find anything I liked.'

'Couldn't find anything you liked?! Which shops did you go to?'

Catherine stuttered; her tongue felt like it was filling her mouth, not allowing her words to escape. 'I can't remember.'

'You can't remember?' He laughed again. 'How can you not remember where you went?' Catherine looked at him, her skin flushed. Before she had a chance to respond, Patrick asked if she was lying to him. Asked if she was with another man.

Catherine took a deep breath. She spoke carefully, sensing a trap. 'Why would I want another man when I have you?'

'Why were you at your old bar? That's where men go to pick up women, not a place for my pregnant wife to go. Unless you were looking to be picked up – we all know it's not hard.'

'H-How do you know I was there?'

Patrick smirked. He reminded her that he could see every penny she spent and where she spent it. 'Why would you be at a bar if not meeting another man?'

'I just went to say hello to my old friends. I haven't seen any of them since before the wedding. Ashleigh was there.'

Patrick's eyes flickered at the mention of Ashleigh's name. His jaw clenched, accentuating his bone structure. He said nothing. The second hand of the kitchen clock ticked loudly against the hum of the refrigerator. Catherine picked at her nail varnish.

'I think it would be best if I put a tracker on your phone now you are pregnant. If you are going to be cavorting around London with my baby, anything could happen. What if there was an emergency and I needed to find you?' Patrick stared at her.

The second hand filled the silence until Catherine mumbled that she didn't feel comfortable with a tracker on her phone.

'You what? Speak up.' Patrick raised his voice, the challenge clear.

'I don't feel comfortable with a tracker on my phone.' Catherine raised her voice and looked him in the eye.

'I don't feel comfortable with you lying about where you are all day. I don't feel comfortable with you gallivanting with God knows who. I don't feel comfortable with you taking risks running around London with our baby, but God forbid I show a little bit of concern about the welfare of our child in case YOU don't feel comfortable.' She remained silent. Her brief moment of confidence was gone as she sagged into the chair. 'Aside from being your husband, I'm a barrister, for fuck's sake,' Patrick continued, 'surely having me knowing you are safe would make you feel more comfortable? Many women would kill to be in your position.'

Catherine thought of Ashleigh. She looked at Patrick and nodded, pulling her phone from her pocket and handing it to him.

'Good girl.'

16
CCTV

The morning after Patrick put a tracker on her phone, Catherine awoke to an empty bed and the sound of drilling outside. Pulling on a dressing gown and slippers, she gave her swollen stomach a gentle rub and padded down the stairs. Peering into the kitchen, she saw a ladder outside the window and a pair of boots firmly planted near the top.

She wrenched open the front door. 'What the hell do you think you are doing?'

The man turned from his position up the ladder and looked her up and down. 'Just following orders.'

'Whose orders? What are you doing?'

'CCTV.' He pulled a piece of paper from his back pocket. 'Been hired by a Patrick Walker to install a top of the range home security system on the property.'

Catherine stared at him. Her mouth opened, and then she closed it again, tears threatening to spill from her eyes. Catherine's shoulders slumped as she turned back to the house.

The man called after her. 'I wouldn't say no to a cuppa.'

17
The Charity Shop

Catherine's eyes drifted to the open wardrobe, and the box inside containing her mother's wedding dress, and a few other sentimental items, of little value. Lifting the lid off the box, she sank her nose into the soft fabric, inhaling the scent. The memories enveloped her. Her parents taking her to the park, looking back and seeing her mother's face as she laughed at Catherine running around, her father buying her the biggest ice cream. Her thoughts turned to Patrick's parents; they were so different to the grandparents her own mum and dad would have been.

Catherine started pulling open drawers and throwing clothes into a heap on the bed. Her old skirts landed in the pile, dresses that Patrick described as slutty, a few bags and some other items she no longer wore. She stuffed everything into bin bags, piling them by the front door and ordered a taxi. As she waited for the taxi to arrive, she looked up at the house; the light on the camera flashed persistently. Catherine swallowed and focused her attention on the pile of bags.

At the first stop, Catherine rang the bell. Crossing her fingers behind her back, she waited, receiving no answer. She hastily scribbled a note and left her mother's wedding dress with another small bag in the porch. *Look after these for me. I can't talk about it now, but one day I will. Trust me and, please, never ask why.*

The bell on the door tinkled as she pushed it open with her back, her hands filled with bags of donations for the charity shop. Two older women rushed to greet her, taking the bags, one giving her a wink, saying she shouldn't be carrying them in her condition. Catherine looked down at her stomach.

'How did you…'

'You don't get to my age without learning how to spot the signs. There really are some pretty dresses in her,' she held the blue dress up, 'are you sure you want to get rid of it all?'

Catherine nodded. 'It's not really me anymore. I don't go out like I used to, not since I got married, even before this.' She glanced down at her stomach, her eyes filled with sorrow.

The older woman put the dress down, her forehead wrinkled as her eyes met Catherine's. She softly offered her a cup of tea. Catherine looked at the window; the taxi driver idled on the yellow loading lines. She turned back to the lady, taking in her soft eyes and gentle features and nodded, unable to speak.

'You go through that door and make yourself comfy, and I'll let the driver know you'll be stopping here, so he can go on.'

The driver pulled away, and Catherine jumped as her phone chimed. She pulled her phone out of her pocket and let out a breath as she saw it was just junk mail arriving in her inbox.

'Come on then, I told you to go on through.' The older woman left her colleague to man the shop and steered Catherine through a door to the back of the shop.

18
Ashleigh

I miss you too. Catherine hit send and rubbed her temples while she waited for the little blue ticks to appear. The subsequent exchange of messages between Catherine and Pia was instant.

I'm sorry.

No, I'm sorry.

I love you.

I miss you.

Pia's name flashed on the screen as the vibrations of Catherine's phone echoed on the kitchen table. Catherine answered, and they both spoke at once, then laughed. They arranged to meet for lunch on the sea front. Any awkwardness from their lack of communication was quickly forgotten, and the old friends clung to each other.

Over lunch, they caught up on each other's news. Catherine filled Pia in on her visit to the old bar, then exclaimed over the latest photos of Pia's nephews. Empty plates pushed in front of them, they paid their bills, Catherine requesting cash-back. Her smile momentarily slipped when the waitress advised they couldn't give cashback. The sky was clear, facilitating an opportunity for a meander around the labyrinth of alleyways that made up The Lanes shopping area. Pia pointed out a cash

machine. Catherine hesitated; using a cash machine would mean a record of the transaction.

They pottered from shop to shop, posing in front of the mirrors in quirky hats, sunglasses and other apparel. They sprayed perfumes and lathered up their skin with moisturisers. They sampled chocolates, cheeses and all sorts of other delicacies. The quirky shops in The Lanes were filled with a rich and diverse variety of goods.

'Look!' Catherine exclaimed, pointing to a sign in a barber shop window. The barber is doing his show today. The owner of the barbershop was a hobby singer known locally for putting on shows, singing from the balcony of the flat above his shop. He raised huge quantities of money for charity and attracted crowds with his Motown crowd pleasers. 'Let's head over to Churchill Square for some baby shops, then we can come back and get hot chocolates to drink while we listen.' Churchill Square was a modern, purpose-built shopping centre at the edge of The Lanes filled with chain shops, offering anything you couldn't find in the little independent stores in The Lanes.

They were greeted by a cheery assistant as they entered Baby & Me. She looked from Pia to Catherine and back again, trying to decide which one of them was pregnant, choosing her words carefully before scuttling away again.

'How long before you will be showing properly?'

'The books say around six months, but I can already see my body has changed. Patrick has noticed the weight gain.' Catherine looked down.

'Weight gain?! You are pregnant. It's not weight gain, its fuel to help you grow another human.'

'Yes, well, however you wrap it up, I am bigger than I was. I really should start a list so I know which of these things I actually need.' She picked up a plastic bottle and put it back down again as the shop assistant appeared, brandishing a pamphlet for expectant mums.

Pia looked at Catherine, giving an exaggerated smile and waggling her eyebrows, mimicking the girl's peppy and overkeen face.

Catherine selected a few neutral items that kept drawing her gaze, and took them to the till, grabbing a vat of stretch mark cream on the way. The shop assistant handed her the bag and cashback she requested. She crumpled the receipt and zipped the cash into the inside pocket of her coat.

'You should have got cash out when we passed the machine before.'

Catherine laughed. She waved her hand and blamed baby brain. They visited a few more shops and picked up a few more pregnancy and new born must-haves. Catherine's eyes followed an older woman in the shop as she waved a stuffed elephant in the air, making faces at a girl who Catherine estimated was a few years younger. The two women had the same eyes, the older of the two with a few more crinkles in the corners. They laughed and shared a joke, then both stopped, putting their hands on the younger girl's stomach and sharing the tender moment. Catherine watched. A single tear rolled down her cheek. Pia linked her arm through her friend's, squeezing. 'Come on, let's go get drinks and get a good spot to listen to the show in The Lanes.'

Catherine took the money from her coat pocket, looking around the kitchen. Her eyes ran over the cupboard, then towards the hallway. Opening a cupboard, she scanned the boxes, looking for something Patrick wouldn't use. The kitchen clock ticked, urging her to make a decision. Running upstairs, she pulled the lid off a tube of hair serum, running the tap and watching the white gloop run down the plug hole. Wiping it dry, she put the money inside and screwed the lid on, replacing the tube as Patrick shouted that he was home. She smoothed down her shirt, pasted a smile on her face and descended the stairs, trailing her hand along the bannister and accepting a kiss from Patrick as she reached the bottom.

His eyes lit up as she showed him the bits she had purchased for the baby. He kissed her on the head. 'This baby is a fresh start for us. A new beginning'.

Catherine smiled, warmth radiating through her body. Patrick put his arms around her and held her in the way he used to. He inhaled the smell of her hair, and she giggled. She took his hand and put it on her stomach, looking up at him.

'I have a client meeting in London tomorrow morning. Why don't we meet in the afternoon and look around some shops to get ideas for the nursery and what other bigger baby things we need to get? Actually, I have a better idea. Mum wants to take you for lunch at some point - she is so excited about the baby. Why don't you and Mum have lunch and I'll come and meet you after. Then we can all go round the shops?'

'You told your mum? I thought we were going to tell them together?' Catherine lifted her head off Patrick's chest and pulled away from him.

'What difference does it make? They know now, and they are so excited to be grandparents. Come on, don't spoil the moment.'

Catherine let her head fall back onto Patrick's chest. He stroked her hair as she watched the hands of the clock tick around, second by second.

The following morning, Catherine woke to a text from Myra letting her know to be ready at 10.30 am as Dick would drive them into London. She sighed. Surveying the clothes in the wardrobe, Catherine considered what would be met with the most approval by her mother-in-law.

Myra booked them a table at a Women Only Club she belonged to. The club operated a strict policy where new members could only apply if an existing member referred them. Catherine looked around at the women occupying the other tables. She was one of the youngest in the room. She snorted, picturing herself there with Pia.

'Something amusing, Dear?'

'No, not at all. It's all quite lovely. Thank you for inviting me here.'

Myra eyed Catherine suspiciously. 'Right. Well, Patrick will be here soon. He is going to meet us outside, so shall we head down? It won't do to keep him waiting.'

'But it's okay to leave his mother and pregnant wife outside waiting for him.' Catherine muttered under her breath.

Patrick whistled as he approached them. He gave each of them a kiss on the cheek, asking how lunch was. Catherine produced the list of things they needed to get for the baby that they had written out over lunch.

'The baby can have your old cot, Patrick. And we still have a lovely old rocking chair for when you are nursing Catherine. Your dad is going to get everything out of the loft so you can go through it. We kept everything from when you and your brother were little.' Myra clasped her hands together, looking at Patrick.

'Of course, Mum. We wouldn't want it any other way.'

Catherine opened her mouth to respond, and Patrick gave her a look. She closed her mouth and said nothing. Of course, Myra hadn't mentioned any of that over lunch.

With Myra delivered to where Dick was waiting to pick her up, Patrick and Catherine moved from shop to shop looking for nursery ideas. They booked an appointment with a top nursery designer to come to the house and talk through their ideas. Catherine watched Patrick as he charmed shop assistants everywhere they went - the proud father-to-be. They giggled and played with their hair, as did most women who entered his orbit. Catherine was invisible; she rolled her eyes.

'I have a surprise for you.'

Catherine eyed Patrick warily.

'I've booked a table at your old club for dinner. I know you enjoyed visiting there last week, so thought we could go together.'

She tensed. 'Why?'

'What do you mean, why? You can be so bloody ungrateful sometimes. Come on, or we will be late.'

Catherine's friend seated her and Patrick and gave them menus to look at. Catherine smiled awkwardly, feeling uncomfortable at being waited on by her old colleagues. Patrick sensed her discomfort and told her to lighten up. He extravagantly studied the menu before ordering a steak for himself and a salad for her. Her friend raised an eyebrow at the salad order, and Catherine obediently patted her stomach.

Ashleigh's laughter rang across the room as she served the table of men in her section. Catherine watched Patrick as he studied her until she turned and looked directly at him. Catherine shivered at the look that passed between them. Ashleigh turned away, laughing at something someone said. Catherine looked around the room, anywhere but Patrick, seeing a few familiar customers in the restaurant seats and at the bar area.

'Patrick! How lovely to see you again.'

Catherine jumped as Ashleigh appeared at their table.

'Catherine.' Ashleigh nodded in Catherine's direction, her body angled towards Patrick.

Patrick smiled, running his eyes over Ashleigh's body. He licked his lips. Catherine cleared her throat noisily, and he glared at her.

'I'm covering Cara's tables while she is on break. What do you fancy for dessert?' Ashleigh's eyes remained focused on Patrick, like a Walker targeting its prey.

Ashleigh let the question hang in the air.

'I think we will leave dessert. For tonight...' Patrick's voice trailed off. 'Catherine, I need to use the bathroom. Can you settle the bill?' He opened his jacket and tossed his wallet on the table. A wad of notes sticking out of the side.

She nodded, ignoring the fact that Ashleigh had disappeared along with Patrick.

19
The Baby

Catherine's reflection in the dark windows appeared ghostlike and eerie, reminding her to draw the curtains. She moved from room to room, looking at the clock in each, her ears straining for the whir of the gates. She looked at her phone - no messages. The evenings alone were becoming more frequent.

Feeling flutters in her stomach, Catherine smiled. She watched the kettle, her hand on her stomach, cradling her baby, until steam began to hiss from the spout, the piercing whistle bringing her out of her reverie. She poured the steaming water over a ginger tea bag and rummaged around at the back of the cupboard for some biscuits. She would replace them tomorrow.

Hands full, Catherine carefully navigated the stairs. The lullaby she hummed to her bump cheered the silent atmosphere.

'You don't even bother to wait up for your husband anymore?'

Catherine stopped mid-stair. 'I was just going to read in bed while I waited for you.'

'While you waited for me? So sorry to inconvenience you.' Patrick snorted. He climbed the stairs briskly until he stood on the landing, his bulk looming ahead of her.

Catherine looked down and made to step up and around him. Patrick sidestepped, blocking her way again. Her hands shook.

'Nothing to say for yourself?'

'I'm sorry.'

Patrick stared at the mug Catherine held, hot liquid threatening to spill onto the carpet. His focus moved to the biscuits, and he scoffed. 'Still not bothered about the baby weight, I see.'

'I am within the healthy range.' Catherine spoke quietly.

Patrick's laugh echoed in the hallway. 'Thank goodness our child will be off to Fitzpatrick's as soon as he is old enough. God knows what sort of mother you will be if you can't even look after yourself.'

Catherine's body tensed; she clenched her teeth, not trusting herself to speak immediately. Patrick's laughter resounded in her head. 'You know I don't want our child to go to boarding school.' She spoke slowly, choosing her words carefully, 'I want him or her to be at home with us.'

'The decision is made. He will go to Fitzwilliam's. It's tradition. Now, I've had a long day. Go and put the kettle on while I have a shower.' He turned towards the bedroom.

Catherine finally finished her ascent of the stairs as Patrick spun around. 'I thought I told you to put the kettle on.' He lurched towards her, and she jumped, spilling her tea. His eyes met hers, and she shrank back, her foot meeting with air where the floor should be. Her wide eyes locked with Patrick's as her arms flailed, a finger glancing off the bannister.

Time slowed as Catherine fell through the air, Patrick watching as her body landed and crumpled at the bottom of the stairs. Neither of them moved until the grandfather clock broke the spell. Catherine stirred and cried out, pain shooting through her stomach. She curled into the foetal position.

'I'll take that drink when you're ready.'

She watched her husband's back as he disappeared into the bedroom before she closed her eyes and let her body succumb to the pain.

~

The distant voices were all around. Catherine's thoughts were jumbled in her head, and she attempted to fight through the fog and put them in order. She tried to move her head, and the voices told her to stay still. Her arm throbbed, her lower back ached, and her stomach was clenched in an iron vice of pain. She was pregnant. She fell. She opened her mouth, but the words wouldn't come out. The far away voices kept saying her name. *Where was Patrick?* She blinked a few times. His voice was in the distance, talking to the others. She made out him saying he woke in the night and found her at the bottom of the stairs. *What time was it?* The voices were saying something to her. They were going to take her to hospital. There was a sensation like when a rollercoaster ride lifts you up into the air, followed by the bumpiness of the ambulance ride. She watched the scene from above. Her body lying in the ambulance, the looks exchanged between paramedics, the siren blaring. *Where was Patrick?*

'Your husband is following in his car.' Someone squeezed her hand.

Had she asked them the question out loud?

Catherine woke in a hospital room, the strong stench of disinfectant and the bright lights jarring to her senses. Patrick stood with his back to her, looking out of the window, his phone pressed to his ear. His voice was low, and she strained to make out the words. When the call ended, she opened her mouth to speak and heard a croaky squeak. Her mouth was dry, her throat sore. He turned and strode to her side. Catherine flinched as his fingers wrapped around hers. Her pulse quickened. She searched her brain for a memory of what happened.

Patrick pressed the bell for the nurse. 'You must have got up to get a drink in the night. I woke up, and you weren't there, and then I found you at the bottom of the stairs.'

Catherine frowned. It sounded like a well-rehearsed story. Is that what happened? She couldn't remember. 'The baby?' she croaked as the nurse stepped into the room.

The nurse explained that the fall had caused a complete placental abruption. She had been at the bottom of the stairs for some time, and it had been too late to save the baby. Catherine had undergone surgery to remove the foetus. She explained that Catherine may find it difficult to conceive in the future, but a doctor would be able to answer any specific questions.

A carnal wail filled the room, and tears ran down Catherine's cheeks. Patrick kissed her forehead, muttering soothing words.

'You've got a good one here,' the nurse nodded towards Patrick, 'he has been so worried about you. Hasn't left your side.' She held a glass of water with a straw to Catherine's lips. 'There you go, just take some slow sips.'

Catherine looked from the nurse to her husband and back again. She frowned, trying to remember, the tears still running down her cheeks. The memories were just out of reach.

The hospital discharged Catherine that evening. She clutched a bag of medication as Patrick pushed the wheelchair to the car. Neither of them spoke. His mother was at the house when they got back. She fussed around Catherine, tucking her into bed and bringing her a hot water bottle and warm milk. Myra and Patrick spoke on the landing in hushed voices. Eventually, Myra left.

'You left me,' Catherine whispered as Patrick stepped back into the bedroom.

'What?'

'I didn't get up in the night. We were arguing. You left me.'

Patrick's eyes flickered, but he didn't miss a beat. 'You must still be confused after surgery. Your mind is playing tricks with you. You are on quite a lot of painkillers.'

'Don't do that. My mind is fine, and I remember what happened. We were talking about…' Catherine's voice broke, '…the baby, and Fitzpatrick's. You were standing over me.'

Patrick's voice turned to steel. 'You had better watch what you are saying, Catherine.'

'Not so keen on the truth now?'

Patrick's hollow laugh echoed in the quiet room. 'Who do you think people would believe? The bored housewife or the award-winning barrister? I'm warning you, Catherine. This is not a road you want to go down.'

'Or what?' She glared at him, her chin jutting out, jaw set, holding eye contact.

'Don't test me, Catherine.' His eyes flashed.

'What if I want out? I'll walk away. I won't ask for anything.'

'You ungrateful little bitch. Till death us do part. Remember that.'

'You can't keep treating me like this. I… I'll speak to someone, tell them how you track my phone.'

'You are so clumsy; you fell down the stairs and killed my child. YOU fell. YOU killed my child. I think it is perfectly reasonable for a husband to care about his wife enough to put a tracker on her phone to help keep her safe, especially when she is prone to being clumsy and forgetful.'

'But, I'm not…'

'That's not what my colleagues think. They saw you fall drunkenly at the Awards last Christmas. I have told them all I worry about you and how your behaviour can be… difficult. Like I said, no-one will believe a word you say. So, you had better start acting like the obedient wife I know you can be.'

Catherine looked down. She nodded, a single tear sliding down her cheek as Patrick closed the door on the way out.

20
I'm Sorry

Catherine stared straight ahead. The grassy clearing of Beachy Head was scattered with people – runners, walkers, pushchairs. Catherine watched people going about their weekend. She didn't flinch at Patrick's touch, not outwardly. It was getting easier to control. Her stomach turned as he squeezed her hand. She fought against the urge to pull her hand away.

'I do love you, you know. I know I can be short at times, but it's because I love you. I want the best for us.'

'I know. I love you too.' Catherine stared ahead, her voice level.

'Hot chocolate?' He didn't wait for an answer. He returned a few minutes later with two takeaway cups. He pulled open Catherine's door and held his hand out. As they walked along the cliff, Patrick talked about work and his family. She listened dutifully. They reached a sign warning not to go too close to the cliff edge. There was a second sign with the phone number for The Samaritans.

Catherine stopped, staring at the signs.

'Isn't it awful they need to put those up?'

Catherine agreed, taking a sip of her hot chocolate, her brow furrowed, deep in thought.

'Although, I know I couldn't go on without you, Catherine. If you ever left me… I just couldn't live without you.'

Catherine's eyes widened, brought back from her reverie.

'Do you understand what I'm saying?'

Catherine linked her arm through Patricks. 'Why would I ever leave you? You are so good to me.' She injected just the right amount of warmth into her tone.

Patrick smiled down at her, kissing her on the head. He reached into his pocket, producing tickets for a West End Show. 'Dinner and show next week, Mrs Walker? I have booked a hotel. I thought it might be time we try for another baby.'

Catherine smiled up at him; the smile didn't quite reach her eyes.

21
Not Pregnant

The plastic stick clattered into the sink. Catherine bit her lip to keep from smiling with relief.

'Well?'

Patrick pushed the door open. He looked from Catherine to the pregnancy test in the sink and back again. She swallowed and shook her head, then looked down, focusing on a piece of lint on the floor. Patrick picked up the test, then threw it back in the sink, slamming the countertop with his palm. He breathed in deeply through his nose, his facial expression rigid, before marching from the room. The wardrobe doors opened and closed with a bang. Catherine watched the bathroom door, waiting until Patrick reappeared. He didn't look at her. Her eyes found the piece of lint on the floor again, and she heard the spray of Patrick's aftershave before its crisp masculine notes filling the bathroom.

'I'm going for work drinks with a client. Don't wait up.'

Catherine looked around the room, her body tense until the front door slammed. Her body sagged back into the bathroom chair, her head falling back into the tall back onto the headrest.

In an act of defiance, she grabbed her phone from the side, sending a message to Pia, *Patrick out. Takeaway at mine?*

Pia tapped back, *Come here if you want? I'll cook.*

'Best I don't go out without letting Patrick know. I don't want to worry him.'

Catherine watched the dots appear on the screen, then disappear. The pattern repeated a few times until the ping announced a reply.

'See you in an hour. I'll pick up an Indian on the way.'

Catherine deleted the text exchange.

The friends talked about Pia's job and her family. Catherine lived vicariously through the escapades of Pia's nights out and her foray into online dating. They huddled together, giggling as they swiped yes or no to prospective partners. Pia sighed and declared herself eternally single, pledging to fill her home with cats. Catherine looked at her.

'Never settle.'

Before Pia could reply, Catherine poured more drinks and demanded to see more potential matches, maintaining there must be someone worth messaging.

The grandfather clock in the hallway chimed 11 pm. Catherine looked at the door, pressing the button on the side of her phone to check for messages. She swallowed, making eye contact with Pia, her eyes pleading.

'It's getting late. I'd best head home.' Pia opened her mouth as if to yawn, stretching her arms overhead.

'I'll follow you out. I need to put the Indian boxes in the outside bin.'

Before crawling up the stairs to bed, Catherine opened the windows in the living room and kitchen. The cool night air diluting the lingering aroma of curry.

~

'Bloody freezing downstairs, and stinks of curry.' Patrick slurred, clambering into bed. Catherine pretended to be asleep. His noisy return to the house had woken her, affording her a glance at the clock before he stumbled up the stairs.

'I said, it's bloody freezing downstairs,' Patrick repeated. His voice lacked its earlier antagonistic tone. She squeezed her eyes firmly closed until the bed dipped and rose as he rolled away from her, loud snoring indicating he would no longer bother her.

Tiptoeing around in the semi-darkness of the early morning, Catherine used the light from the landing to gather Patrick's clothes from the floor for washing. She crept down the stairs with the laundry basket and began sorting the colours. Shoving the first load into the machine, a splash of colour caught Catherine's eye. She saturated the lipstick mark on his collar with stain remover and pushed it back into the drum, her expression impassive. Checking the pockets of his jeans, she pulled a crumpled receipt from her old bar.

Catherine jumped as a shadow appeared across the floor, Patrick's bulk blocking the light. She balled the receipt into her hand and turned to smile at him.

'Good night last night?'

Patrick frowned.

'Why? What are you getting at?'

'Nothing. Just asking if you had a good night.'

'Not as good as you by the smell of things. The place stinks. I know you didn't go out, and you didn't order a curry using your bank card.' Patrick tutted. 'Naughty Catherine. How did you pay for it? Have you been hiding money from me?'

Catherine remained silent, weighing up her options. Patrick stepped through the utility room door to the kitchen, and she held her breath at the clatter and crashing as Patrick pulled open drawers, searching. He growled, his face stony.

'Come on then. Where is it?'

'I don't know what you are talking about.'

'I don't know what you are talking about,' Patrick repeated in a high-pitched tone. 'You didn't use your card, so you must have money hidden somewhere. MY money.'

Catherine yelped as his fingers dug in around her wrist and pulled her behind him. She stumbled on the stairs. Patrick's vice-like grip remained, her skin scuffed on the stair carpet as he continued relentlessly. He pulled open drawers, rummaging around. Holding a bra between his thumb and forefinger, he laughed, asking Catherine who she thought would want to see her wearing that. The dressing table drawer slid open, revealing her jewellery, carefully displayed in velvet trays. Patrick's eyes rested on the photo of Catherine's parents. He scoffed. She stepped toward him, opening her mouth and closing it again as he looked at her, daring her to say something. He pulled the picture from the drawer and dropped it to the floor, the glass crunching under the rubber sole of his slipper. His quest continued, powder from Catherine's makeup dusting the sink as he tipped her makeup bag upside down. The colours bled and ran as they meshed with the standing drips in the sink. She glanced at the shelf containing her tubes and pots of lotions and potions. Patrick followed her almost imperceptible gaze, raising his hand to the shelf.

'It was Pia!' Catherine blurted out.

His hand froze in the air. 'What do you mean it was Pia?' He lowered his arm.

'Pia came over last night. She bought the Indian.' Catherine's heart pounded. 'I would never try to hide anything from you. I am so grateful for all you do for me.'

'You lied. You know I don't want that woman in my house.' Patrick's eyes narrowed. He looked at Catherine. 'Are you lying to me again?'

Catherine's eyes widened as she shook her head, the rest of her body frozen to the spot.

'Because, you know, I take our marriage vows seriously, Catherine. You promised to love, honour and obey me,' his emphasis on the word obey. 'Until death, remember, Wife?'

She nodded.

Patrick instructed her to clean up the mess she made him make. 'And you are not to see Pia again. Understood?'

Catherine nodded, dropping to her knees beside the crushed photo of her parents, their smiles watching her through the cracks in the glass.

22
Christmas

Catherine woke on Christmas Day to an empty bed. She smiled, savouring the moments of solitude before real life caught up. She slowly stretched with a groan and felt around on the bedside table for her phone to text Pia. With another stretch, she rolled out of bed and padded to the dressing table, taking out the photo of her parents and wishing them a Happy Christmas. She closed her eyes, taking a moment to consider how different her life would be with them still in it. The peace was shattered by Patrick bellowing up the stairs to be ready in 10 minutes, or he would go without her. Catherine looked at the clock, weighing up her options. It was easier to go. She pulled on one of the cashmere polo necks he bought her last Christmas and teamed it with a long skirt.

Christmas at The Walker's followed a set format. Catherine learned quickly that this world had little room for change. She followed Myra to the kitchen, automatically standing by the simmering pots and pans, waiting for instructions.

'You've lost weight,' Myra judged, 'you need to keep your strength up. Patrick said you are trying for another baby.'

'Patrick prefers me like this.' Catherine's smile didn't reach her eyes.

Myra sniffed.

'A toast,' Patrick raised his glass, 'to Mum and Dad for hosting a wonderful Christmas, again, especially you, Mum, for cooking. To Max, for being the brother that always makes me look good. And to my wife, I know this isn't how we planned our second Christmas. There should be one more around the table, but hopefully, one day, we will have another chance.'

Catherine raised a glass of elderflower cordial in a champagne flute. Patrick didn't want her to drink whilst they were trying to conceive, and she always did her best to obey his wishes.

23
The End

Catherine took a deep breath before opening the car door. There were two other cars in the car park, but no people around. She reminded herself she was just an ordinary person going for a walk. The wind blew around her as she retrieved her backpack from the boot of the car. Her long hair whipped around her face, and she allowed herself a moment of sadness at what would have to be done. She took one last look through the car window. The cream envelope sat on the passenger seat bearing a single word, 'Patrick'. As she walked away from the car, she dropped her keys into the bin and strode across the open common to the edge of the cliffs. The wind was strong now, and she concentrated on not getting blown sideways as she stepped one foot in front of the other. The white cliff edge was breathtakingly beautiful, and she could see why people chose this view to be the last thing they would see before jumping. She looked around; she was still alone. Catherine removed each of her shoes and threw them to the crashing waves below. She took off her bright pink cashmere scarf, running the soft wool through her fingers, remembering the day she bought it as a newlywed all those years ago. As close to the edge as she dared, Catherine dropped the scarf, watching as it snagged on the cliff face below. In a final move, she removed one diamond stud from her ear and dropped it on the soft grass at her feet. She dropped the other into the water.

Her trail laid, Catherine needed to move quickly. She pulled a new pair of shoes from her bag and slipped them on her feet, then pulled a black beanie on and a khaki coat over the plain sweatshirt she wore and started walking. Once at Eastbourne Pier, she locked herself in a toilet cubicle and set about cutting her long hair off, fighting back tears as she covered it with paper towels in the bin. She tossed her head upside down and tried not to breathe in the fumes of the coloured hair spray until she had emptied the can. Dark mascara on her eyebrows completed the change of appearance. She removed her wedding and engagement rings, cursing the visible mark they left, rubbing the indent. She put her hand in her pocket to check her phone, then remembered she had to leave it in the glovebox of the car. She would get a new one when it was safe. Pulling the cheap watch from the pocket of her charity shop coat, she checked the time. The bus would be here in five minutes. Her heart was racing now. Could she do this?

The bus pulled up, and she put on a pair of sunglasses before boarding. Keeping her face angled away from the cameras, her heartbeat quickened as she handed over the cash for a ticket and took her seat. She just had to make it to Dover, the ferry, and they would be free.

'My Darling Patrick.

I am sorry I have not been able to be the wife and mother you deserve. I wish more than anything that things could have been different and I could have given you a child, but it was not to be.

I hope my leaving this way gives you the chance to have the life you wanted. I want you to meet someone else, to be happy.

To have children and to be the dad you have always wanted to be.

This was the only way.

Till death us do part.

Your Catherine.'

A Matter of Perspective

BRIGHTON WEEKLY: EMINENT BARRISTER APPEALS FOR INFORMATION

The wife of Patrick Walker, a distinguished Barrister decorated with Awards for his work, is missing, presumed dead. A note was found in her car at Beachy Head, a well-known suicide spot. Police are not looking for anyone else in connection with her disappearance. Personal items believed to belong to Mrs Walker were found at the cliff edge. At the time of going to print, Mrs Walker's body has not been found.

Patrick Walker is offering a generous reward for anyone with information about her last known movements. He has given the following statement:

'I urge everyone to look out for my wife. I know she is out there somewhere. She may be hurt or confused and need help to find home. Catherine, I love you. If you see this, please know that I just want you home safely with me. Till death us do part.'

Ashleigh: 'That poor man, he doesn't deserve to be alone'.

Max: 'My poor brother, I know he can be difficult, but he doesn't deserve this.'

Dianne & Bill: 'That poor man, he doesn't deserve this heartache.'

Dick & Myra: 'Our poor son. How could she do this to him.'

Pia: 'It should never have come to this; I should've done more.'

The Older Lady from the Charity Shop: 'I hope she made it.'

Patrick: 'She won't get away with this.'

PART 2: OLIVA

1
Oliva

Catherine turned the sign on the door to closed and began methodically stacking the chairs atop the Formica tables. The chilled display cabinet, filled with cakes, emitted a gentle hum and a light glow in the dusk. As she lifted one of the chairs, there was a clatter as a book fell to the floor – a guidebook for visiting England - not one she recognised. Catherine put it on the little white painted bookshelf with the other used paperbacks for customers and continued stacking the chairs.

When Catherine wandered into the café nearly 20 years before, pregnant and alone, Maggie took her under her wing. Maggie, it turned out, had spent some time living in Catherine's hometown in England before her emigration to Spain. Maggie had a kind spirit. She asked no questions but seemed to know what Catherine and her unborn child needed. They bonded over unspoken troubled pasts, being alone, and spending their hard-earned money on imported English biscuits. *There is nothing that can't be dealt with by talking it through over a cup of a tea and a chocolate hobnob,* Maggie would say. Catherine smiled at the memory of Maggie with her never-ending words of wisdom. Maggie gave Catherine a place to stay and a job. She and Catherine didn't have family until they found each other. Anyone who didn't know their stories assumed they were grandmother and granddaughter. When Maggie passed away a few years earlier, she left the café to Catherine. It wasn't until Maggie died that Catherine learned her true story in a letter left with her will. Maggie was forced to leave her home in the coastal town of Plymouth in Devon after being a witness in a high-profile court case. She lived in the shadows in a witness protection programme for a few years before deciding to move to sunnier climes, where she bought the run-down café and turned it into the thriving business it was when Catherine walked through the door.

Catherine smiled at the picture of her and Maggie, taken many years before. It had pride of place behind the counter, their sun-kissed faces frozen in the laughter of a shared joke. When Josie was born, Maggie adopted the role of great-grandmother. Despite Catherine's good-natured protests about rotting her teeth and lack of adequate dental services in Europe, Maggie spoiled Josie with ice creams and cakes and all the imported English confectionary she could get her hands on. *It's good for her to have a taste of the culture of her home country,* Maggie would say with a twinkle in her eye. Josie's teeth were never a problem, and she and Maggie were as thick as thieves.

Catherine shook her head at the memories and deftly swept the café before filling the bucket with a strong citrus cleaner to mop the floor. Josie was out this evening, so she made sure to leave the chain off the door before she retired to the flat above the café. The stairs were dim, with just enough light coming from the nightlight on the landing to guide her way. Catherine slipped her shoes off and sighed as she wriggled her toes into her fluffy memory foam slippers. Putting the kettle on, she shuffled silently to Josie's room, where her grandson slept. At not yet two, Mateo's head was full of dark curls; his skin a deep olive complexion. His cheeky smile came from his father, but his nose and eyes were his mother's; and Patrick's. As Catherine pushed the door open, his gentle snoring caused her heart to contract. She leaned over the cot, unable to resist the urge to stroke his thick hair. His snore skipped a beat, and Catherine froze until he turned over and resumed his rhythmic snuffling. She retreated from the room and settled down on the old sofa, her legs curled up under her, with a cup of tea and a paperback book.

The little flat was full of bookshelves stuffed with battered paperbacks. Maggie used to say Catherine liked to rescue them. She once suggested Catherine get a Kindle. Catherine's eyes darkened, filled with memories. *I had one once; never again. Nothing beats the smell and feel of a real book*, Catherine responded firmly. And so, the paperback collection continued to grow.

A few hours after checking on Mateo, Catherine woke suddenly. She was still on the sofa; her book lay on the floor where it landed when she fell asleep, her tea cold. She blinked rapidly, looking around, her heart beating faster than it had been only moments earlier. Rubbing her eyes, she pulled herself to standing, expecting to hear Josie coming up the stairs any minute. She rolled her shoulders and gave her neck a rub; *she was too old to be falling asleep on the sofa.* The room was quiet, and there was no sign of Josie appearing. Catherine pulled her cardigan around her and shuffled down to the door, expecting to find Josie outside, having forgotten her key. The café remained in darkness, the glow of the chiller illuminating the shadows cast by the furniture. A steady ticking drew Catherine's eyes to the clock – before midnight. The café was just off the main street of Oliva, so it benefited from a steady flow of customers during the day, but they weren't disturbed by partygoers in the evening. Catherine unlocked the side door with a smile and glanced at the empty stoop. The side alley leading to their private door was deserted. She stepped back inside, pulling the door closed and automatically moved to check the café entrance, finding it locked. She yawned, rubbing her eyes and gave one last glance around the café, frowning as she spotted a book on the floor; the guidebook for England lay beside the bookshelf. She put it firmly back on the shelf with the other books, jumping at the knocking on the front door.

'I saw you lurking in the shadows, so thought I'd come in the front. What are you doing up?' Josie stepped into the café as Catherine held the door open to let her in. She gave her mum a peck on the cheek and pulled a takeaway container from her bag with a flourish, 'chips *and* a burger, want some?'

Catherine chuckled and shook her head. 'No, you enjoy it, love. Do you want a cuppa? I'll put the kettle on.'

Josie chattered about her night as she staggered up the stairs. Catherine sighed and scooped up the escaping chips that landed on the floor in her wake. Josie settled at the opposite end of the sofa to where Catherine slept earlier, tucking into her burger and animatedly filling Catherine in on what she and her friend Javi had been up to. Javi and Josie had grown up together. Javi's family owned a guest house in the village. Ever since they were little, they had been as thick as thieves. Catherine once hoped they would end up together, but Javi preferred his partners male. They were still as thick as thieves, and Catherine loved to hear about their adventures. She studied her daughter's features as she listened to her speak; she inherited her bone structure from her father's side of the family - the Walker nose and jawline; but the way her emotions lit her face up and shaped her expressions were from Catherine's side of the family.

'What?'

'What do you mean, what?'

'You were staring at me.'

Catherine laughed. 'I was thinking about how much you remind me of my mum sometimes. You have her energy and her facial expressions.'

'I wish we had more photos of her. We must go to England one day. We could do one of those online ancestry tests and find all sorts of long-lost relatives over there!'

'One day, mi vida, one day,' she said, adopting the Spanish term of endearment for her daughter, 'but now, it's late, and time for bed.' She swept the takeaway wrappers from the sofa and pushed them down into the bin, heading for her room, 'Good night.' She smiled softly at her daughter.

Catherine and Josie shared a room while Maggie was alive. The rooms were a good size, and Maggie suggested splitting theirs to give them each their own space, but they never minded. When Maggie died, Catherine moved into her room, and Josie now shared with her son, Mateo. They planned to finally split the second bedroom to give Mateo his own space. They got as far as choosing paint before realising neither of them quite knew where to start with building a partition wall, and that would need to be done before they could start painting, so the project hadn't quite gotten off the ground yet.

2
The Kindle

Josie appeared in the café looking sheepish mid-morning. She waved her hand at a couple of regulars who sat reading their morning papers with their breakfasts and greeted her mum, 'You should have woken me.'

Catherine waved her hand. 'Ah, you work hard. You deserve a lie-in now and then. When you are ready, though, Mateo could do with changing.'

Mateo was in the brightly coloured children's corner, his dark head down, tongue poking out, and a crayon in his hand. His eyes lit up as he heard Josie approaching. 'Mamá!'

Josie scooped Mateo up and carried him upstairs to change, returning ten minutes later in a coral-coloured sun dress with a big floppy sun hat, flip-flops and a seagrass tote over her shoulder. Mateo rested comfortably on her hip, his little fingers wrapped around her long beaded necklace. 'We are off to the beach with Javi. Do you need anything while we are out?'

'Oooh, perhaps a hunky Spaniard to whisk me off to a private island on his yacht?' One of the locals looked up from his paper, cleared his throat and winked at her. Catherine laughed, topping up his coffee.

'Yeh, alright, Mum,' Josie rolled her eyes, 'but do you need anything?'

'Actually, yes. Can you ask Javier if they can recommend someone to do the partition in your room, and I will give them a call later to get it started? Oh, and can you grab me a couple of touristy postcards to send to Pia, please. If you see any.'

'Done, and done. And don't let him hear you call him Javier! See you later.' Josie pushed the café door open and stopped, then closed the door and opened it again. 'Where's the bell, Mum?'

'Oh, I hadn't noticed! I don't know! I haven't taken it down; it must have fallen off. I'll have a look in a minute. You go on.' Catherine waved Josie off, looking around on the floor to see where the old cowbell had fallen. It was nowhere to be seen. She shrugged as a new customer entered, 'We do table service, so find a seat, and I'll bring you a menu,' Catherine instructed breezily, glancing around once more.

The café was busy throughout the morning, with a steady stream of customers. Oliva was not as busy as the nearby resorts of Benidorm and Alicante, but was still a popular tourist destination. Oliva was more laid back, with its white-washed buildings, pretty churches, and views of the mountains. It provided a charming and authentic taste of Spain. There was a good ex-pat community, but it retained its quaint Valencian attraction. The walk from the café to the beach could be done in 15 minutes, but beautiful views and orange groves challenged even the keenest beach-goer not to stop and appreciate the simple beauty. Catherine settled in Oliva because it served her purpose – it offered both anonymity and a sense of community. It was a wonderful place to raise Josie, a far cry from the metropolitan areas of Brighton & Hove. Catherine often pondered what their life would have been like if she stayed. *Would she have ever been able to leave? Would Josie have survived? Would*

Catherine have survived? Perhaps Patrick would have changed his ways once he became a father? As her mind drifted to these thoughts, Catherine felt the familiar pang of guilt at the *what ifs?* These thoughts intruded upon her mind less often these days, but they still lurked beneath the surface. Maggie would say, *you did what you had to do to survive, Pet. You can't worry yourself with What If? You have to look to the future now.*

Catherine wiped down the tables as the trade began to slow for the day. A movement outside the shop caught her eye, or rather, a lack of movement. The person stood on the corner of main street, facing the café. Catherine waved her hand in greeting to the tourist, who appeared to be holding a map. In a split second, they turned and melted into a passing crowd. Glancing at her watch, Catherine scanned the street for signs of Josie and Mateo. The spring weather was not too humid but was sunny nonetheless. Josie and Javi often made a pit stop at the café after the beach and would sit on the benches outside, enjoying the late afternoon sunshine. The sound of Mateo's laughter heralded their arrival.

'Nana!'

'Nene!' Catherine scooped Mateo into her arms, showering him with kisses. 'I missed you! Milkshake?'

'You spoil him, Mum.' Josie smiled.

'Did someone say milkshake?' Javi joined in the conversation.

'You guys go enjoy the last of the sun and I'll bring you out a round of milkshakes. Javier, if you are staying, I'm doing omelettes for dinner,' Catherine looked at her watch, 'they will be a few hours yet, though, if you guys can keep yourselves occupied.' She watched as Javi scooped Mateo into his arms and carried him out to the bench. The lack of bell was resoundingly loud in the quietening café.

Mateo was a surprise addition to the family. Catherine hadn't expected to be a grandparent when her daughter was still a teenager herself, but as Maggie used to say, *life is what you make it.* Much like Josie, despite the lack of family, the love Mateo was surrounded with by their little community more than made up for it. Mateo's father spent the summer in Oliva with his family. He was Josie's first love, a teenage romance. He neglected to mention to Josie that he already had a girlfriend at home in Madrid, a fact carefully concealed by his lack of online presence – this in itself should have rang alarm bells, but Josie was besotted. Catherine and her daughter, it turned out, both share the same poor taste in men, and he made it clear he wanted no part in Mateo's life, promptly blocking Josie's number. She never had his address. After a few hormonal months of crying and soul searching, she had no choice but to accept his decision. Javi stepped up and gave Mateo a male role model in his life. Catherine couldn't be prouder of how the teenagers had risen to the challenge and raised a beautiful toddler. Javier spoke to him in Spanish. He was already well on the way to being bi-lingual. Catherine watched her daughter laughing with Javi and Mateo and smiled. She was so mature in some ways, so responsible, but still only a child herself. Catherine had to remind herself of this at times.

Milkshakes delivered to their smiling and sun-kissed recipients; Catherine set about looking for the missing doorbell. She pulled out the umbrella stand to no avail and scratched her forehead, looking around. Distracted by the bookcase, Catherine spotted a Kindle nestled among the paperbacks. She pulled it from the shelf, looking inside the cover for a name or any indication of its owner. It was an old one, the same kind Patrick bought her. No matter how many years Catherine had been free from him, her memories still had the ability to trigger a racing heart and a rush of adrenaline. Catherine fell into the nearest seat, focusing on her breathing, a skill she picked up from reading about hypnobirthing in another life. She looked at the screen of the Kindle, her finger hovering over the on button, before snapping the cover shut and dropping it into the lost property box under the counter. As she did so, she spotted a bright blue and white scarf. Her heart began to race again as she pulled it from the box, the wool scratchy against her fingers. The sight of the seagull on the Brighton & Hove Albion scarf assaulted her senses, triggering the smells of the beach in England. She was sitting on the beach with Patrick, eating fish and chips, watching the seagulls as they screeched and swooped upon unsuspecting tourists, not quick enough to protect their chips.

'Mum? Mum, what's wrong? You look like you've seen a ghost. Actually, you look like a ghost; you are so pale!'

'Where did this scarf come from?'

'I dunno.'

'How did it get into the lost property box?'

Josie shrugged. 'Someone left it behind a couple of weeks ago. I chucked it in the lost property in case they came back.'

'Did you see who left it?'

'No. Why's it so important? What's wrong?'

'Nothing. I – I'm just being silly.' Catherine gripped the counter, her knuckles white. 'Ignore me. I'm just being paranoid. Old age is stirring up old memories in me.' She forced a laugh.

'Why don't you go upstairs and lie down? We can finish up here. It's not long until close anyway. I'll send Javi up with a cup of tea and a hobnob.'

Catherine nodded and let Josie take her hands from the counter. 'I'll be okay. I don't know what came over me. You go back out with the boys. I'll be fine.'

Josie's face was etched with concern, her brow furrowed. Catherine held up a hand, blocking any protest. 'Go on, off you go. Oh, did you get my postcards?'

'Balls. Completely forgot.'

'Well, that will keep you occupied until dinner. You can go grab them for me now. And don't say balls.'

'We don't mind!' one of the regulars chipped in, winking at Josie.

'Shush, you'. Catherine gave him a mock whip with the tea towel. 'Just because you have a mouth like an old English sailor, that doesn't mean I want my beautiful English Rose to have one.' She laughed and shoo-ed Josie out of the door.

3
The Bell

Catherine woke suddenly again. She looked around, her senses on wide alert, eyes quickly acclimating to the darkened room. The moonlight cast shadows through the gap in the curtain, giving every item of furniture a sinister appearance. She rolled out of bed and pulled on her dressing gown, reaching behind the curtain for the old cricket bat she kept there. Carefully creeping through the flat, stepping over the creakiest of floorboards and avoiding toys Mateo left on the floor, she paused at Josie's door. Straining in the silence, she moved to the top of the stairs, seeing nothing but the dim light of the chiller stretching across the linoleum floor beyond the hallway. Feeling for the wall, Catherine slowly edged her way down the stairs into the café. She held her cricket bat high, like a baseball player, ready for action.

'Mum!'

'Madre Mia! Josie!' Catherine lowered her weapon; it did nothing to slow the beating of her heart that was threatening to burst out of her chest.

'What on earth are you doing?' Josie laughed. 'Why are you wielding a cricket bat like an extra in a B-Movie?'

'I heard a noise and came to investigate. You gave me a fright. What on earth are you doing sneaking around in the middle of the night?'

Josie held up her fork. 'Busted. I couldn't sleep and was craving something sweet. All the good stuff is down here.' She pulled a second fork from the tray and passed it to Catherine. 'Join me for a moonlit gateau.'

The almost full moon was high in the sky, creating shadowy monsters in the street outside the café. Catherine moved closer to the door to look up at the bright yellow orb. The moon was the same wherever you were, but the stars – Catherine always thought the stars shone brighter in the Spanish sky. The sky, perfectly clear but for its shimmering moon and twinkling stars, reminded Catherine she was safe. She breathed in deeply, allowing her heart to return to its normal rhythm. She moved back to take a fork from Josie, and mother and daughter ate in silence; co-conspirators in the night.

~

No worse off for their nocturnal adventures, Catherine and Josie rose early, ready for a day's trade. Friday was the day the town would be busy with the weekly market, and the main road would be closed ready for stalls and tents to be erected. Tourists and locals would flock to the main street, eager to find a bargain. The market was diverse in its wares, and you might find anything in your shopping bag when you got home. Local vendors offered an array of fresh fruit and vegetables, all locally grown. The ripe oranges and lemons from the local groves would be sold fresh from the trees, baked into pies and cakes and even as juice drinks. Vendors travelled from further afield, offering handmade ceramic items and decorative pots. There were jewellery sellers with both used and new trinkets. There were also stalls selling beautiful handmade shawls and tablecloths. Along with the handmade items and homegrown produce, there were market stalls full of mass produced clothing. Tourists sifted through piles of fast fashion clothing, keen to pick up a bargain. The vendors were a mixed bag – some going for the hard sell and looking to bargain with tourists and locals alike, others would step back and let the customers browse at their leisure. Local tour companies brought tourists from Benidorm and Alicante. Catherine and Josie baked extra cakes and pies the day before to keep up with the extra footfall. They both loved the market, so they took it in turns to sneak out and have a look around.

Ready for the morning of baking ahead, Catherine passed Josie her apron from the hook by the kitchen and looped her own over her head before making her way to turn the sign on the door to open. They didn't officially open until 9.30 am, but didn't want to lose any opportunistic early trade when they were there baking anyway. As Catherine turned the sign to show they were open and unlocked the door, the slight tinkle stopped her. She frowned. The bell was hanging from the café door.

'So that's what you were really up to last night.'

'What?'

'You were putting the bell back. Ok, you got me. I looked everywhere for it!'

'What do you mean?'

Catherine faltered, 'The bell. It's back on the door. Didn't you put it there?'

'No. Why would I hide the bell?'

'Well, how did it get there then? Maybe Javier did it as a joke when he dropped you here last night. Ring him and check.'

'He won't be up yet. I'm sure one of the regulars just spotted it on the floor and hung it back up.'

'It wasn't there last night when I closed up.'

'You probably just didn't notice it. You weren't quite yourself yesterday afternoon.' Josie said gently.

'Don't do that.'

'What?'

'Make out I'm crazy. I know what I saw, and that bell wasn't there last night. Please, just give Javier a call.'

'Alright, alright.' Josie held her hands up, waggling her eyebrow at Catherine.

Catherine didn't move; staring at Josie until Josie pulled her phone from her apron pocket. They held eye contact as the phone rang, broken only when Javi's voice told them he was unable to get to the phone. Josie left a message asking him to call as soon as he was awake.

'Happy?'

'I will be when I find out how that bell got there. Maybe someone got in overnight… but I just unlocked the door. You saw me, didn't you? The door was locked.' Catherine moved to the side door, rattling the handle.

'Why would someone want to break in and return the bell?'

Catherine shrugged. She looked around the café for signs of an intruder. Everything was in its place. The scarf in the lost property box caught her eye. Snatching it up, she unlocked the side door and strode into the street, looking up and down, before stuffing it in the bin on top of yesterday's empty packets and cans.

'What the hell, Mum.'

'Right, we have baking to do. And watch your language.' Catherine said brusquely. They baked undisturbed, in companionable silence, until the regulars began to arrive for breakfast.

Catherine wasn't much of a cook until she met Maggie. She wasn't a bad cook or a bad baker, but she had never found enough joy in it to hone the skills. Everything changed when

Maggie gave her the job in the café. Catherine began by washing dishes and doing all she could to stay out of sight and avoid customers. As the weeks passed, her confidence grew along with her bump. Patrick was looking for a slim blonde, and Catherine was now a pregnant brunette. She began taking a few orders and gradually built up a rapport with the customers. As long as no one asked about home, Catherine blended in like she had been in Oliva all her life, apart from the Brighton accent. Whilst her confidence in the safe confines of the café grew, Catherine still rarely left the premises. The locals would try to coax her out to the markets or to see the beauty of the orange groves and the ruined castle that presided over the area. Her initial reaction of panic soon gave way to a practiced smile and a light-hearted quip to redirect the well-meaning individuals. From the safety of the café, she began to pick up bits of the local dialect, keen to learn some of the lingo. It was this desire to learn that eventually coaxed Catherine out into the Olivian sun. A retired school teacher who used to visit the café for 'cake and company' was the one to make it happen; *I teach you Spanish, non, not Spanish, I teach you Valencian, but only if you let me take you to the Castillo de Santa Ana. The castle at the top of the hill. The only way you can learn to speak our language is when you have truly appreciated the beauty of our country.* Catherine agreed to accompany María to the castle. No longer used to the exertion and carrying her Josie bump, Catherine puffed and panted her way up the hill. They reached the top, and Catherine bent over double, wiping sweat from her forehead. When she regained control of her breathing, she looked up and felt her breath taken away from her again. The castle provided views over the Olivian town, the old buildings linked together by winding roads and alleys. The orange groves and its trees connected the town to the beach in the distance. The sun bounced off the water, creating a glittering blue carpet beneath the skyline. The winding path that led them up above the village created a sea of colour; trees that flourished year-round and beautiful, vibrant pink Bougainvillea flowers. Catherine and María said nothing. The silence settled peacefully around them, and Catherine's hand rested on her stomach. From that day, Catherine began her Spanish lessons and her true immersion into the way of life. She spent hours with Maggie - watching her bake and digesting the methods and tricks to make the perfect lemon drizzle cake – now Catherine's speciality. She learned the knack of cinnamon rolls and breakfast pastries, and how to make traditional omelettes and paellas. Maggie watched Catherine, letting her join at her own pace and never asking anything from her. After work, Catherine began going for walks on her own, and Maggie later described to Catherine that this was when she saw the light appearing in Catherine's eyes. Catherine's skin glowed with pregnancy and the Spanish sun. It was soon time for Josie to be born. In the early days, if Catherine heard an unfamiliar voice, or a Brighton or London accent, she scurried to the back. Maggie would take over the tables without question.

The doorbell tinkled, announcing the arrival of María, who shuffled to her usual table.

'Hola, bon dia.' Catherine shouted in greeting. She immediately put down the napkins she was folding and poured a cup of strong coffee for María, putting it in front of her and exchanging pleasantries in Spanish.

'Just because you are speaking in Spanish, I still know when you are talking about me!' Josie interrupted.

'María was saying it isn't too late to teach you to speak Spanish.'

Josie held her hands up. 'I know, I know. I've been thinking about it more since Mateo started to learn. You'll be the first person I come to when I'm ready!'

A group of tourists pulled their attention back to the counter, and Josie busied herself handing out menus and taking orders. The group of girls were showing Josie the jewellery souvenirs they bought at the market, and Catherine began preparing homemade lemonade and tostadas.

'Mum, the girls are renting a villa and were asking about places to visit. I recommended the hot springs. They've asked me if I want to go with them. It might be fun?'

Catherine paused before answering. Josie didn't have many friends growing up. The local school was small, with some of the children travelling for up to an hour from villages surrounding Oliva. This, coupled with Catherine's wariness, meant she sometimes regretted that Josie never got to experience the joy of having a group of girlfriends. Javi to Josie was what Pia was to Catherine, but sometimes, life was more fun as a gang. She smiled. 'Why not?' and turned to the girls, 'Are you here alone or with parents?' Having ascertained they were on a parent-free girl's holiday, Catherine checked the details of the trip and made sure they all had her phone number before approving the plan. They were a little older than Josie and put Catherine's mind at ease.

'You must come by in the morning before you all head off and I'll have packed lunches ready for you all.' She smiled and hummed to herself as she returned to attend to the orders piling up.

4
The Earring

Pia was due to arrive in the next few days, and Catherine went into overdrive checking stock levels, scrubbing the café to within an inch of its life and double-checking shift rotas. They had a local girl who helped out two days a week and a couple of casual workers who would cover extra shifts to allow Catherine some time off with her friend. Her excitement, combined with recent events leaving her stomach twisted in knots, resulted in an emotional rollercoaster. Due to the size of the flat, Pia rented a room in Javi's family guest house. They were offered a reduced rate, and Catherine reminded herself she must take them a tray of cakes to show her appreciation.

After Patrick's death, Catherine's emotions spiralled. For all her anxieties when she first landed at Maggie's café, this was when she truly fell apart. Catherine kept an eye on English news, using a pay-as-you-go phone with a VPN to block all traces of her accessing the articles. She searched the Brighton Argus for any articles mentioning Patrick or his family. At first, the case of his missing wife had garnered not only local newspaper attention but the tabloids. After the first reported sighting of Catherine in France, some European papers also cashed in on the story. As time went by, the pictorial articles were reduced to a small mention on anniversaries or a paragraph when there was another article about Patrick. When he remarried, her picture became national news again, placed side by side with his new bride's smiling photo. Catherine was no longer painted as a lost soul; she was now cast as the one who abandoned him. And his new wife – she was the saviour who helped Patrick find love and happiness again. It was two years after Catherine's 'death' that the new Mrs Walker walked down the aisle. Upon seeing the article, Catherine ran to the bathroom and emptied her stomach contents. Her whole body shook as Maggie held her. *What if he does the same to her?*

During the years since she left, Catherine desperately missed Pia. They did everything together for as long as she could remember. The two of them were inseparable. Until Patrick. She followed Pia's career using the VPN. Pia still worked as an Editor. During the years they weren't in touch, Catherine bought everything that credited Pia as an Editor. This raised Maggie's eyebrows more than a few times – there was the time Catherine received a delivery with a book on tantric sex and the autobiography of a Brighton drag queen; she quite enjoyed that one, and one on the history of Dartmoor. Catherine devoured them all. The knowledge that Pia had read the same words made her feel closer to her estranged friend. If Maggie ever spotted the connection between the books, she never said. Catherine found the tantric sex book in Maggie's room after she passed.

It wasn't until after Patrick's death that Catherine felt able to reach out to Pia. An email to which she received an almost instantaneous response accusing her of being a fraud and a fake, followed by the blocking of her email address. Catherine debated her next steps for a few days before declaring to Maggie she had to try phoning Pia. True to form, Maggie gave no judgement and no opinion. She simply smiled, her wrinkles deepening with sincerity. By now, Catherine was familiar with every comforting line, crease, and expression on Maggie's face. The first time she called Pia, Pia told her to *fuck off and leave me alone.* Catherine looked at the phone, then bent over double laughing, tears streaming down her face. Maggie looked on, bemused. 'She hasn't changed a bit,' declared Catherine. The next attempt, she managed to get Pia to listen long enough to hear her voice.

The emotions ran high in those first weeks of contact - they hit every cliché on the rollercoaster. They cried, they talked, they cried some more. Sometimes, Pia shouted and hung up. The Catherine that left would have called and called, pleading. Catherine was older and wiser. She waited, giving Pia the space and time she needed. She cried her tears of helplessness to Maggie; held her until the tears dried up, and she was ready for a cup of tea and a greedily large plate of chocolate hobnobs. The first time, it took a few days and a few more packets of biscuits before Pia broke the silence and reached out to Catherine. Their initial contact remained tentative, terse at times; Catherine's interactions with those around her swung from elation at having her friend back in her life to the anxiety of being found. She would be serving a customer with a smile and then suddenly have the breath knocked out of her at the thought of Patrick or his family finding her. Finding out about Josie. Pia didn't ask Catherine where she was, and Catherine didn't volunteer the information until a year later. By this point, Catherine and Pia were texting and speaking as if they had never been apart. The drawn-out trial for Patrick's murder passed, and the headlines died down. They didn't discuss Patrick - that came later. Catherine didn't tell Pia about Josie, not yet. The first time they met up, Catherine travelled to Alicante. They had been before when they were younger. It felt nice to be reminded of their old memories, but they were both hyper-aware of how much had changed.

The first time Pia came to Oliva was five years after Catherine's 'death'. The first time she met Maggie, Pia hugged her as if she would never let her go; an immediate bond formed. The first time she met Josie, Pia swore. Josie took some time to warm to Pia after this. Pia explained to Catherine she was not prepared for how much of Patrick she would see in Josie's face.

Nearly 20 years after Catherine left the UK, and Pia was a regular visitor to Oliva. Catherine couldn't risk a return to the UK or for anyone else to know she was alive. It broke her heart, asking Pia to keep the secret from her family, but Catherine didn't trust Patrick's family not to look for her. She never said it out loud, but she still couldn't quite believe he was dead. Each time Pia visited, Catherine's eyes searched the streets, her senses on high alert for anything out of place or anyone unusual – worrying Pia was followed. She never saw anything - until these last few weeks.

The day of Pia's arrival, Catherine was assembling a welcome hamper of local goodies in the café when she spotted the book on the table again. Her forehead wrinkled as she recognised it as the English guidebook. There was something on top of it. Catherine picked up the small item and held it in the palm of her hand. The light danced off the many flat edges of the multi-faceted earring. She let out her breath with a rush of air and dropped it as if it burned her hand. Catherine dropped into the nearest chair, her heart pounding, threatening to burst out of her chest. The silence in the closed café was stifling, and she struggled to catch her breath. The safe familiarity of the café dissipated - the counter now yielded a hiding place for an intruder, the stairway to the flat was a lair to lure Catherine to, and the glass windows with the pretty views now left her exposed, visible for anyone to see. Catherine remembered the day Patrick gave her the earrings; it was after he sent his assistant, Elsie, to take her shopping for a suitable wardrobe. He gave her the earrings to go with her new clothes. She looked down where the earring landed on the old tiled floor and back at the book on the table. Snatching it up, she flipped open the cover and scanned the first page for a clue, then spotted the post-it note sticking out of the book. She flipped to the marked page and gasped; Brighton.

5
Theories

'What's wrong?' Pia took the metro from the airport to Valencia and a train to Gandia, where Catherine picked up her to make the short journey to Oliva itself. As soon as Pia sat in the car and clicked her seatbelt in, she picked up on Catherine's demeanour. Glancing sideways at Catherine, she noticed her friend's teeth clenched and saw the lines in her forehead. 'Come on. This is me. You know you can tell me anything.'

'It's Patrick. He's back.'

Pia took a deep breath. Then pursed her lips as she considered her response.

'He's back, Pia. He's back, and he's come for me.' Catherine's hands gripped the steering wheel as she spoke, her knuckles white. Her voice increased a few octaves as she spoke again, the words tumbling out at speed. 'He's coming for us, and he knows about Josie, and he is going to take her from me. She will hate me forever.'

'Pull in as soon as you can; Oliva can wait. I think we need to stop and talk. Somewhere we won't be known, somewhere with a bar.'

'No. We need to get back. I won't be driven away from my home again. Or should I? Should I run? Maybe I should just find somewhere new. What should I do? What if he has found me, Pia?

Pia covered her friend's hand on the gear stick and squeezed. 'I don't know what's happened, but we will get through this. We will.'

They sat in silence for the rest of the journey, Pia stealing glances at her friend, who stared straight ahead. Leaving the parked car at an angle, they grabbed Pia's bags and hurried up the alley to the side door and straight up to the flat. Catherine moved from room to room before closing the door at the top of the stairs and turning the rarely used lock.

'What about Josie?'

'She won't be back until late; she's out with friends. Mateo is with Adriana for the night – I think you met her last time?' Pia nodded. Catherine moved to the kitchen, stretching up and pulling a box from atop the cupboards. She systematically laid the items on the coffee table; the guidebook, the earring – now housed in a small plastic pot, the Kindle, the scarf she had retrieved from the bin. 'Look at these things; someone has been leaving them for me. The book, look at the book.' Catherine's voice became raised, in pitch and volume, as she pushed the book into Pia's hands, open at the marked page. 'The bell, the noises. Someone has been in the café putting this book on the table for me to find. They took the bell from the door; I lost my mind wondering where it was, and then they put it back.'

Pia frowned, looking at Catherine. 'Sit down. Let me make us both a drink, and we can talk it through.' Pia glanced at the items, recognising the scarf, having seen similar flapping around the necks of many football fans over the years. She moved to the kitchen, putting the kettle on and methodically searching the cupboards for biscuits before giving up and unzipping her suitcase. 'Ta-da!' she winked at Catherine, brandishing the packet of chocolate digestives. 'Honestly, you move to another country with all their wonderful foods, and *then* you develop an obsession with English biscuits.'

Catherine risked a smile. 'Blame Maggie.' Her voice caught in her throat as she said Maggie's name.

'You really lucked in with her, huh? I still wish you would have spoken to me before leaving. I could've helped, found a way to get you out of there.' Catherine sighed as Pia spoke. 'I know, I know, but there must have been a way. You shouldn't have had to give up your whole life.'

'He would have killed us both. You didn't live my life, Pia. There are things you don't know, things no-one knows. No-one ever really knows what goes on behind closed doors.'

'That's my point, I *should* have known. I knew he was a dickhead, but I didn't realise to what extent. When I saw those bruises on your body in the hospital that time… I should have pushed you to talk to me.'

'There's no point going over this. It's done. And I didn't give up my life. I love my life here, and I'm so grateful for meeting Maggie.' She saw Pia bristle. 'Of course, I missed you and your family, but it was safer for everyone this way.'

'I went to your funeral, Cat.'

'I know. I'm sorry.' Catherine looked down, reaching out for a biscuit from the packet and nibbling at it. Pia handed her a cup of tea, and she dunked the biscuit, opening her mouth and fitting the whole biscuit in, leaving streaks of chocolate on her lips. They made eye contact and burst into laughter.

'I'm sorry. I know it was hard for you. It's just – fuck, it was hard for me. So hard for me. And that box you left with your mum's dress for me to look after. It all makes sense now. Anyway, it's done now. What's going on with you? This isn't like you.'

Catherine spoke, an outpouring of the series of events – being woken in the night, the objects reminding her of Brighton and the feeling of being watching. Pia listened, really listened. She didn't say a word, just let Catherine explain her feelings. 'It all sounds so silly hearing myself say it out loud. I feel so foolish, but I just can't shake the feeling that someone's out to get me.'

'Let's think about this rationally. Not that you aren't already rational, but we need to look at it from all angles. Who would want to harm you? Have you fled from any other husbands?' Catherine gave Pia a wry smile. 'Too soon?' Catherine allowed herself a brief grin. 'Ok. So there are no other husbands and no-one that you've fallen out with?' Catherine shook her head. 'And we know Patrick is dead. There is only one explanation!'

'There is?'

'Yes! It's his ghost. He has unfinished business and has come to haunt you because you are living a good life without him.'

'Very funny. Maybe he faked his death.' Pia looked at her. 'Okay then, what about Max or someone else in his family?'

'Dick and Myra can't be particularly agile these days. They weren't exactly spritely back in the day, let alone twenty years later – that's if they are even still alive. And even if they did manage to track you down, I can't see them pulling off undercover tactics like hiding books and making noises in the night. This is all probably just a weird coincidence.'

Catherine's shoulders dropped as she let out a breath. 'I'm being paranoid, aren't I?'

'I don't want you to be going through this and feeling like you are going mad or paranoid. Equally, I don't want it to be real. I don't know what to think, but I honestly don't see Dick and Myra coming over here to scare you, and Max always liked you. Don't you remember how jealous Patrick was when Max danced with you at your wedding?'

'He never liked it that me and Max got on. You're right. It's nothing. Thousands of people have earrings like that, and there are guidebooks for so many countries on that shelf. I'm sorry.'

She brushed the crumbs off her lap, where she sat on the sofa. 'This is your holiday, and you have been met with a rambling, suspicious, biscuit monster. I should be greeting you with an Agua de Valencia, not raiding your luggage for snacks before you even make it to the guest house.' Catherine swallowed and forced a smile. 'My emotions are like Jekyll and Hyde these days.'

'It's not too late. Let's down these cups of tea and show the town we're still young.' She slurped her tea and took Catherine's empty cup, passionately singing the words to Love is a Battlefield. She turned and stopped mid-serenade at the sight of Catherine standing in a floppy hat, with a bikini top hanging around her neck, a bottle of wine in her hand and a small suitcase beside her.

'Surprise! I booked a room for two. It's gunna be just like old times!'

Pia shrieked and began singing another 80s hit. Her singing was interrupted by the doorknob rattling. Both she and Catherine screamed.

'Why's the door locked?' Josie shouted from the hallway, rattling the handle again.

Catherine and Pia unfroze, making eye contact as they let out their breaths. Catherine unlocked the door and swept her arm theatrically, summoning Josie in. 'You're back early?'

'Wasn't feeling well, so came back to have a bath and get some rest. Why are you guys acting weird? Why was the door locked?'

Catherine and Pia looked at each other and burst into laughter.

'God, you two are so embarrassing. I'm going to my room.'

~

Pia and Catherine checked in at Javi's and planned to walk up to the castle. Catherine stashed the bottle of wine she was still clutching in her seagrass tote, along with the plastic tooth mugs from the room and the crisps and dips from the welcome basket she had made for Pia. They gulped bottles of water as they climbed the dry dusty path, their talk waning as the incline increased. As they reached a rest stop, they paused to admire the view. The sun sparkled in the distance, and they debated what to do the next day before silence fell once more as they continued their ascent. Upon reaching the summit, they made their way around the derelict walls and found a sunny spot to set up their picnic. There was a light breeze on the hill, and they drank their wine from plastic cups, catching up on each other's lives, the earlier worries forgotten for now.

'When are you working this week?'

'I forgot to tell you – I managed to get cover for the whole week, so I'm all yours! Beach tomorrow, then I thought we could go out to the hot springs one day. I have a couple of spa passes for the Playa de Pechuán as well.'

'Ooh, is that the posh hotel down by the beach.'

'Yup. We can use the pool and all the facilities, and we have a massage each. The other days, we can just see how we feel.'

'What day's the market? I want to make sure I go to it again; I want to get some gifts to take back for everyone. They seem to think I have a secret boyfriend out here that I visit each year! They keep threatening to tag along.' Pia glanced at Catherine. 'Don't worry, I won't let them. They still don't know you are alive.'

Catherine hesitated, recent events still playing on her mind. She swallowed. 'I miss them. I know I get to see photos and hear your updates, but it's not the same. Do you think they could ever forgive me?'

'I *know* they would forgive you. They would just be so relieved that you are alive. They all went to your memorial service. Patrick made sure the wake, or whatever you call it when it's a memorial, was family only, but at least they got to go to the memorial. Although I know they would be happier still to know you are alive.'

'Maybe. Maybe I'm being over-cautious. Look at the mess I got myself into earlier. I need to move on. Patrick's dead.' Catherine's voice grew firmer. 'Patrick is dead! He can't hurt me anymore.' She smiled and tapped her plastic cup against Pia's.

'Yes, Girl!'

'Ok. Let's do it.' Catherine drew a deep breath in. 'Let's plan it. Bring them with you on your next visit.'

'All of them?!'

'Yes! We can book one of the holiday chalets down by the beach – some have housekeeping and a private pool. It'll be the perfect way to get to know each other again.'

~

The following day was spent at the beach, talking and planning the rest of the week. Patrick's name wasn't mentioned again. The items Catherine had been collecting as evidence of someone out to get her had gone when she popped back to the flat; she suspected Pia had put Josie up to that. Their time together flew by, and it was soon time to drop Pia at the airport.

'I love you.'

'I love you more.'

'Don't fake your death again.'

'Don't make me want to.'

Catherine and Pia hugged, exchanging familiar words and laughing. 'Right, let me go. I need to pee, and you are squeezing me tight enough that I might wet myself.' Pia pulled away from Catherine and picked up her case. 'Love you, Girl.'

Catherine watched Pia's back as she dragged her case through the glass doors into the airport, disappearing amongst the other travellers. A flight must have not long landed; Catherine could always spot the arrivals from England when she dropped Pia at the airport. Their pale skin and look of desperation when they saw there was little more than a coach trip between them and the beach gave them away. Catherine had spent almost as much of her life in Spain as England, and most of her adult life. The airport reminded her of what she left behind and the life she could have ended up with. Her skin had acclimatised over the years; the year-round tan kept it glowing and youthful. This was a life she couldn't have dreamed of growing up – she certainly wouldn't have ever left her life in England to try it, even if she never met Patrick. As Catherine stood by the car, it occurred to her that if it wasn't for Patrick, she wouldn't have this life she loved at all. She shuddered at the realisation. Suddenly cold and uncomfortable, Catherine let Josie know she was heading back to the café.

6
The Unlocked Door

Catherine finished cleaning the counter top and wiped her hands on her apron before tapping out a text to Josie suggesting they eat out at one of the local restaurants that evening. In the days since Pia's departure, Catherine had been busily catching up on supply orders and banking. The little café ran well without her, but there were always things that only she could do. Catherine had been working hard to put some money aside to make some improvements to the café, and she looked around, appraising the décor. The café was stuck in a time warp, and they hadn't changed much since Maggie died; a combination of finances and respect for Maggie, but it was time to start putting their own stamp on things. The decision to have Pia's family visit had got Catherine thinking it was high time that she and Josie put themselves out there. She had lived in a shadow for nearly 20 years, and it was time to let go of the past. Catherine's phone chimed, a reply from Josie suggesting they eat at Grub. A restaurant owned by ex-pats - Grub was popular with tourists, locals and ex-pats alike. It served traditional English pub grub – lasagne, bangers and mash, ham, egg and chips, with desserts such as trifle and Eton mess. Catherine rolled her eyes. Josie loved Grub. When she was little, Catherine tried to avoid talking about England with her. She later regretted keeping her heritage from her, and it soon became a ritual for Maggie and Josie to go to Grub once a week. Maggie would fill Josie's head with stories about England, fuelling a fascination for Josie to dream of visiting. Catherine occasionally joined them. When Maggie died, the tradition died with her, but they still tried to go when they could.

They closed the café early once a week – another tradition from when Maggie was alive. They would use the early finish to spend quality time together, just the three of them. They often went on little road trips to neighbouring towns and villages, to the beach or walking in the orange groves. There were a couple of donkeys in the olive groves, and Josie loved to pet them. Despite their stereotypically grumpy reputation, these donkeys knew how to get attention and loved an ear rub in exchange for a carrot. As Josie got older, she went off and did her own thing, and Catherine and Maggie would sit and put the world to rights. Today, Catherine planned to catch up on paperwork. She looked towards the main street, watching the steady stream of people going about their day. It was cool standing beside the chiller fridge, and Catherine rubbed her arms - *perhaps a cup of tea and biscuit watching the passers-by before making a start on the paperwork.*

~

Dinner at Grub lived up to their expectations. The popular restaurant was always busy with a lively atmosphere, even for the early dinner crowd. Adriana and her partner, Carmen, were already seated and waiting to order. They made space on their table, and Josie, Catherine and Mateo joined them. Adriana and Mateo high-fived, and he abandoned his mother for their friend.

'Little traitor,' Josie laughed.

'What can I say? My girlfriend is the toddler whisperer! Hopefully, it won't be too long before we have our own little cariño.' Carmen squeezed Adriana's hand; her eyes filled with love as they made eye contact.

'Wait – you're not –'

'No, no, no. We are, how you say in English?' Carmen looked to Adriana.'

'Adopting, adoptando. Nothing is final yet, but hopefully it won't be too long. Who knows, maybe we will end up with a little one the same age as Mateo. Wouldn't that be fun?'

After dinner, Mateo fell asleep in his buggy, and they walked home, chatting in hushed tones, careful not to wake him. The air was warm, starting to heat up before the summer, and the sound of chicharras chirping gave a vibrant foreground to the music and voices drifting from various gardens and eateries.

'You forgot to turn the sign to closed.'

'Whoops! I'm sure I did, although I think anyone walking past can tell we aren't there.' Catherine veered toward the main door to change it.

'I know, I know, but it has our opening times on it.'

As Catherine opened her mouth to reply, she stopped.

'What?'

'The door. It's open.'

What do you mean it's open?'

'It's not locked. I definitely locked it. Wait out here with Mateo while I go inside and look around. Have you got your phone on you?'

'Don't be daft. You probably just forgot to lock it.'

'I didn't forget to lock it.'

'You forgot to turn the closed sign.'

'Yes, but I know I locked the door.' Catherine stepped into the empty café. Nothing looked out of place, but the silence was deafening. Something felt amiss, but she couldn't put her finger on it. The rhythmic sound of the buggy wheels on the floor caused her to whirl around.

'You keep an eye on Mateo and make sure he doesn't wake up. I'll run upstairs and check everything to put your mind at ease.' Josie gave her mum's arm a squeeze and moved to the dark doorway leading to the flat.

Catherine pulled a chair out and sat beside the buggy, her hand resting on the edge, with one finger gently stroking her grandson's little hand. Her heart rate gradually slowed and aligned with his gentle snoring. Josie thundered back down the stairs, declaring everything was fine, forgetting Mateo was sleeping. He lifted his head, his sleepy eyes looking around; his surroundings different from where he fell asleep. As he screwed his face up and opened his mouth, Catherine scooped him into her arms, uttering soothing sounds. She followed Josie up the stairs to the flat and handed the sleeping toddler to her daughter.

~

'Mum, I'm worried about you.' Josie put a cup of tea on the bedside table, watching as Catherine ran the straighteners over her wayward hair.

'Me? Why would you be worried about me? I'm fine.'

'You don't seem yourself lately. Freaking out over the scarf the other week, forgetting to lock the door. I didn't want to say anything when Pia was here, but I am worried about you.'

Catherine clicked off the straighteners and pulled the plug out of the wall, propping the hot irons on top of the metal radiator. 'You don't need to worry about me. I'm fine. Although it is weird that the door was unlocked last night.'

'Exactly. Who else would have left it open? I just don't want you taking on too much. We can get some more shifts covered, give some more hours to the casual staff. You don't have to do everything.'

'I don't know, but I know it wasn't me.' Catherine patted Josie and leaned down to kiss her on the head. She grabbed the tea and headed for the door. 'I'll go on down and get the coffee machine on. The regulars will be setting off soon, heading our way.' Catherine got halfway down the stairs before her nose wrinkled. When she got to the bottom of the stairs, the smell was unmistakable. She put her cup of tea on the side, not caring as the hot liquid sloshed over the edges, forming a pool on the table, and rushed to the source of the smell – the chiller cabinet. 'No! No, no, no, no, no.' Catherine's eyes went to the wire and moved along until it reached the plug socket at the wall – only it didn't. The plug lay on the floor in front of the socket. As she plugged it back in, Josie appeared.

'What's that smell?!'

Catherine indicated the chiller cabinet as she crouched to plug it back in. With a sigh, she began taking out the cakes and creamy desserts ready to bag up and dispose of. 'Can you get the doors opened to get some air circulating and maybe bring down the fans from upstairs.' Josie hesitated as if to say something. Catherine took charge, 'Now, please.'

Customers began trickling in, initiating a break in the tense silence to exchange pleasantries and encourage them to take their drinks to the outside seating. Catherine wrote a list of produce and ingredients they needed to buy in, and asked Josie to pop to the wholesalers. María shuffled into the café, the tinkling bell heralding her arrival. Catherine hurried to pull out a chair at her favourite table.

'You might want to sit outside today. The smell has nearly gone, but we had a problem with the chiller overnight, and the place was stinking this morning.'

María smiled, her eyes crinkling at the corners. 'I'd rather be in here with you, churri. Just a coffee, por favor. Do you have time to sit and have one of your English teas with me?'

Catherine looked at the clock, the baking equipment laid out ready to restock the counter and the empty chiller, then back at María's hopeful face. Her shoulders dropped, and she smiled at the older woman. 'Of course, que tal, how are you?'

The two old friends drank their respective drinks and caught up in a mixture of Spanish and English. Catherine filled María in the events of the previous night.

'But, churri, we are all forgetful sometimes.' She patted Catherine's hand.

'I'm not forgetful, and I didn't unplug the chiller.' Catherine immediately regretted her sharp tone. 'I'm sorry, I just feel like I am going mad. I know I didn't unplug it, and I know I locked the door, but why would someone break in and unplug the chiller?'

'There is an old saying, hay un cierto placer en la locura, que solo el loco conoce.'

'There is a certain pleasure in madness that only the madman knows?'

The older woman nodded as the bell tinkled, and Josie backed into the café laden with bags. Catherine rushed to take some from her, carrying them straight to the kitchen area to unpack. She re-tied her apron and started stacking the ingredients they needed for baking on the counter top.

'Right, María, muchas gracias for the chat, but we have cakes to create. Can I get you a top up before the mayhem starts?'

'No, I am going to walk up to the castillo.' Catherine frowned. The older woman was still active for her age, but Catherine worried about her walking up the hill on her own. 'Don't you pull that face, young lady; I have been walking up that hill since before you were born. And you,' she turned to Josie, 'go easy on your mother. Everything is not always what it seems.'

Catherine smiled at her gratefully. 'Well, come by for a drink when you get back down. We might even have some of your favourite almond and olive oil cake for you by then.' She winked as María stood to leave, 'adéu'.

Earlier tension dissipated as Catherine and Josie worked to bake and create food to fill the counter; almond and olive, magdalenas, fartons – pastry fingers designed to be dipped in a nutty drink. Maggie had always stocked a traditional Victoria sponge as a nod to her heritage, and they kept this going. The ex-pat community loved being able to get sweet treats for a taste of their homeland. It was a careful balance to make sure the stock was a balance of pastries, cakes and cream cakes that attracted natives, ex-pats and tourists.

'Did I tell you Pia is going to bring her family over?'

'No, that's great. I'd love to meet more people who knew you when you lived in England. I still don't see why we can't go and visit them. Whatever you were running away from 20 years ago, surely it's been long enough.'

'Don't start going down that road again. One day, I'll tell you everything, but I can't go back there.'

'I know, I know, cue cryptic excuses and a promise to tell me more, that will never happen.' Josie rolled her eyes.

'You don't know what my life was like.'

'No, I don't, because you won't tell me, Mum!'

'Let's focus on the positive that Pia's family will hopefully visit.'

'Is that what all this is about? Is that why you are being forgetful and twitchy? Are you nervous about speaking to them again? What did they do that made you abandon them.'

'They didn't do anything. It wasn't them. It will be so lovely for you to meet them. When my parents died, Pia and her family looked after me. I had my grandmother for a few years, but when she died… well, they are my family. We talked about renting a chalet down by the beach.'

'Oooh, can we get one of the posh ones with the private pool?'

'Oh yes, we will be going all out.' Catherine laughed at her daughter's excitement.

'I keep telling Javi I only made friends with him as I thought his parents' place had a private pool we could use. By the time I found out it doesn't, it was too late.'

'Lesson learner, next time, do your research before you extend the hand of friendship!' Catherine's tone became serious, 'You have a good friend there, though. I am so pleased you had a happy childhood. You did have a happy childhood, didn't you?'

'Of course I did.' Pia wrapped her arms around her mother's waist for a hug.

'María is right, though; I should have made sure you learned Spanish properly. I am not sure how I managed to raise such an English rose when you have never set foot in the country, but I wouldn't have you any other way.'

'What's that? I heard my name.'

'Perfect timing, María! Slice of almond and olive oil?'

7
Hove, actually

Market day was busy, but not so much that Catherine and Josie weren't able to step away from the café to browse what was on offer. Catherine returned from her walk with some earrings from a designer who lived between Oliva and the nearby coastal village of Bellreguart. Her unusual jewellery attracted people from many neighbouring towns and villages, keen to purchase one of her unique designs. Catherine held up the pair of sea glass earrings for Pia's birthday.

'What's in the other bag?'

Catherine held up a large Cornish pasty. 'It's the visit from Pia, I think. And the excitement of seeing her family again soon. I've started craving things I haven't missed for years!'

'Either that or you're pregnant!' Josie quipped.

'Ha! Why would I want any other children when the one I have is perfect?'

'Kiss-ass. Is it my turn to go shopping now?'

'Go on then, off you go. What time is Adriana dropping Mateo back?'

'I said I'd let her know when I have escaped and meet her at the market.'

'Escaped? How rude!'

Josie untied her apron and dropped it on the counter, where it fell to the floor as she slipped out from behind the counter. Catherine picked it up from where it landed and hung it up, taking her own from the peg next to it and fastening it around her waist. They each had their own apron hook with their name above it – a gift from Josie for Mother's Day last year. They always celebrated Mother's Day on the fourth Sunday of Lent, as per UK tradition, until Mateo came along. El dia de la Madre was traditionally on the first Sunday in May, and Josie chose to celebrate Mother's Day with Mateo, then to celebrate his Spanish heritage. Both UK and Spanish Father's Days went without celebration. Olivia often had events and offers on for both dates for Mother's Day, given the large ex-pat community, and the town's penchant for using an excuse to have celebrations and get togethers.

This was something Catherine loved about Oliva. There were times when the UK came together to celebrate, usually bank holiday weekends when the entire nation went out drinking, but generally, the English kept themselves to themselves. At first, Catherine saw this sense of community, this knowing of each other's business as a threat to her anonymity, but she soon saw the caring and support that this group of people had for each other and was welcomed as one of their own. Many neighbours knew Catherine's past hadn't been straightforward but no longer questioned it. She got the occasional questions when asked why she wasn't on social media or why they didn't have pictures of staff on the café website – but Catherine remained steadfast in her objections that not everyone had to live their life on social media; Maggie was the same. Catherine did allow Josie to have social media when she was old enough. It was the cause of many sleepless nights and discussions with Maggie. She didn't want Josie to be different from her peers, but she had to understand the risks. Josie followed the rules; not without rolling her eyes at her mother whenever the subject came up. They had an agreement in the early days that Catherine would look at the profile of anyone who requested to follow or make friends with Josie on social media. Now, Catherine trusted her to be aware of the risks of social media – as much as she could when Catherine didn't tell her the full story.

A few years ago, a magazine did a feature of the town. The travel photographer spent a week enjoying the city and immersing himself in the culture. He photographed the café, and Catherine made it clear no photographs of her were to be included in the article. Josie kept an eye out for the photos on their Facebook page, excited to see the café and spotted the photograph with Catherine in the background. After numerous lengthy calls with the magazine's editor, who said it was too late to pull it from print, followed by threats of legal action from Catherine and Maggie, the magazine agreed to remove the photo with Catherine. They since turned down any promotional opportunities, choosing to advertise locally instead.

Josie left the café with a tinkling of the bell, leaving Catherine with a steady flow of customers to tend to. Catherine knew she was lucky to have the relationship she did with Josie, but also knew she must have a chat with Josie at some point about spreading her wings if she wanted to. Just because Catherine loved this café, she didn't want Josie to feel obliged to work there. She was a smart girl; she came from a bloodline rich with Judges, even if she didn't know it.

As trade began to slow for the day, Josie, Mateo and Adriana appeared at the window. Mateo, having been lifted out of the buggy whilst Josie folded it up, was pressing his nose on the glass window and pulling faces at Catherine. Catherine laughed, waggling her eyebrows and sticking her tongue out in playful retaliation. As they all swept into the café, she scooped Mateo up in her arms, smothering him with kisses and spinning him around.

'Yaya! Yaya!' Mateo giggled with joy, shouting Grandma in his native tongue as she twirled him in the air.

Setting him down, Catherine noticed Mateo holding something tightly in his small hand. Seeing her eyes on his hand, he proudly presented the package to her.

'What have you got there, Nene?' Catherine took the little package. 'Is this a present for Yaya?' Mateo nodded, smiling. Catherine looked at the paper packet and then at Josie, who shrugged and continued her conversation with Adriana. For reasons unknown, Catherine's heart pounded with anticipation as she unfolded the wrapping until she held a hanging ceramic ornament in her hand. She gasped as she turned it over, revealing the words, 'Hove, Actually.' The ornament clattered to the floor as Catherine's hands shook.

'No like?' Mateo looked at the floor with concern.

Catherine looked at her grandson's innocent face and breathed deeply, willing the dizziness to pass.

'What's wrong, Mum? You look like you've seen a ghost.'

'I think I have. Where did that come from?'

'I don't know. Adriana, did you give it to him?' Adriana confirmed she hadn't, and he hadn't had it just before meeting Josie, so she assumed Josie gave it to him. The three women turned to look at Mateo. 'Mateo, bebé, where did the present come from?'

'Lady.'

'What lady?'

'Lady say give to Yaya.' Mateo's eyes filled with tears.

'It's okay, Bébé, don't cry. We just want to know who gave you the lovely present?' Josie scooped Mateo into her arms, wiping his cheeks and bopping his nose with her forefinger.

Catherine took a couple of shaky breaths before fixing a smile on her face. She clapped her hands. 'Right, I have a couple more hours to do down here, but I think I might know some people who would like milkshakes!' She scooped up the ornament, dropping it into her pocket and headed behind the counter, pulling ingredients out to prepare drinks. Upset quickly forgotten, Mateo's face lit up, and he struggled down from his mother's arms to wait by the counter for his milkshake.

~

Café closed for the day, chairs up and everything restocked for the morning, Catherine sat and pulled the ornament out of her pocket. She looked at the door to the flat and paused, listening. Confident she was alone, Catherine ran her fingers over the ceramic surface, feeling the bumps where the text stood out on the flat background. It was warm in her hands. Memories flooded her thoughts; the wedding and the way Patrick looked at her when they first met. How safe she felt when she was first with him, and how proud she was to become Mrs Walker. The house was luxurious compared to her life before, and she had felt she finally had a purpose. That wasn't why she married him - she loved him, and she believed he loved her. Thinking of their wedding day, she remembered her pride as she walked up the aisle towards his handsome face. She smiled at the memory of Max's supportive arm linked through hers as he walked her up the aisle – he was so careful, worrying he would stand on her dress. The dress. Catherine squeezed her eyes shut, gripping the ornament tightly in her hand. *When did it all go wrong?* She gave so many years of her life to him – not just the years they were married, but the years after. Even after hearing of his death, she never truly felt free. He still managed to consume her thoughts at times. He always told her she could never escape him – she thought by physically leaving, she had, but he was right; he would always have some power over her. A single tear rolled down her cheek at the realisation.

Catherine looked down at her white knuckles gripping the little plaque. As she loosened her hold, she thought back to the day she bought it, newly married and full of life – a life worlds away from her life today. She remembered the shop with the cashmere scarves, running them through her hands and using the credit card Patrick gave her, the one embossed with Mrs Walker, to buy one of the beautiful creations, the scarf she left at Beachy Head a few years later. Her thoughts turned to the day she left; the windy day that would have otherwise been a wild and beautiful coastal visit, and the nauseating fear for the days that followed. She folded the ornament into a paper bag and tucked it into the bottom of the lost property box. The shrill sound of her phone ringing in her pocket made Catherine jump. She glanced at the screen, *Pia.* Taking a deep breath, she pressed the green button.

'Hola.'

'What's wrong?'

'Hello to you too. What do you mean, what's wrong?'

'Your voice sounds funny. I've known you long enough to know when something's wrong.'

'Ugh. It's just. No. It doesn't matter.'

'Don't do that. This is me. Has something else happened with your *stalker?*' Pia lowered her voice as she said the word.

Catherine hesitated. 'How do you know? Where are you?'

'I'm at home. Why?'

'How do you know something else happened? Are you still in Spain?'

'Of course I'm not still in Spain. Why would I let you drop me at the airport and not get on the plane?' Pia laughed. 'What's going on, Catherine?'

'I have to go. I'll call you back later.'

'Wait – you can't –'

Catherine dropped the phone back in her apron pocket, placing her palms flat on the countertop to steady herself. The room began to spin, and she stumbled backwards, sliding down the cabinet until she met the cool floor. Leaning her head back against the hard surface, Catherine breathed in through her nose and out through her mouth until the spots disappeared from her vision. *Pia. It was Pia.*

Hearing footsteps above her, Catherine checked her watch. They would soon be tramping down the stairs, looking for her. She stood, untying her apron and hanging it carefully on her peg. A clatter outside caused her to whirl around; she saw no one. Her skin prickled with unease. She double-checked the doors were locked and scanned the empty street, unable to shake the feeling of being watched.

8
Pia

Catherine woke to Josie shaking her. She blinked rapidly. The room was in semi-darkness; the dim light that told you night had finished, but it wasn't yet daytime. The realisation Josie was at her side jolted her awake.

'What's wrong? Mateo?' Her eyes searched Josie's face for clues.

'It's Pia.'

Catherine rubbed her eyes. 'What about Pia?'

'I thought I heard a noise, and with all the strange goings on lately, I thought I had better check it out. I saw your phone on the side, and there were eight missed calls from Pia. Something must be wrong for her to try you that many times.'

Catherine sank back into the bed. 'Oh.'

'What do you mean, Oh?'

'Just, oh, that's all. What were you doing going downstairs on your own when there might have been someone down there?'

'Don't change the subject. What's going on?'

'Nothing's going on. I'm just taking some space from Pia, that's all. You don't need to know everything in my life.'

Josie recoiled at her mother's tone. She dropped the phone on the bed and stalked out of the room.

Catherine glanced at the phone and sighed. Josie was so grown up for her age, a mother herself, but it was easy to forget she was still a teenager. She bit her lip, running her palm over her forehead. The clock ticked on the bedside table, reminding her it was still too early to get up. Adrenaline coursed through her body; she would never get back to sleep. When Josie was little and up in the night, she would take her for a walk through the orange groves, walking until sunrise. The red and yellow hues stretching behind the trees and into the distance almost made up for the lack of sleep. *Surely if Pia is behind all this, she wouldn't actually hurt me? Why would Pia be behind it? who else could it be?* Spurred on by her thoughts, Catherine put on her walking shoes and resolved to go and see the sunrise.

~

Upon her return to the café, Catherine immediately noticed the brown envelope on the floor. There was no other post. She stooped to pick it up, turning it over in her hands; no postmark or return address. *Hand-delivered.* Stepping out into the empty street, Catherine looked around. 'Hello?' Feeling braver, she stepped out further and ripped open the envelope, pulling out a postcard showing Brighton Pier. Scrawled on the back were the words, *wish you were here.* 'What do you want?' Her words echoed in the daybreak. Ripping the postcard into four pieces, she dropped it into the bin and switched on the coffee machine. Catherine's phone chirped with a message from Pia. Her fingers deftly tapped a reply, saying she needed space. Three dots appeared on the screen. She held her breath, watching them until they disappeared. They were replaced with the vibration of an incoming call, which she quickly rejected.

'Buenas Catherine. Una carta para Josie y dos para ti.'

'Gracias Rafa.' Catherine smiled at the postman and took the letters; bills, by the look of it. Deleting the notification of a voicemail left by Pia, she began getting the little café ready for customers.

~

'I'm sorry, Josie. I didn't mean to snap at you. It's just – it's complicated.' Catherine handed Josie a mug of tea as a peace offering and nodded toward the letter addressed to her on the counter. She watched as Josie stuffed it in her pocket without looking at it. 'What are you up to today?'

'Me and Javi are taking Mateo to the park this morning. Oh, and don't forget, the handyman is coming by later to look at the bedroom partition.'

'Javi and I.'

'What?'

'You said, me and Javi, it's Javi and I.'

'Whatever.' Josie rolled her eyes. 'Did you get that about the bedroom?'

'Yes, perfect, thanks for sorting that. I have some other bits of work I want to talk to him about as well.'

Josie sat at one of the café tables sipping her tea. 'So, are you going to tell me what you and Pia fell out about? You know you'll feel better for talking about it. I know you like to be all independent woman, but you can't always do everything on your own.'

'How did I raise such a beautiful *and* wise daughter?'

'Don't change the subject. Oh, and I'm beautiful because I have your genes, Mamá.'

'It sounds crazy now I am going to say it out loud, but I just started thinking about all the strange things that have been happening and wondering if it might be Pia behind them.'

Josie put her mug down with a thud, hot tea spilling onto the plastic table top.

'You think I'm crazy?' Catherine swallowed. 'I shouldn't be putting this on you. It's not fair.'

'You are always saying we are a team. You can always talk to me. I don't think you're crazy; I just think you have a lot on.'

'I know, I know. I haven't told you everything. There have been a few more strange things happening. There was the scarf I asked you about – that was the scarf of the football team in my home town in England, then the Kindle – just like one I used to have –'

'The scarf is just a weird coincidence, and Kindle do make more than one of each item! Also, since when would you ever have a Kindle? You hate Kindles. For all my life, you always go on about the sanctity of books.'

'It was the same model, the same one, I just know it. I don't know how, but I could feel it. The earring – exactly the same as a pair I had many years ago when I first met your father.'

Josie's eyebrows raised at the mention of her father.

Catherine continued. 'The feeling of being watched, the door being unlocked, the chiller being unplugged.' Josie opened her mouth to speak, and Catherine held her hand up. 'Don't tell me it's all a coincidence and that I am overtired or imagining things. The ornament yesterday - I had one just like it in my house in England, and who gave it to Mateo?'

'OK, I admit, that is weird.'

'And there's more.' Catherine looked at the door as the bell tinkled, pausing their conversation to serve a takeaway coffee and lemon cake to one of their neighbours.

Josie watched until the customer had left and looked expectantly at Catherine.

'Where was I? Oh, yes. The postcard.'

Josie watched as Catherine left the café. She waited a few minutes, frowning, before following her. 'What are you doing?' she asked incredulously as Catherine rifled through the contents of the bin.

'It was here.'

'What was? Mum, you are worrying me.'

'I got a postcard this morning. It was hand delivered and had a picture of Brighton, where I used to live, on it. It just said wish you were here on it. I ripped it up and threw it in the bin, and now it's gone.'

'What do you mean gone? Mum, no one is out here stealing things from our bin.'

'Well, what other explanation is there? Someone's messing with me! I didn't imagine the postcard.' Catherine's voice rose as Javi appeared.

'Everything okay, Señoras?'

'Morning Javier. Yes, gracias. Just looking for something. All ready for your morning out?' Catherine brushed her apron down and smoothed her hair.

Josie interjected. 'Mum, I don't think I should leave you on your own. Not when you're upset like this.'

'Don't be daft. Come in and let me cut you some sandwiches and pack you a lunch to take to save you having to buy anything.'

Josie hesitated, exchanging a look with Javi.

'I might be old, but I'm not blind. Don't look at Javi like that. Now, come on, let's get lunch sorted, and you guys can be on your way.'

Catherine busied around cutting sandwiches and wrapping cake between serving customers while Javi and Josie disappeared upstairs. When they reappeared with Mateo, she handed them a takeaway bag each.

'Thanks, Mum.' Josie gave her mum a kiss on the cheek. 'Oh, and I was thinking about Pia. If you are that worried it's her, why not ask her to send a picture of herself somewhere you know, holding today's paper? That way, you'll know she isn't in Spain.'

Catherine stared at Josie. 'I wouldn't have even thought of that. Great idea, thanks love. Now, go on, on your way.' Catherine held the door open and shooed the trio out of the café. 'Adios.'

'María, do you mind letting any customers know I will just be a couple of minutes?'

'Only if you ask me in Spanish.'

Catherine laughed and disappeared up the stairs before María could make good on her request. She showed the handyman, Ron, to Mateo and Josie's bedroom, explaining what they were hoping for. Ron was a fellow ex-pat; a Scotsman who settled in Spain with his wife when their children grew up and moved out. Catherine glanced at the door as he settled on the arm of the sofa with his mug of tea.

'Aye, Lassie, we were supposed to be living our dream. Unfortunately for me, the wife's dream turned out to be a string of affairs with sexy Spaniards. Only Nessie knows where she is now.' He winked, then saw Catherine's face. 'Well, the kids probably have some idea, but I've not seen hide nor hair of her. You didnae think I killed her, did you?!'

Catherine forced a laugh. 'You weren't tempted to go back to Scotland then?'

'Och, no. I love my life here. Be nice to see the grandchildren more, but I'm too old to go back to the highland weather now. What about you? No husband or boyfriend?'

'Not right now.' Catherine glanced at the clock.

'Did you move out here with someone then? What made you move to Oliva?'

Catherine shifted, her eyes darting between the clock and the door.

'Not on the run, are ye?'

For the second time in the conversation, Catherine forced a laugh. She held her hands up. 'You got me! I killed my mobster husband and fled to Spain to avoid being caught.'

'Well, Lassie, whatever the reason. We both picked a beautiful part of the world to settle in.'

'Sorry, Ron. I don't mean to be rude, but I think I heard the shop bell. I must run back down.'

'Aye. You go do what you need to do. I'll be down to measure up for those blinds once I've looked at where you want this partition wall putting.'

Catherine escaped to the café where María stood behind the counter. She wore an apron and was handing a slice of cake to one of the other regulars. Catherine giggled as it struck her that they reminded her of children play-acting shops, only it was pensioners instead of toddlers. She watched as María took the euros, declaring that she hadn't cracked the till yet, so couldn't give any change, but she would make sure Catherine put it in the charity box when she had finished with her handyman.

'Hey! Enough of that, You! There will be talk all over town about me if you carry on like that.'

'You could do a lot worse.' María winked.

'What makes you think I'm looking for a man?'

María raised one eyebrow.

'I'm not looking for a woman either. Come on then, out of my kitchen.' Catherine shooed María from behind the counter.'

'Sold three pastries, a slice of cake, one can of pop and a coffee. Oh, and I helped myself to another coffee. Pardon. I hope you don't mind.'

'Of course, I don't mind. What would I do without you?' Catherine gave the older woman a hug. 'A slice of cake to say thank you?'

'If you insist.'

Catherine put the small pile of money in the till, removing coins for the charity collection pot. This year they were collecting for the Spanish Red Cross, the Cruz Roja. She jiggled the pot, frowning, and made a mental note to put on some promotions to raise some more money for the cause. María continued to let Catherine know that she was too young to give up on men and that once Josie grew older and moved out, she would appreciate the company. Their conversation stopped when Ron appeared in the doorway with his toolbox and an empty mug.

'Look, he even tidies up after himself.' María declared loudly, smirking at Catherine.

'Right, that's it. I'm sure you have things to be getting on with.' Catherine took María's empty plate from the table. María, taking the good-natured hint, stood to leave, delivering a parting shot in Spanish. Something Catherine couldn't quite catch, but whatever it was, it caused Ron's face to flame bright red.

9
A Suspect

The next day, Ron returned to fit the blinds, much to the delight of María, who was conveniently back for '*more of that lovely cake*'. María's face dropped when Catherine announced she was off to the bank and informed Ron he would be in safe hands with Josie if he needed anything. Josie said nothing when Catherine filled her in on Ron's visit and the plan for him to fit blinds. Catherine knew her daughter well enough to know the silence meant there would be some sort of unsolicited opinion coming her way later. She sighed and stowed the cash bag in her satchel, ready to go to the bank.

The bank was busier than Catherine expected, and she was forced to stand in line waiting for a cashier to become available. She shuffled between feet, always uncomfortable standing with a large sum of money on her. Adjusting the satchel so it rested against her abdomen, she pulled out her phone, remembering she hadn't yet texted Pia. *Sorry for radio silence, can you send a selfie with today's paper? Somewhere in Brighton.* She waited for the message to show as delivered and received Pia's confused reply. *Humour me, please, just send the picture.* She received a reply that Pia would go buy a paper and would send it later.

Leaving the bank, her bag considerably lighter, Catherine took a detour on the way home to sit in the sunshine. She leaned against an orange tree, her face tilted up to the sun. The air was rich with the citrusy scent of the fruit. Catherine wrinkled her nose as she noticed the breeze also wafted the smell of donkey manure in her direction. The groves were unusually quiet, and Catherine sighed, her legs stretched out in front of her, appreciating the solace; moments like this allowed time to stand still while she cleared her mind. After what felt to Catherine as though hours had passed, her bag vibrated against her thigh. Rummaging for her phone, Catherine opened the pictures from Pia. In the first picture, she stood posed against a plain wall, the newspaper held with both hands, her face solemn as if posing for a mugshot. Catherine swiped through the pictures, laughing as Pia posed with the beach and Brighton Pier in the background and another with an ice cream in one hand and the newspaper in the other. She sank back against the tree, letting her shoulders drop and closed her eyes with relief. *It's not Pia.* Her phone vibrating again caused her to smile as Pia sent a series of texts asking for explanations with a series of confused face emojis; Pia clearly thought there was some sort of joke she wasn't yet in on. Catherine's relief was quickly forgotten. *If it isn't Pia, who is it?* She looked around. The earlier solace of the orange grove suddenly changed to a feeling of isolation, the silence became eerie, and she shuddered as she hurried back through the trees, a sudden chill in the air. A noise behind her caused Catherine to spin around, her heart racing and her mouth open in a silent scream. The approaching donkey was undeterred by her sudden movement, continuing towards her as if he knew his warm fur would help to calm Catherine's racing pulse. She let her hands run over his coarse coat, inhaling the familiar musky smell, murmuring an apology that she hadn't brought him a snack. His tail whipped at a fly buzzing around his flank, hitting Catherine.

'Right, Donkey. I can't stop here all day; I have to go find out who has it in for me.' She said the words softly, trying to convince herself, as much as the donkey, that it was no big deal.

The café was bustling when the bell tinkled, announcing Catherine's return. A coachload of tourists had descended on the main street, and Josie was busily preparing lunches. With a quick assessment of the situation, Catherine pulled her apron on, scrubbed the smell of donkey from her hands and asked where she should jump in. Given instructions on where to deliver plates, Catherine and Josie worked together to serve the lunches and send the coach trip away with cakes for later before working on cleaning up the aftermath that came with a sudden flurry of business. The tables were soon cleared, and Catherine set about vacuuming the dust under the windows Ron had finished.

He looked at his watch. 'I need to get off soon, Lassie. I promised I'd finish up some jobs for a wee lady up the road. Is it OK to finish up tomorrow?'

'Of course, of course. They look fab so far! Thanks so much for getting started so quickly.'

'Well, you said it was urgent, and I don't like to leave a damsel in need.' Ron winked at Catherine as he began tidying his tools. 'Just the last one. I'll leave it in the corner and get it done tomorrow.'

As soon as the door closed behind him, Josie wasted no time in teasing Catherine about his desire to return the next day.

'Don't be daft. He's just doing his job.'

'Yeh, of course.' Josie winked. 'Mum, you know I'd be happy if you met someone, right?'

'I know you would. I'm just not interested.'

'He does like you, though.'

'You've been spending too much time with María! I think we've earned ourselves a cup of tea and a plate of hobnobs.'

10
The Wedding Photo

'Mum, I can't find my keys. Have you seen them?' Josie rummaged in her bag, then looked around her, scanning the sofa and the coffee table.

'No, but I'm sure they will turn up. I'm home all evening anyway.'

'I might be back late, and I don't want you to have to wait up for me.' Josie picked up sofa cushions and toy dinosaurs, looking for them. Exasperated, she grabbed the corners of her bag, tipping the contents on the coffee table.

Catherine spotted the unopened envelope. 'What was in the letter you had the other day?'

'Oh, I don't know, I forgot it was there. I'll look later.' Josie scooped the collection of items back into her bag, leaving the envelope on the coffee table. 'Can I take your keys?'

Catherine unclipped the back door key from her keyring and handed it to Josie, telling her to have a good evening.

~

'Mum!'

Catherine woke immediately to the sound of Josie's scream. Throwing back the covers, she stumbled in the darkness in her haste to reach Josie. Josie stood in the living room, looking at something, her face white.

'What's happened? What is it?'

Josie's hand shook as she passed the envelope and its contents to Catherine.

Catherine looked at the photograph in her hand; her breath caught in her throat as she fought the weakness in her legs.

'Where did you get this?' Her voice was barely audible.

'Is that my dad?'

'Where did you get this?' Catherine's voice rose as she grabbed Josie's arm. Her fingers dug into her daughter's flesh as she shook her. 'Is it you? Have you been doing this?' Josie shook herself free, rubbed her arm and took a step back. 'How could you?' She whispered.

'What are you on about? I haven't done anything. I was sent the photo in the post. Is it him?' Tears flowed down Josie's cheeks as she worked to keep her voice low. She snatched the envelope from Catherine and held it out, both of their eyes scanning the rectangle for clues. The heavy silence was broken by the familiar tinkle of the bell.

Catherine blinked. 'I'm sorry. What am I saying? Of course it wasn't you.' She searched Josie's face for forgiveness. 'Did you lock the door when you came in?' Catherine's voice was back to a whisper. She looked at Josie, her eyes wide. Josie's eyes darted to Mateo's door. 'Now, listen to me. I want you to barricade yourself and Mateo into your room and call the policía – tell them there has been a break-in.' Josie swallowed and nodded. Catherine shoved Josie in the direction of her room, spurring her daughter into action. She crept to the stairs, cocking her head. The darkness was still, quiet. Her bare feet allowed her to slip down the stairs without a sound. Her skin prickled as she reached for the light switch, the click of the button illuminating the café. 'Wh-what the –.' The room was covered in photocopies of the wedding photo. They were taped to the windows, the walls, on the chiller, and spread over the tables. Catherine bent to pick up one of the pictures from the floor, looking into the holes where her eyes had been. Her eyes travelled around the room; the pictures were all the same – her eyes had been poked out in each of them. The café was empty, and both doors were locked when she tried the handles. Working quickly, Catherine began gathering the pictures, grabbing at them and ripping them from their positions, all the while aware of Patrick's eyes watching her, judging her. The pictures were in a pile on the table as the flash of blue light crept into the room. She let out a breath and shouted up the stairs to let Josie know the police had arrived.

The shadow of the officer at the door preceded his knock, and Catherine moved to let him in. As she passed the pile of photos, her hand reached out and grabbed a tea towel to cover them. 'Officer, gracias.' She stepped aside and gestured for him to step into the restaurant. Apologising, she said she thought it might have been a false alarm. She glanced at the table, wringing her hands. The officer offered to check the property.

'Oliva very safe. No crime. No need to worry here, not like England.' He smiled at Catherine. 'I check upstairs to be sure.' She followed him up the stairs. The wedding photo lay on the coffee table, and her nostrils flared as the memories flooded her consciousness yet again. Clenching her jaw and saying nothing, she waited for the officer to give the all clear and followed him to the front door, thanking him and locking it safely behind him.

~

It felt like only a few minutes after falling into bed that the sun woke Catherine. The morning routine passed by with a companionable silence between Catherine and Josie, broken only for light-hearted conversation with Mateo. The adventures of the night before forgotten, Mateo was excited to be spending the day with Adriana. His eyes gave away his interrupted sleep, but his toddler energy took more than a few nighttime shenanigans to impact his morning. He sat at a table with his breakfast while they opened the café and waited for Adriana to arrive.

'Buenos días!'

'Hola, Adriana.' Catherine smiled in greeting as Josie handed Adriana two packed lunches and Mateo's day bag. They filled Adriana in on the suspected intruder so she knew to expect Mateo to crash at some point. The concern showed on her face, causing Catherine to reassure her it was probably just their imagination. She exchanged a look with Josie and shook her head gently. They waved goodbye to Mateo through the windows as he and Adriana left, hand in hand.

'It wasn't nothing. We both know it wasn't nothing.' Josie murmured her concern, keeping her head down to avoid attracting the attention of customers.

'I know. We need to talk. We will. I promise.'

'You can't keep fobbing me off. I need to know if it's safe for me and Mateo to be here, because if it's not –' Josie broke off, not finishing the sentence. She looked at Catherine for reassurance, her eyes searching Catherine's in vain. Catherine stepped away, a plate of breakfast in each hand, a smile pasted on her face as she delivered the plates. As she swept the café for empty plates and cups, Catherine heard a gasp. She squeezed her eyes shut, knowing what Josie had found. She chided herself for not emptying the bin, getting rid of the evidence of the photocopies of her wedding photo. Standing in front of Josie, Catherine put her hands on her daughter's shoulders.

'Look at me. We will talk about this later. I promise. I need to speak to Pia. There are some things we have never spoken about, not since I moved to Spain, and I think it's time we did. And then, we are going to talk. Just you and me. We will close the café and ask Adriana to have Mateo for a bit longer.' She looked into her daughter's worried eyes and gave her shoulders a gentle squeeze. 'We will get to the bottom of this. Now, can you look after the café and text Adriana?' Josie nodded. 'I'll be just upstairs if you need anything.' Josie nodded again, and Catherine pulled her into her arms, squeezing her tightly. She hung her apron on its hook and grabbed a croissant from the pastry stand, giving Josie a wink.

With the door to the flat closed, blocking the sounds from the café, Catherine sank onto the sofa, her head in her hands. Her body shook as the sobs escaped her mouth. Loud choked sobs. She allowed herself to sit like that for a few moments before taking a deep breath and dialling Pia.

'Sup? You okay?'

'Not really. We need to talk. There are things – there are questions I need to ask, things I've been avoiding.'

'Sounds serious.'

'It is. I want to know everything. Everything you know about the Walkers, then and now.'

'Okay. Can you give me five minutes? I'm due on a conference call with a magazine about some editing work in 20 minutes, but I can push it back. I'll call you right back.'

Catherine disconnected the call and remained seated, watching the phone in her hand. Her eyes drifted to the croissant, and her stomach turned. She jumped as the phone rang in her hand and watched Pia's name flashing on the screen. Fumbling, she swiped to answer the call and took a deep breath, ready to face her fears.

Nearly two hours later, Catherine hung up the call to Pia. She leaned back on the sofa and laughed. She laughed and laughed until tears streamed down her cheeks. When she thought she could laugh no more, she felt another wave rising inside her. Not hearing a knock at the door, the first she knew of Josie coming up to the flat was the door opening.

'Mum, are you okay? What's happened?' Josie's face was etched with concern.

'I don't know. I don't know why I'm laughing. The whole thing is bloody awful. The prime suspect is batshit crazy, and we have no idea what the motivation behind all this is, but I can't stop laughing.'

'Okay, well, shout if you need me.' Josie tactfully retreated from the room, pulling the door closed behind her.

Catherine sobered up as the click of the door left her surrounded by silence. She stood to flick the kettle on, reflecting on her conversation with Pia. She already knew Patrick had remarried from searching the local news in Brighton. When she first left, she looked daily. She watched as his appeals for her whereabouts dwindled until it was just anniversaries. Her 'suicide' was always mentioned in any media about Beachy Head due to her marriage to Patrick. She knew he remarried, but he always said he would find her if she ever left – Catherine had lived in fear of these words since the day she got on that boat, even after his death. She didn't think him remarrying would make him any less of a threat. Patrick was nothing if not true to his word. If he had ever found out she took his child from him… she shuddered at the memory. Pia said his second wife had accused him of being abusive. Pia testified at the murder trial; said he was abusive to Catherine – without evidence, the court said it was hearsay. The jury didn't believe it. The courts said Ashleigh was trying to tarnish the reputation of a good, law-abiding man. Catherine confided in Pia that she suspected Patrick was having an affair with Ashleigh before she left. It was a quick wedding; Patrick and Ashleigh spun it to the papers that Ashleigh was a close friend of Catherine's, and they fell in love through their grief, something positive to come from their shared loss. *Lying tramp* Catherine spat bitterly to Pia, immediately regretting her harsh words when reminded of how it all ended.

Pia said the house was surrounded with flowers when Patrick died. It became a shrine until Patrick's parents sold it. The campaigners for male victims of domestic abuse used it as a backdrop for their campaigns – filming press statements and promotional videos with the flowers in the frame. Catherine expressed to Pia she wished she had been stronger. She wished Patrick didn't die a hero. That Ashleigh wasn't in prison, and she hadn't had to put her friends through thinking she was dead.

'You did what was best for you and Josie. Nothing else matters. I forgive you.'

A single tear ran down Catherine's cheek at those words. She avoided the conversation for all these years, didn't want to face the chain of events her running had started, couldn't face what she put her friend through. The rush of emotions as she ended the call left her feeling as if a weight had been lifted from her shoulders. The release that led to Josie finding her mother crying with laughter in an empty room.

COMMUNITY ROCKED BY STABBING OF LOCAL JUDGE

Brighton & Hove residents were shocked to wake up to news of a stabbing in the Hove area of Brighton. The victim has been named locally as The Honourable Mr Justice Walker. Tributes are flooding social media, and flowers have been left at the gates of his residence in Hove.

Residents report a significant police presence, followed by a female being led out of the property and taken away in a police vehicle. Police have not yet confirmed the woman's identity, but say they are not looking for anyone else in connection with the incident.

More updates as we receive them.

JUDGE WHO HELPED MALE DOMESTIC ABUSE VICTIMS STABBED IN SUSPECTED DOMESTIC DISPUTE

Local stabbing victim has now been formally identified as The Honourable Mr Justice Walker. It is understood that his wife, Mrs Ashleigh Walker, has been charged with his murder. She will be detained in custody until a trial date has been set.

The community is saddened by this sudden end to an already tumultuous life. Mr Walker's first wife disappeared five years ago, leaving a suicide note at well-known local beauty spot, Beachy Head. Mr Walker pleaded to media outlets throughout Europe for information, believing that she would one day be found alive. He went on to find comfort with a former colleague of his first wife, who he later married. It is believed that the second Mrs Walker also comes from a troubled background. Those close to Mr Walker report periods of instability and erratic behaviour from Mrs Walker. A colleague of Mr Walker's said to reporters, 'It was only a matter of time before something like this happened.'

JUDGEMENT DAY FOR WIFE OF MURDERED JUDGE

The Honourable Mr Justice Walker was a respected Judge, quickly rising through the ranks with a promising future ahead of him. Today, justice was served for his murder. Mrs Ashleigh Walker was tried in front of a jury of 12 men and women, who gave a unanimous guilty verdict for the charge of murder. Ashleigh Walker will be remanded in custody until sentencing.

Ashleigh Walker was the second wife of the late Judge Patrick Walker KC. Ashleigh's defence barrister cited mitigating circumstances outlining a catalogue of controlling and abusive behaviours. There was no evidence to support these claims. The prosecution presented witness statements from esteemed hierarchy in the legal profession supporting the Judge's good character and noting his concerns about his wife's increasingly erratic behaviour. A colleague who asked not to be named said, 'After the difficulties with Catherine, it is sad that Patrick found himself in the situation again. He always wanted to help people. Perhaps his biggest fault was choosing to love broken women, women beyond help.' Judge Walker's first wife disappeared in an apparent suicide at Beachy Head, leaving a note saying she could no longer live with her inability to bear children.

Judge Patrick Walker KC won numerous awards for his work in the legal profession. He was involved in high-profile cases such as the conviction of Henrietta Forbes for the domestic abuse of her husband, Charles. This was a ground-breaking case in its time, being one of the first successful convictions of a female abuser. This paved the way for several further cases to be brought before the courts. Domestic abuse charities in support of women continue to campaign for the re-trial of

Henrietta Forbes, believing the wrong perpetrator is behind bars.

The sentencing hearing for Mrs Ashleigh Walker is expected to be set for a few months' time.

11
England

'I never told you the full story of my life back in England, and I'm so grateful that you never pushed me for answers.' Catherine gave her daughter a weak smile. 'You must have so many questions, and I think it's time I answer some of them.'

Josie squeezed her mother's hand across the table.

'You have your uncle's eyes.' Catherine squeezed her hand back and then withdrew, putting her hands safely around her coffee cup, cradling its warmth. Looking at her daughter's eyes, she let herself be transported back in time. 'I've told you before, I ran away. That was only partly true. I had you, and you were the most precious thing in the world. Of course, you were just a bean at that point, but the moment I knew you existed, I knew I would do anything to protect you. I was married to your father at the time.' She looked to Josie before continuing. 'He wasn't a nice husband. He was a brilliant man in so many ways. He was dazzling, dreamy, and good looking. He was like a drug; he swept me off my feet. He was my Prince Charming, and I was his Cinderella. Or his waitress working in a cocktail bar. Catherine gave a wry smile. He was a pillar of the community, an upstanding citizen, but they always say you never really know what goes on behind closed doors. Anyway, I found out I was pregnant, and I wasn't going to let him take another child from me –'

'Wha –'

Catherine's knuckles turned white as she gripped the mug. 'Please, just let me finish the story. As I was saying, I wouldn't let him take another child from me. You would have had a little brother or sister, but there was a fall - the baby didn't make it.' Her voice cracked, and she took a deep breath. 'I found out I was pregnant with you, and I knew I had to leave. I had been putting money away for a while, putting plans in place for if – no, *when* I needed them. I had a fairy godmother, you see. She was not unlike Maggie. She worked in a charity shop, and one day, when I dropped some bags in, she spotted how desperately sad I was. This was during my first pregnancy. She listened. She never judged me, and she helped me plan my escape. Patrick, your father, was monitoring my every move by that point. He tracked my phone; he tracked my bank account. I had to get cash back when I bought anything and carefully hide it away. I had to be so careful, just small amounts, here and there.'

'Why didn't you tell someone?'

'No-one would have believed me. Patrick made sure to cover his tracks. Little comments to his colleagues and family implying I had a drink problem to explain the injuries.'

'But someone –'

'Please. Every day I regret not being stronger, not forcing someone to believe what he did to me. Maybe if I had, he would still be alive, and another life wouldn't have been ruined in the process. Anyway, I waited until he was working in the city, and I left. I drove my car to Beachy Head, a well-known suicide spot.' She patted her daughter's hand at the gasp. 'No, I wasn't thinking of that. I already had you on the way – my precious, precious girl. I didn't know you were a girl at that point, but I already loved you more than anything else in the world.

Pretending I was dead was the only way I could get away. It was the only way he would let me go. He used to say to me *until death do us part*, he said it to taunt me. He made sure I knew he would find me if I ran – he was rich, powerful. I suppose that money should have been yours now. I left a suicide note in the car, threw my scarf and an earring over the cliff edge, and I ran. I cut and dyed my hair; I took off my wedding rings, and I got out of the country. It was easier back then, so I managed to get to France on a boat. Of course, he suspected it was all fake. I saw appeals on TV and in the newspaper where he asked people for information. He made sure my face was in the media all over Europe. Everyone loved him even more – *poor Patrick, can't accept the death of his terrible wife, who abandoned him.* I stayed in France for a few days, but then someone recognised me, even with my new hair. The information got to Patrick, and I read online that he went to France, looking for me. I moved on, but I hadn't managed to save as much money as I would have liked. I had a few bits of jewellery; I sold those, but I knew I had to find a job and somewhere safe, and fast. I had you growing inside me, and I was so tired. This should have been exciting, a new start, but I was so anxious. I worried I had done the wrong thing for you, taking you from your father. A part of me felt guilty for taking his child from him. Many times, I nearly gave in and phoned him, but the fear of what he would do to me stopped me. And I was right. If I had stayed, it would have been me that ended up dead. Or in prison.'

Catherine stood and put their cups on the side.

'Oh, Mum.' Josie stood and put her arms around her mother's waist. Turning her head so her cheek rested on her mother's back. 'You could have told me. I would have listened.'

Catherine flicked the switch on the kettle. 'Go get the biscuits, and I'll make us some more tea.'

They sat at the table again, a packet of chocolate hobnobs between them. Catherine smiled at the imported English snack habit that she hadn't been able to shake despite not setting foot on English soil for nearly 20 years. 'What I told you about my parents was true. They did die in a car accident, and my grandmother, who was the most wonderful lady, raised me. If it wasn't for Pia and her family, I don't know how I would have gotten through it. When I moved to Oliva and met Maggie, it was like I suddenly had family again. I know she wasn't my blood family, but she was like another grandmother. She took me in; she gave me a job and somewhere to stay. The rest - you know.' Catherine broke another hobnob in half, dunking it in the hot tea until the chocolate softened and the biscuit soaked enough to melt in her mouth.

'Can – can I ask about my Dad? You don't have to, but I would like to know about him. Did he have any family? You said he died?' Josie spoke slowly, choosing her words with care as she saw her mother's forehead wrinkle.

'Another time. For now, we need to focus on getting cover for the café so we can go to England. We should have gone years ago.'

PART 3: THERAPY

My Journal?!

Sally, my therapist, said it might be helpful to write a journal. Said writing my thoughts down might help me process them. I don't even know who I am writing this to. I can't believe I have a therapist. But then, I can't believe a lot of things about my life. How did I get here?

I should have seen the signs. They were always there. He made me feel so special - like I was the only one he had eyes for. But he was controlling, so controlling. He hated when other men even looked at me, let alone spoke to me. At the time, I felt flattered he cared so much. I thought the dark look that flashed in his eyes was a sign of how much he loved me.

Before

Sally thinks it would be helpful for me to start at the beginning. She said it will help to put my thoughts and experiences in order. I am not sure what good it will do - It won't change anything, but at least I can tell her I'm trying. I can't remember the exact dates things happened, so I'll just tell my story as I remember it, from the beginning.

I always wanted him. I can't believe I was stupid enough to be jealous when he chose her over me. Her relationship with him is as much a part of this story as mine is. This story begins with a group of neanderthal men in a bar. I fucked him in the toilets the first time they came in. And then they came back when she was working, and he acted like I never existed. All he saw was her doe eyes and innocent act. He was mine before he was ever hers to take. I'm not jealous of her, though. I despise her. I don't want to be all childish about this, but I saw him first. Perhaps if he chose me, things would have been different. He didn't. He chose her, and I had to watch as they started dating and he came into the bar, flashing his cash around and flirting with her. Of course, Miss Goody Two-Shoes can't have been that great because it wasn't long into the marriage before he started sniffing around me again. She had the big white wedding, the local newspapers celebrating their fairy-tale romance. She went to all the events with him, on his arm, as his wife. But me? I was only good enough to fuck in the bathroom of the club. I was sure she caught us once - the look she gave us when we came back to the table wasn't what I expected, though. She almost looked pleased. Looking back, maybe all this is what she wanted. Maybe this was all a very clever game.

The Affair

When the affair started, he would come in with friends and give me a look, signalling to meet him in the bathroom. God, he was just so good looking. His eyes had the power to draw you in, to make you feel like the only person in the room. I thought I was in control. I thought I knew what I was doing. I didn't want to work in a bar; I wanted to make something of my life. Well, I sure did that. I made a bloody mess of it. I escaped the estate, growing up with Mum and having no money, and he was supposed to be my new beginning. She never contacted me when *it* happened. Shows I was right to leave her and her filthy house, not much better than a squat.

As time went on, I pushed him for more. I played the game and had him eating out of the palm of my hand. I never knew my father, but I must have got my looks from him because Mum was never much of a looker. Back then, I could attract men like a moth to a flame, and he was the moth I wanted. We would go to posh hotels and out for fancy meals. He worked in the city, so as long as we were never seen, he could get away with the late hours and overnight trips. If anyone saw us, they never said anything. She never said anything. He bought me expensive presents, jewellery, and flowers. I didn't stop seeing other men – they paid me cash for my time. Cash that kept me in the nice flat I had. I used them all for their money. They all thought I meant it when I told them how young they looked and how their wives must be so grateful to have them – that one always got them opening their wallets. Of course, there was always a quid pro quo – I had to endure ten minutes of them pawing at me now and then. I knew that once I had him, I wouldn't have to do it anymore. But at the time, I had a great figure and just thought it may as well make me some money. ~~He was different, he liked me for me as well as my body.~~ I thought he liked me for me. He never offered cash. He was my fairytale, not hers. Mine. Some fairytale he turned out to be – I didn't know back then that fairytales don't exist. There is no such thing as a happy ending, not in real life.

He told me he would leave her. He kept saying that he loved me and as soon as he could, he would leave. Then she got herself pregnant - not as dumb as she looked that one. He said he couldn't leave her while she was pregnant; it wouldn't look good. I kept thinking how unfair it was - I saw him first. I thought if only I could be patient, he would stay true to his word. I had to see them on the front of local newspapers at events together – the golden couple of the legal world.

Her

She played a good game; I'll give her that. Making out she wasn't interested, making him chase her. She was no different from the rest of us back then. We were all broke, none of us had the best home life, and we were all just trying to make as much money as we could until something better came along.

It didn't quite go to plan, though. After he knocked her up, she had a fall and lost the baby. He was telling everyone she was drinking too much and not looking after herself. He still used to visit the bar. Of course, we were careful – he couldn't have people seeing us together. He would finish work, come to the bar for a few drinks and pass me a note with a hotel key and suite number. It was exciting. I got a buzz out of it, wanting my shift to be over so I could go to his suite, knowing he would be waiting with champagne. Anyway, the baby. She lost the baby. He lost the baby. Whatever you call it, the baby was no more. I'm not sure what happened. With what I know about him now, it wouldn't surprise me if he beat it out of her. Only the two of them know the truth.

After they lost the baby, he said he couldn't leave; she was too fragile. He told me she drank and that she was abusive to him, blamed her fragile mental state. I believed it all. I ended up more like my mother than I ever thought I would.

Ding Dong! The Witch is Dead!

One day, she was gone. She disappeared; vanished into the sea. Just like that. I was with him on the day it happened. He wasn't lying when he said he was working in the city. He just spent more of the day in a hotel room with me than actually working. Those days of lazing around naked on expensive sheets are a world away from my life now. When I think of how he could make me melt with just a look or the touch of his skin against mine… it still makes me shiver - in a different way now. Of course, he never believed she was dead. He was determined to keep looking for her. He became obsessed with her – newspaper appeals, private detectives, hours scouring the internet.

Either she is desperate not to be found, or she really is dead. Either way, he always believed she was out there. I know she's dead; she can't not be after all this time. If she wasn't, surely she would have come back after it all happened. I still talk about her as if she is out there, but she can't be, not anymore.

I knew there was something different about him. I thought it was exciting, a bit of danger – I didn't realise the full reality of it until he told the story of her going missing – there was an almost imperceptible smirk as he relayed the events and played the grieving widower. He knew how to showcase the right emotions, but I saw the anger beneath the surface. The anger came out when it was just him and me. He paced the hotel room, furious that she had got one up on him. He said we couldn't see each other for a while after that, said it wouldn't look good for him.

His female clientele increased with women throwing themselves at his feet. They had no shame. No shame at all. He was supposed to be mine.

Sally says I must stop focusing on her. She says it isn't healthy. Sally didn't have to live in a house where the woman was immortalised. Some days he worshipped her photos - she was a saint that I could never live up to. Other days, usually after he had been drinking, he would rant about how she tricked him, and no one made a fool out of him.

Us

Why am I even writing this? I don't know what good it will do. It won't change anything. It won't turn back the clock. Nothing can change things. This is my life now, if you can call it a life. This is my shitty, shitty existence. Even when I'm back on the out, I'll be tainted. The papers will have a field day. They thought nothing of splashing my face all over the papers for everyone to see. After what I had to put up with at his hands… I'm the one suffering. I'm the one who has lost my freedom – not that I had that when he was alive anyway.

When the press died down a little, he started coming back to the bar. He said we still had to be careful, but gradually, we started meeting at the hotel again. Things were starting to get back to how they were, when one day, one of his drunk ass friends asked me out. I saw the fire in his eyes; the jealousy flashed like a burning rage. I thought he was going to knock his friend out then and there. Before I could answer, he pulled me to his side and kissed me. It was like being in a romantic film – until you find out that he isn't Brad Pitt after all. Brad Pitt, is he still a thing? I feel like I've lost track of what's going on in the real world.

Anyway, in those days, I felt protected when he displayed his masculinity like that. He was a caveman, and I was his girl. We were lucky most people accepted our relationship quickly. The press helped – his friend at one of the local papers span the story as me helping him find happiness again, a second chance. I made out that she and I were closer than we were, and everyone thought we were brought together by our shared loss. Shared loss my ass. He drove the woman away, and as for me, well, if it wasn't for her, I wouldn't be in here. This is all her fault.

~~The Wedding~~
The First Punch

Our wedding night. Isn't your wedding day supposed to be one of the happiest days of your life? By then, I already knew he was an asshole. It was too late. I knew when I went dress shopping. I knew when I did the place settings. I knew when we chose the food. I knew when I looked in the mirror, wearing what should have been the dress of my dreams. How easy it is for the dream dress to become something that would signify the end of my life. Because that's what it feels like. My life ended. I'm jumping ahead again. Sally always says I get over-emotional. I act without thinking things through, and I jump all over the place in my stories when I let my emotions control me. Fucking Sally, always with the rational thinking.

I don't know why I wrote the wedding at the top of this page. I wanted to start this part of the story before the wedding. After we become an 'official' couple, when everyone knew about us. Things moved very quickly. He asked me to move in within a year of her disappearing – I don't remember when it was exactly. I suppose I was unofficially living there already. When he asked me to move in, it was more of a formality. I hoped it meant I would be able to change the place a bit. It was very 'lawyery bachelor pad', but her presence was definitely there – mostly in tacky ornaments clearly bought by her. I remember one that said, 'Hove, Actually on it'. She was always trying to fit in, always conscious that she would never really be accepted into his world. I suppose we weren't too different in that way, but she lacked the confidence to brazen it out. Of course, all her belongings were still there. Patrick hadn't bothered to clear any of it. Did he think she was going to come back for it? If she ran away like he thought she did, she sure as hell wouldn't be coming back to pick up her favourite dress. Her jewellery was all there, exactly as she left it. Her Kindle was on the bedside table as if she would be back the next day to finish her book. Weirdly, I found paperbacks in random places. I found a couple amongst the towels in the pool-house, and another time I found a few in a shoe box at the back of the wardrobe. Yes. I snooped through all her stuff. How often do you get a chance to nose through everything belonging to the woman before you? Never. I wasn't going to pass that opportunity up. I think he liked her things being around. It was a reminder to me to behave. Eventually, he had to give in a bit, and he let me box up most of it and put it in the garage. He tried to make me get rid of some of my stuff, things he said weren't 'befitting of a judge's wife'. I managed to hide them in amongst her stuff – it felt like a game, and it was one small round that I could win. I couldn't win very often. I rarely tried.

At first, his controlling behaviour was flattering. It was when we were around other people. He would get jealous if another man spoke to me or if he thought I even looked at someone else. I remember one time he left my wrist bruised with how tightly he squeezed it. At the time, I was making polite chit-chat with the cashier in the supermarket. It soon became easier not to speak to anyone. I must have come across as so rude.

It wasn't long before he started to suggest my clothes needed changing. He ordered things for me and told me what to wear to his fancy work parties. Some of my favourite clothes went missing. A top here, a skirt there. It was always the skimpier outfits. He denied all knowledge. Of course he did. The parties were dull. So dull. I just used to take advantage of the free champagne and try to find at least one other normal person. They were all such Stepford wives. At this point, even though I noticed he was a bit controlling, the sex was still mind-blowing. Looking back, I overlooked so much because I was still drawn in by those eyes, those deep pools of sexual attraction. His body was never less than perfect – toned and tanned. He was always a bit kinky. I knew that from his days with her. He used to say how boring she was in bed. I used it as my opportunity to show him what he was missing, a way to lure him to me – blindfolds, leather paddles, the odd whip. He liked to spank me, show me who was in charge.

So there we are, attending boring parties but having mind-blowing kinky sex. He got a bit jealous, and I started going out a bit less – there was a pool at the house, and we converted one of the rooms downstairs into a gym. I didn't need to go out, and he was happier if I was home. Then one day, I was getting a bit bored. He was working on a big case, so I went into the city to meet a friend. A female friend. We went to a few bars and stayed out late dancing. When I came home, he was weird. He was sitting in the dark, waiting for me. I thought it was a joke at first – him sitting looking creepy. Until his fist hit me in the face. It was just the one blow - that was enough. He said I shouldn't be out displaying myself to other men and that maybe I would think twice when I looked in the mirror and saw the state of my face. He told me to sleep on the sofa. I was drunk, but not drunk enough that I don't remember crying myself to sleep. The next morning he acted as if nothing had happened. He made us both coffee and asked what I had planned for the day while he was at work. I remember asking him if he was going to say anything about last night. He asked if I meant about me going out and embarrassing him. He completely ignored the fact that he had hit me. It felt like he had slapped me across the breakfast table; that's how it felt when he pretended nothing happened. There was this moment where it hung in the air between us as if he was challenging me. When the moment broke, he told me he thought I understood how I was expected to behave.

My Chance to Leave

Looking back, I am mad at myself for not leaving when I had the chance. I say I had the chance, but I don't know what he would have done if I took him up on his offer. It was after that first time he hit me. He asked if I wanted to leave. Before I could reply, he said that now was my chance. He talked about how he thought we had an understanding, that we got on, knew how to please each other, and we both got something from the relationship. It was so cold, so calculating. At the time, though, it came across as perfectly reasonable. He said he was going out to a business meeting and that if I wanted out of the relationship, to get my things and be gone by the time he returned. I felt panic. I remember the feeling rising inside me. I didn't know where to go or what to do. At that point, I didn't have credit cards in my name or any money I could access. I could spend whatever I wanted whenever I wanted, but it was using his cards, his online accounts, and his name. I didn't have enough savings to rent somewhere and had given up my flat. I suppose I could have phoned one of my old friends, but I didn't. I have had to live with my decision to stay. The worst decision of my life. Actually, there is probably an argument that plunging a knife into his body was the worst decision of my life. Anyway, I couldn't leave. I felt like I couldn't leave. Perhaps, if I was really ready to, I would have seen that none of those things mattered

– deep down, a part of me still loved him and hoped it was a one off; even after all the other warning signs. How fucked up is that? I have never been a stupid person, but I feel stupid writing that. I can hear your voice now, Sally, telling me that it isn't my fault, rationalising my decision to stay. It's not that simple though, is it? If I had left at that point, perhaps he would still be alive. If he was still alive, though, I would probably be dead.

He came home that evening and the house was spotless. He was greeted with the perfect wife. I was dressed how he liked me, and dinner was in the oven. He said he was pleased to see me and that I would want for nothing in life. That was it. That was the moment I signed a contract with the devil. The wedding came later, but the deal was already done.

The Wedding

Our wedding was around two years after she disappeared. She was still everywhere in the house, even though her stuff was gone. Her presence, or lack of it, hung between us. I know people talked about how quickly we got together, and I was always seen as some sort of predator who swooped in and bagged myself a vulnerable widower. Looking back, it was the opposite. He didn't tell me that being a punchbag was part of the deal. After the night I agreed to stay, he didn't lay a finger on me again until our wedding night. I don't know if it was because I was so desperate to please him that he didn't have any reason to, or if he was worried I would leave. Although he was never worried - he always got his way, so maybe it was just luck.

We got married in Brighton Registry Office with a selection of his friends and family. I didn't have many people to invite. We had photos on the seafront afterwards and a hotel reception. It was a beautiful day, and to everyone looking in from the outside – I was a princess. I didn't get much say in the wedding. I didn't even get to choose my dress. He phoned the dress shop and told them what sort of dress he wanted me to have, so there was a shortlist for me to choose from. They were all beautiful, but surely a bride should get to choose her dress? His mother had a big say in the guest list and the music, and everything else. In the end, I just let her get on with it.

His brother was pleasant enough. His brother was so much like him in some ways, but so different in others. He was a softer version, less striking and without the edge. He kept his distance.

Anyway, where was I? I was going to tell you about the wedding. We got a mention in the local paper, of course. People love a happy ever after, and that's what a second wife was – a second chance at his happy ending. I smiled for the photos, and in some moments, I was truly happy. I was on an emotional rollercoaster. On our wedding day itself, I felt like maybe things would be okay. I remember thinking, *if mum could see me now*. Ha. Mum didn't come to the wedding, she wasn't interested even back then, but some small part of me felt smug that I had left behind that life with her for good.

We stayed in the hotel where our reception was, so at the end of the wedding reception, we just had to climb the stairs. Our guests gathered at the bottom of the grand staircase, and he scooped me into his arms and carried me up the stairs. I felt weightless and nuzzled into his neck. All these years later, there are some moments that are still so vivid. I remember the smell of his aftershave and the smiling faces of our guests. I remember the way his jaw clenched as we got to the top of the stairs, out of sight of the guests, and he put me down. I tried to put my arms around him, to draw him in for a kiss, and he turned away from me. It felt like a punch to the gut, or what I thought a punch to the gut would feel like. I would find that out later. He went into our room and swept the petals off the bed, put the lights on and blew out the candles. I was so confused. What was happening? What was wrong? I tried to talk to him. It was our wedding night, for fucks sake. It should have been the happiest day of my life.

Apparently, I spent the whole evening flirting with other men, and I embarrassed him. I don't have any idea what he was talking about. I spent the night lying awake, racking my brains trying to figure out what I had done wrong. I was always so careful about who I talked to and how I came across that I couldn't see what I had done that had upset him so much. Whatever it was, apparently it warranted a blow to my stomach. I slept in my dress. I couldn't undo it myself and didn't dare ask him for help. I woke the next morning to him unlacing the dress and kissing the back of my neck as if nothing happened.

Our marriage was consummated.

Even though our relationship was toxic, I think I told you before our sex life was always good. We knew how to please each other in the bedroom, most of the time. Over time, he got rougher and rougher; he seemed to like it if I resisted. I don't know if he thought I was role-playing or if it was a way of punishing me, another way he could get off on the power and control. Eventually, I started zoning out and just let him get on with it.

Catherine - BITCH

I came home one day to find wedding photos on the kitchen table. Not my wedding photos, HER wedding photos. What the fuck? I know it was to get a reaction from me. He said he was just reminiscing. I didn't react. He watched me and spoke about his wedding to her, saying how he just hoped she was happy, wherever she was. Again, what the fuck? He tried to goad me into a reaction. It was little things like that all the time. He liked to remind me that she was the perfect wife and that I would have to try harder if I didn't want to always live in her shadows. He was the one who managed to get her declared dead so we could remarry – when it came to her, he was so unpredictable.

Other times, he would call her a slut and say that at least he had trained me to behave better. He would say it as if he was joking, but I knew it was a warning. I noticed that if her name was mentioned around friends, he would make comments implying she had a drink problem. I didn't like the woman at the time, and now I fucking hope she is dead, but I'm pretty sure she didn't have a drink problem – I can't see him lettering her get away with it, for a start! At the time I first heard him say it, it seemed weird that he fabricated that. It made sense later when I found out at the trial he had told people all sorts of lies about me – at least he was consistent, making all his wives out to be unreasonable. Anyway, this is supposed to be about her. Sally said she thought I showed some feelings of resentment toward the woman, and writing things down might help me to process them.

He was Jekyll and Hyde – some days, he would say he couldn't wait to be reunited and that she must be living somewhere with memory loss; other days he said she had better be dead because if he found out she was alive, he would make her wish she was. It was as if a darkness consumed him. Those days, I had to tread carefully. Some days it felt as if the beatings were her punishment, dished out for me to take. I asked him once if he hit her. I was feeling brave, or maybe stupid because I remember I referred to her as his Precious Catherine. He told me that he doesn't know how he managed to choose two useless wives and that neither of us ever got anything we didn't deserve.

What's the Point?

I don't see the point in all this. I told Sally today that it just makes me hate her more. And nothing will change. Seriously, what is the point? They will both still be dead, and I will still be stuck here.

Release

The thing is. Some days, I like writing all this – in a way, I do feel like it helps me think things through better. Other days, it makes things more real. It brings back everything that happened, and I have to deal with my reality all over again. I have to remember that I had a life before this one. I've been here so long now that this is normal. How pathetic is that? Prison is normal. When I get out, I will have spent almost as much of my adult life in prison as I did outside. I don't even know what to expect when I get out. Things are different. The world has changed, and if I am honest, it bloody terrifies me. What have I got to get out for anyway? I don't have any family. I don't even know if Mum is still alive. The house and everything of his were inherited by his family under the Forfeiture Rule. Fucking Forfeiture Rule doesn't take into consideration the suffering I had to go through living with him; how much I put up with. Because I snapped and couldn't take it anymore, I'm the one who has to lose everything. I should have known no one would believe me. Even in death, he managed to manipulate everyone and outsmart me. He always said he never loses. He was right. He will be somewhere up there, or wherever you go when you die, laughing and gloating at my predicament.

I keep thinking about my release. That's what this is all for, anyway. That's why I am keeping this diary and having the extra sessions with Sally. She is going to assess me and prepare a report on if she thinks I am ready for release. They have to decide if I am a risk. Of course I'm not a bloody risk. The people I feel anger towards are both already dead. And I do feel anger. I can acknowledge my feelings and recognise anger. I feel very angry. Angry towards her for not fighting. For not telling the world what he was like, and making them listen. Maybe then, I wouldn't have ended up where I am now. Angry with him for all he put me through. But I can't be a danger to ghosts. And I can't hurt myself any more than he already did.

The Abuse

I don't see what good can come from reliving the abuse he put me through. I talked about this with Sally, and she said it might be useful to write it down and burn it. She said I could burn this whole journal if I wanted to, and that might be healing for me. I asked if she wanted to read it, and she said in her usual calm voice that it was my journal and she would do whatever I felt was best. We will see. I won't burn the rest of it, but I might give it a go burning these pages. Maybe when I re-read this, there will just be missing pages after this bit.

Where do I start with the abuse? I have been through it all. Punches and slaps, the odd kick to the stomach once he had floored me. Rarely where anyone would see, of course. Not that it mattered much, as I didn't go out much. If there were no events coming up, my face was fair game. If I did go out, it was always agreed by him. He knew where, when and who with. He put a tracker on my phone.

~~When my arm was broken.~~ When he broke my arm, he told everyone I fell when I was drunk. Fuck knows what else he told people about me. I remember getting sympathetic looks from a whole table of his friends once when they were talking about family. One of them said he had told them I had a difficult childhood. Fuck off, you pretentious twat. Perhaps I won't share this with Sally. I'm not sure I should be swearing. Maybe I'll rewrite it. Actually, it's my journal, and I can write what I want.

I have scars on my body from times he went too far. He would hold my hand under boiling water or hover the flame of a candle near my skin. Waiting to see when the heat was hot enough to make me squirm. He usually let me move before there was any lasting damage, but I do have a shiny patch on my forearm where he didn't move the candle quick enough, and the burn left a permanent reminder. It still itches sometimes as if he is reminding me that he has marked me forever. He told his mother I did it trying to cook for him – she never let that one go. Any chance to show up any inadequacies that she thought I had and she would be singing the from the terrace.

I could go on. What more do you want to hear? How he made me have cold showers for weeks at a time? Or the time he decided I was fat and made me eat nothing but vegetable peelings because that's what pigs eat? There was never anything that would do too much long-lasting harm – I think it was more the control. He liked to see my fear. Besides, he still wanted a baby, so he had to keep me in a state where I was still able to have his child. That's definitely a story for another day.

In the early days, he would bring home flowers after a particularly bad temper flare up. He smiled and turned on the charm, expecting me to forgive him and tell him it was okay. For me to apologise for winding him up. Eventually, he didn't even bother with the pretence – not unless anyone else was around of course. Then it was all smiles. Any events or work occasions we went to, he made sure to tell the world how much he loved me. One time, he presented me with a spa day voucher, and everyone said what a wonderful husband he was. That night, he told me they had their work cut out for them, but someone had to try to make me presentable.

No-one Gave a Shit

The worst thing about the abuse is that no-one noticed. Not one person saw what was happening, how broken I was. I don't know if they didn't care or if they only saw what they wanted to see.

Children

I never felt a burning desire to have children. Many women say they always knew they wanted children from a young age. Others used to say to me that my maternal instincts would kick in one day. They never did. I don't know if I'm just not cut out to be a mother or if my maternal instincts knew it wasn't safe for me to bring a child into the life I lived. It wouldn't be much better than my own shitty upbringing.

He wanted children. He told me we would start trying for a baby as soon as we were married. No. Actually, he didn't tell me. He told everyone we spoke to. He told them all as if it was something we had discussed and something I had agreed to. We discussed children, and I said one day I might want them, but we never agreed on anything. After the wedding, he started ordering baby and nursery catalogues. I carried on taking my pill until one day, it must have been around six months after the wedding, he asked if I was still taking it. We never discussed stopping it, but it seems he had that discussion in his head. The look on his face was so intense. I was terrified he would find out I was still taking it. I told him I had stopped a month or so after the wedding, and the first chance I got, I popped the remaining pills out of the packet and cut the empty packet into small pieces, wrapped them in toilet roll and flushed them. He must have been getting slack – I don't know how he hadn't seen the packet. I wrapped the remaining pills in foil and then hid them in my shampoo.

After a couple of months, we had the first visit to the fertility doctor. He came with me. Of course he did. We told the doctor I had stopped taking my pill a few months earlier, and the doctor suggested running some tests and gave us a leaflet and some websites to look at with supplements and things to improve our chances. She mentioned his age. I saw the control it took for him not to react – his jaw was clenched, and that vein of his was throbbing. I had to go back for the blood tests, and he let me go alone. I was terrified he would walk in, but I knew it was my only chance to make sure I couldn't get pregnant. I asked them for the contraceptive injection. I didn't say much – I couldn't. I was still terrified of him finding out. I just asked if there could be a note on my medical record that it wasn't to be mentioned in front of him. When it all happened – the courts summoned my medical records. The way it was worded made me sound like a deceptive wife who was tricking her husband and pretending she wanted a baby, but didn't. I suppose when it boils down to it, I was.

But it wasn't like that.

IT WASN'T LIKE THAT.

I never did get pregnant, thank God. I managed to carry on with the injection under the pretence that I was having blood tests and getting fertility advice. Luckily, he didn't try to attend appointments. He booked me in with a fertility specialist. I know he rang to check that I attended as she commented on how caring my husband was ringing to talk things through after. She thought he was caring – I know he was making sure I was where I said I was. He was checking up on me a little less during that period, but I didn't dare go anywhere or do anything I shouldn't anyway. He must have known that. The fear of him finding out about the contraceptive injection kept me awake at night. I was physically sick some mornings in the run up to the appointments. Luckily he thought this anxiety was me being desperate to have a child.

He didn't get tested at any point – he said he knew his sperm worked because Catherine was pregnant that time. The comments aimed at me became more and more hurtful – he would say that my body didn't work, and I wasn't a real woman. I can't even begin to imagine how awful that would be to hear if my situation was genuine. For me, it was hurtful but also a relief, because it meant I wasn't carrying his child.

The physical abuse got worse the longer we tried for a baby. He punished me. He didn't even consider the damage he was doing to my body at that point, the same body he expected to carry a child. I was broken. Sex was a mechanical chore. I suppose one benefit was that the kinky stuff stopped. He must have been getting it elsewhere by then. That didn't stop him being rough with me, though. Another way to punish me.

That Night

Sally said it would be helpful to write down my account of what happened that night. I have been over and over it so many times. I sometimes feel like I am telling someone else's story. We had been married for a few years by then. My life was miserable. I know a lot of people have shitty lives, but mine was worse. I barely existed. No-one noticed. If anyone ever did ask if I was okay, he would tell them that I suffered with depression and was going through a bad patch. I would be punished for it later. The next time I saw anyone, I would be sure to paint a bright and sunny disposition on my face.

The night it happened, I was asleep when he came home. I woke at the crash of the front door slamming open and remembered the clock glowing in the darkness. 2 am. He shouted from the bottom of the stairs. I remember him yelling, *wife,* he shouted. He was shouting at first, but then his tone got more playful. Playful was worse. He came up the stairs saying, *come out, come out whereever you are.* I can still hear his voice now, taunting me. Sometimes, I wake in the night sweating, imagining him in the room. The nightmares are less frequent than when I was first here, but I still get them. He opened the door to the bedroom, and I remember seeing his silhouette framed in the doorway. His arms rested on either side of the door frame, staring at me. I froze; I didn't know whether to pretend to be asleep or try to make polite conversation. He knew I was awake. He said he knew I wasn't sleeping. He told me to get ready for some husband-and-wife time. I said I was tired. I told him I wasn't in the mood. He used that playful tone again, *don't play hard to get.* I told him no. I said I wasn't in the mood; I didn't want to. I should have just let him get on with it – I don't know why I antagonised him by saying I didn't want to. I knew he wouldn't take no for an answer. I made it worse for myself because he punished me for saying no. It wasn't the first time he hurt me with his roughness. Afterwards, I lay there shaking until he went to sleep, too afraid to move. I don't know how long I lay there. It felt like hours, but the police records say I phoned them at 4.37 am, so it can't have been that long.

When I was sure he was asleep, I slipped out of bed. I intended to get a glass of water and then go back to bed, but I didn't. I saw the knife block in the kitchen. I remember noticing it. I drank my water, put the glass in the dishwasher, grabbed and knife and went back upstairs. I still don't remember what I was thinking. Even now, they all seem to want me to say I felt angry or I wanted to kill him. I didn't. I took the knife upstairs, and then I remember thinking I would stab him. I was as if the thought was someone else's. I don't recall thinking about killing him or causing him pain. I just went over to his sleeping body and plunged the knife into him. I do remember thinking it took a bit more effort than I expected, but I stabbed him a few times. Then I looked at the blood; it had seeped into the sheets, staining them red. There was so much of it that it couldn't soak in quick enough, so it pooled on the surface of the bed. Anyway, I put the knife on the dressing table and phoned 999. I told them our address and that I had stabbed him.

This is stupid. I've been over and over this – the courts, the doctors, everybody. Everybody judging me, thinking they know what my life was like. Sally, if you are reading this - I don't see what I can gain by going over it again. I can't go over this anymore tonight. I'll finish this tomorrow.

~

The police came and took me away. There was no need for the sirens – they clearly wanted everyone to wake up and see the shame of me being led from the house in cuffs. I'm not saying I didn't do wrong, but they didn't help. The press managed to get pictures from that night. The police all knew him. They treated me like dirt. No-one even considered that I might have a side of the story to tell. The cells were nothing like you would imagine. You see people arrested on TV, read about it in books and films, but nothing prepares you for the reality. Even Sally and all the people who have worked with me over the years – they visit people in police stations, in jails, then see the cells, but they don't really see them. They don't feel the absolute loneliness that hits you whenever the door lock clicks. They don't hear the sounds at night. I don't know which is worse, the shouting and ranting or the crying. At first, I didn't know where other people's wailing ended and mine began. Now, I just lie there waiting until sleep takes over. Often daylight comes first and a new day in my reality begins.

Over the years, I have become better at judging people, although I thought I was good at judging people back then – but now, I trust no one. I'm not sure that's what you want to hear? What do you want to hear? I don't even understand why you want me to go over all this again, but the hoops – I will jump through the hoops, exactly as I have been for most of my life – for different reasons and people, but hoops all the same. When I first arrived in the remand prison, I was allowed to wear my own clothes. The police took what I was wearing as it was covered in blood. I had no one to bring me anything else – so even before I had been sentenced, I had to wear someone else's cast-offs that the charity donated. It wasn't until I came to prison that I learned quite how much women are capable of. I didn't know where to turn – what happened to women sticking together? Very few people believed ~~my story~~ what happened. Some of those women had come across him in the court system – he had helped them in the early days when he was defending petty criminals. I never thought I would be in a place in my life where people would spit at me. Actual fucking phlegm. He would have loved knowing that, anything to degrade me even more, and if others did it on his behalf – even better. I was seen as some sort of black widow. The early days, no, the early years, are a blur. I did what I had to do to survive.

I can hear Sally asking now, what do I mean by that? There are a few times in a woman's life when she will find out what she is capable of doing to survive. I started that lesson in my marriage and continued it in prison. A new set of horrors went on around me. I had to learn to adapt. I started using the gym as much as I could – not because I enjoy it, but because others will see I am strong. I can defend myself if I need to. There have only been one or two occasions I have had to. I have used my time to study – although I don't really see the point. Even if someone did want to employ an ex-con, they will know my name as soon as they put it into Google, and then no one will want to employ me. I have got the certificates because I know it's what's expected. If I have learned anything throughout my life, it is when to do as I am told.

Release

I suppose this is the most important thing to document. They want to know what I am thinking. What I am feeling. They want Sally to get inside my head so everyone can decide if I'm fit for release. After all these years, someone has to put their name on a piece of paper saying they think I am fit for release and am not a danger to the public. I was never a danger to the public. I was a lonely, desperate person who had had enough of her life. Hasn't everyone felt that despair at some point in their life? I know it was wrong to take a life, even after how he treated me. I know that. Fuck. I don't even know if I want to be released. I don't know what there is for me outside. At least I know the routine and system here. I know the screws, and I surround myself with like-minded people. If I don't fight for release, they win. I say they because I still blame her – Catherine. If it wasn't for her, I wouldn't be in this position. If she had spoken out, he wouldn't have gotten away with it, because that's what really riles me – even in death, no one believes he was capable of the things he did – he died a saint. So yes, if I don't fight for release, they win, and it's my turn to win. It's my turn to win now.

Freedom?

I don't know why I am writing this. I don't need to. None told me to, but some days I find myself lost. I don't have a Sally anymore – no-one to talk to and no-one to suggest what I write. I thought writing my thoughts here as if I am talking to Sally might help put my things in order. It has been a while since I last wrote here.

Sally, you recommended my release. You spoke as if you really saw me, and for that, I will always be grateful. I know you will never read this, but I quite liked talking to you in the end and find it comforting to imagine what you would say and how you would help me work through anything that bothers me.

I am out of prison. Free, apparently. The days and weeks blend into one. It's not all that different from prison. I follow my routine and do as I have been told I must. I am pleased I'm allowed to live on my own now. The halfway house did my head in – not in prison and not on the out, like being stuck in purgatory. The bedsit I'm in isn't much, but it's mine. I have nearly finished the Thinking Skills Programme with probation, and I have a part-time job. I don't talk to many people, but to be able to walk along the beach is all I need – to feel the wind on my face and taste the salty air. I have seen Catherine's friend a couple of times. She must work near the seafront because I see her at lunchtime. She always dresses brightly and is often on her phone or having lunch with different people. Even after all these years, I recognised her instantly. She used to come into the club with Catherine back in the day. I thought about approaching her, but I don't know what I would say. She came to the trial – she even gave evidence against him, saying she believed he was abusive to Catherine. The prosecution ripped her to shreds. There was no evidence. They said she was a bitter friend who was always jealous when Catherine got married.

If she knew all along, why didn't she help me after she knew I was with him? Just another person who found it easier to look the other way.

I suppose at least she came to court, but it was too little too late.

Pia

I've started following her. I don't know why. Maybe if life turned out differently, I would have a life like hers – normal. I blend in now, and no one notices me. What a change from the life I had before when men threw themselves at me. Prison has aged me.

~

She has it all. A perfect life. She is always seeing her family or doing fun things with her nephews. I assume it's her nephews – I saw her coming out of the aquarium the other day with children, and I know she doesn't have any of her own. I Googled her to check. There is no sign of a partner either, but she never appears lonely.

~

I sat on the table next to her at lunchtime today. Even being that close, she looked right through me. It gave me a buzz, knowing I could go places and pass people and not be seen. Being invisible felt good today. She was on the phone to someone saying she is going on holiday. I wish I could hear the other side of the conversation, but it sounded like she goes on holiday a lot.

~

I haven't seen Pia for a few days – she's in Spain. I miss her. Even though she's not my friend, it gives me comfort to follow her. Both of us were fucked over by Catherine. Maybe one day we will be friends - sipping cocktails bonded by hate. Catherine abandoned her. Left her to be ripped apart and ridiculed in the dock. Another part of me hangs back, remembering she knew what sort of man I was marrying and let it happen.

~

Pia is back! She looks amazing – tanned and happy. She met her mum, and they had coffee on the seafront. I sat on the wall by the coffee shop they were in. I wonder if she has a boyfriend over there – she was cagey when her mum asked about her trip. It sounded like she has a secret life she is keeping from her family. Maybe one day I will be able to go to Spain and see for myself. Maybe, when my probation officer gets off my back a bit.

~

I heard her on the phone. She answered it with 'Hey, Cat.' I couldn't get close enough to hear anymore because she was walking and there were too many people around. It can't be? That bitch had better not still be alive. How could Pia do this to me? How could Catherine do this to both of us? Maybe there is another explanation. Maybe she has a new best friend called Cat?

~

I have to find out if it's Catherine she is speaking to. But how is she still alive? She is potentially out there somewhere, knowing he got remarried. Knowing he would have done the same to me as her, and she said nothing. Even at my trial, she didn't come forward. If she told the courts what he did to her, maybe I wouldn't have spent more than a decade in prison. I hate her. I HATE HER. THIS IS ALL HER FAULT.

~

I've heard Pia on the phone to her again. I can't get any information, but it sounds like it's Catherine she visits in Spain. It can't be – she's dead. I have to go over there. I have to see for myself. I need to find out where she goes. Somehow, I have to get into Pia's flat.

~

It was so easy. I got on the train at the same time as her and managed to pickpocket her keys in the crowd. I got off at the first stop and went straight back to her place. She must have had her laptop with her, and I was panicking she would come back and catch me, but I went through the flat from top to bottom. There were no holiday photos, nothing. There was an old photo of her and Catherine on the fridge – from when they were teenagers. The only thing I could find was a photo of a beach with a hotel in the shot - the Playa de Pechuán. I Googled it, and there were only two results – one in Mexico and the other in a place in Spain called Oliva. BINGO. I have to go to Spain. I have to check.

Oliva

I've seen her. It was definitely her. She looks older, but it's her. She looks fucking good. This new lifestyle suits her. I hate her even more. Why did she get to escape and have a life in the sun? I'm back in my room, but I'm going to find out more tomorrow. I can't stay long; I have to see probation once a week.

~

There is a girl. She looks just like him. She must have been pregnant when she left. He can't have known, or he would have said something. The spawn has his eyes, his facial features. Even without getting up close, I could see the family resemblance. I had to get a better look - I walked right past her as she left the café they were in. Seeing those features up close – it felt like a blow to my stomach. It was him. I wanted to stab her, to wipe out every part of his disgusting DNA. How could Catherine have his child? How can she bear to look at the girl? She was with a boy – I think his parents own the B&B I'm staying in. I will have to be careful to stay invisible. Forgettable. I feel sick.

~

I went back to the café this evening. I watched Catherine. She was all alone cleaning and putting the chairs up. The lights were on, so I could watch her through the big glass windows. At one point, she looked out, right at me. I squeezed back into the shadows and held my breath. I saw her looking out into the darkness. She couldn't have seen me – it was too dark. I felt my heart racing with excitement as she stared at me without seeing me. See how you like having your life messed with, Bitch. She ruined my life. Why should she get a happy ending? It's time to have some fun.

PART 4: MAKING SENSE

1
Coming Home

The plane touched down, and Josie and Catherine braced themselves as the force of the breaking pushed them back into their seats. As the plane came to a standstill, Josie grinned at Catherine as the passengers clapped.

'Why are they clapping?'

'Because we landed safely. Clapping the pilot.' Catherine shrugged as Josie got in the spirit, standing and clapping her hands.

The summer air was cooler than this time of year in Oliva but still warm as they stepped off the plane. Josie's eyes shone as they disembarked the plane, taking in every detail, looking around the airport.

'Nearly there - have you got your passport ready?' Catherine prompted her daughter, guiding her through her first flying experience. Catherine's nerves twisted her stomach into knots, anxious she would be stopped by border control. She consciously pulled herself taller and jutted her chin forward, ready to justify her right to come home if questioned. They passed through customs with nothing to declare and waited by the carousel for their luggage. Bags retrieved, they made their way through the glass doors at the exit, and Catherine broke into to a large smile at the sight of Pia waiting for them.

'Welcome home.'

'That sounds weird. This is all weird. I never knew if I would ever come back here again.'

'Come on, let's get you both back to mine and settled in, and then we can figure out a plan. I know you came to settle some old scores, but this is Josie's first time in England, and we need to show her the sights!' Pia linked her arm through Josie's and led them to her car.

Catherine flinched as they pulled out of the airport onto the busy motorway, forgetting how it felt to be on the left-hand side of the road. The 45 minute journey was filled with Josie talking about all the things she wanted to do whilst she was there.

'I want to go to London – we have to see all the sights, the Tower of London, Buckingham Palace, Big Ben. I can't wait. And the guards, will we get to see the guards?'

Catherine and Pia looked at each other and laughed. Catherine let herself sink back into the seat.

'Yes, we will do all of those awful tourist things if we really must! Let's make a list of everything you want to do later and decide which days to go into London.'

'I already have a list! I have to make sure I get a Paddington Bear for Mateo.' Josie's face fell briefly. 'This is the longest I have ever been apart from him, and we have only just arrived.'

Catherine twisted in her seat. 'We will Facetime Adriana when we get to Pia's. Anyway, what about Brighton? Have you got any activities to do in Brighton on your list?'

'Well, I want to go to the pier and do some shopping, of course. I want to see your old house and where you grew up.'

Catherine turned to face the road at the mention of her old house. Pia glanced sideways at her friend, reaching over to give her hand a brief squeeze.

'Well, luckily for you, I have made a quick detour, and we have our first tourist attraction coming up.' Pia put on a mock tour guide voice. 'If you turn to your left, you will see Brighton Pier. Brighton Pier was built in, oh, damn, I can't remember. Never mind. Brighton Pier is a historic structure filled with fun fair rides, amusement arcades and all the junk food your heart desires.'

'I know she wants to see all this touristy stuff, Cat, but if we get a chance, we must take her out to see some of the other areas, like Shoreham. We can go down and have an ice cream and a walk along the river. Do you remember, we always used to be out that way for a while? We had that friend from school we hung out with for a while, the one who lived on the herb estate?'

'Oh yeh. I'd forgotten that. What was her name again? Jane? Jill?'

'Jenny?'

'That's it!'

Josie shuffled to the other side of the car, pressing her nose up against the glass as the traffic slowed them to a leisurely crawl along the seafront. The seafront was busy – a mixture of tourists finishing their days on the beach and heading for the hotels lining the streets, early starts for hen and stag groups and people enjoying post-work drinks on the patios. They crawled past the promenade, and Josie exclaimed at a group of rollerbladers whizzing up and down the weathered tarmac.

'Mum, look at them! And did you see the Bride and Groom in the bandstand having their photo taken? The pictures will be amazing!'

Catherine gave a tight smile, reminded of her own wedding day. She swallowed, took a deep breath and twisted to give Josie what she hoped was a smile matching her daughter's excitement. She turned to Josie, 'It's so weird. It's all the same, but different.'

'It has been nearly two decades!'

'I know, I know. I don't know what I expected. I'll be glad of a cup of tea and a chocolate hobnob, though!'

2
Brighton Pier

Catherine awoke to the distinctive aroma of toast and coffee wafting into the room. Her eyes flew open, and she let them close again as she remembered she didn't need to be up for the café. Stretching her limbs, she surveyed Pia's spare room, appreciating the lie in. The room echoed Pia's personality, and Catherine smiled, taking everything in. She had a tour of the flat on FaceTime, but it wasn't the same as seeing it properly. Memories decorated the room – pictures of her family, a corkboard filled with postcards and travel mementoes, row upon row of books. The shelves reflected Pia's work and the varied genres of books she edited. Catherine rolled out of the bed and ran her fingers along the spines on the bookshelf, memories flooding her mind. She and Pia had always bonded over a love of reading, often swapping and sharing paperbacks, spending hours reading side-by-side. Her fingers came to rest on a photo album, and she pulled it from the shelf, sinking back onto the bed to look through it. It was from their teenage years, back when people still printed photos and put them into albums – before everything went digital. She smiled at the group of girls in their school uniform, younger than her own daughter now. They all looked so happy and carefree. She continued flipping through the album, a wistful look on her face.

'What are you smiling about?' Josie appeared at the door, holding out a cup of coffee. 'Coffee. I'll put some more toast in when you guys are up and about.'

Catherine shuffled along the bed, making space for Josie to sit beside her. They looked at the album together, Josie laughing at their hairstyles and fashion choices. Catherine paused to rest her hand on a photo of her on Brighton Pier with her nan. They were both laughing and holding candy floss.

'What's going on in here? Don't start having holiday fun without me!' Pia stood in the doorway in her pyjamas.

'Just looking at old memories. My daughter here doesn't agree with our fashion choices!'

Pia joined them on the bed, looking through the album until they reached the end, and Josie jumped up to pull the second album from the shelf, sliding back in between Catherine and Pia to open the album. The three women laughed as they watched Catherine and Pia grow up, experimenting with various changing hairstyles and dress sense. Gradually, the photos moved to holidays and roundtrips, with family featuring less, and Catherine's Nan stopped being in the photos at all.

They fell silent as Josie turned a page, and Catherine, in a wedding dress, smiled out at them. Catherine stifled a gasp.

'I'm sorry. I haven't looked at these for years. I forgot that was even in there. I'll put it away.' As she went to take the album, Josie tightened her grip, her fingers tracing her mother's image on the page.

'Is that my father?' Patrick's profile was visible in the background. 'I see why you said he looks like me, Pia.' Josie spoke softly. 'Are there more? I want to see them - If you don't mind, Mum?'

Catherine remained silent.

'There won't be any of your father. I never liked the man. Your mum was always too good for him.' Pia firmly took the album from Josie and closed it. 'Why don't just me and you look at these another day?' She briefly made eye contact with Catherine and smiled at Josie as she nodded. 'Right. Toast. I thought you were on self-appointed breakfast duty?! We'll get dressed; you get the coffee made.'

For the first day of their holiday, the trio planned to explore Brighton. Josie armed herself with a list of tourist 'must-do activities,' recommended online. Their first destination was Brighton Pier. Josie made a beeline for one of the kiosks lining the entrance. Armed with hot doughnuts, they made their way through the entrance barriers, ready to experience the busy attractions.

'We must make sure we bring you back at night; it's a whole different experience, isn't it, Cat?'

Catherine's eyes darted around.

'Cat? Hello?' Pia jarred her back to their conversation.

'Sorry, what did you say?'

'I just said we will have to bring Josie here at night.' She turned to Josie, 'We had some fun here, your mum and me. It was a fun place to come, growing up – it still is now.' She turned back to Catherine. 'You okay, Cat? What's up?'

Catherine looked around again. She moved closer to Pia. 'I just feel like he is all around. All my memories are tainted by him and the places we went together. He's everywhere. And let's not forget why we are here. This isn't a sightseeing trip – we came because someone has been terrorising me. They could be watching us now.' Her voice raised at the last sentence, becoming slightly squeaky.

Pia put her hand on her arm. 'Cat, chill out. We're fine. No-one is here; no-one is watching us, and Patrick's dead. He can't hurt you anymore.'

'That's just it, though, isn't it? He can. He still is. Look at me; I'm a mess.'

'Babe, we've got you. We can take it slower if you need to? Or if you need to spend some time on your own, let me know, and I don't mind taking Josie to any places she desperately wants to go that are too painful for you. But remember, all these places have memories from before Patrick; with me, with your nan, with other friends, and your mum and dad.'

'I know. I'm being silly. We do need to find out who has been stalking me, though. Who would bother to come all the way to Spain to put pictures of Patrick everywhere and hide my old stuff?'

'Let's talk about that later. There are things I need to tell you.'

'But –'

Pia looked at Josie, who had wandered over to the barrier at the edge of the pier, looking at the beach and eating her doughnuts. 'Not now. Later, I promise.' She squeezed Catherine's hand.

The two friends made their way to where Josie stood, standing one on each side of her, Catherine's arm around her waist. Josie put her head on her mum's shoulder and held out a doughnut. Catherine laughed, wiping the sugar from Josie's chin. 'I love Spanish food, but there is something special about a warm, freshly fried doughnut caked in sugar.' She took the proffered doughnut and groaned with pleasure at every bite. Licking the sugar from her lips, she pulled Josie away from the edge and tugged her towards the arcade.

They played on the basketball hoops, competed against each other on the dance machines and put endless coins in the 10p machines, watching as the coins jerked down through the pins to land on the moving shelf. Josie's eye lit up as the machine pushed the money closed to the edge; temptation pulled away by the magnet, keeping a pile of coins hanging just over the edge of the prize chute.

'What's that one?' Josie pointed to a mannequin fortune teller in a glass booth.

'Ah! Zoltar! I had forgotten this was here. Do you remember how often we would come and get our fortunes told, determined that they would come true?' Catherine's smile reached her eyes as nostalgia took over her body.

'I think I still have my fortunes in a box somewhere!'

'What is it?' Josie interrupted their memories.

'There was a film called –'

'Big.' Catherine finished. 'And Tom Hanks, that's the actor in the film, was a little boy who told the Zoltar machine he wanted to be a grown up, to be big.'

'So you make a wish?' asked Josie, frowning.

'Not really. It's a fortune teller, but I guess you can make a wish as well. Anyway, the next day, he is an adult, but he still has the mind of a ten-year-old, or whatever he was.'

'We should watch it. Your mum and I used to watch it all the time. It's a great film.'

'If you say so. So, can we get our fortunes now?' Josie rolled her eyes and looked for the coin slot, sliding her money in the hole and waiting for the animated character to tell her great things were coming her way. A little card came out of another slot, and Josie snatched it out. 'Great things are coming your way,' she read. See the world, and you will be truly happy.' She looked between her companions. 'It knows I am travelling! How do they do that?! You do one, Mum, and you, Pia.'

Pia smiled and inserted her coin, retrieving a yellow card with her own fortune. She handed it to Josie to read out.

'Enjoy the simple things in life. Meaning will follow.' Josie frowned. 'What does that mean?'

Pia shrugged and smiled, handing a coin to Catherine. Catherine's hand hovered over the slot for a moment before she pushed the coin and waited for her fortune. Josie snatched at the third yellow card and read it out.

'Don't let the past hold you back. The future is yours to make of it what you choose.' Josie smiled delightedly and handed it to Catherine. 'Let's do them every time we visit, and we can keep them as mementoes!'

The women left the arcade and made their way further along the pier, Catherine and Pia steering Josie away from the sweet shops, promising that she would get to try everything before they went back to Spain.

'Patrick!'

Catherine's stomach flipped, and her head whipped around. She looked from bench to bench and scanned the walkway.

'Patrick, there you are.'

She saw a woman scoop up a young dark-haired toddler as he ran around the corner.

Catherine's shoulders dropped, and she let out a breath. Squeezing her eyes tightly shut for a moment, she shook her head and caught up with Pia and Josie.

'Mum! Shall we go on the big wheel?'

'I think I'll sit this one out. You two go on, though. Just make sure you aren't sick after all those doughnuts!' Catherine laughed and handed over the cash for two tickets. The attendant clipped the pod closed, and Josie and Pia gradually rose higher and higher until they were out of view. The wheel moved slowly at first, then picked up momentum as it spun; Josie and Pia giving excited waves each time they passed Catherine. The fairground music blasted around them; the pier busy with heavy footfall in the sunshine. As the opening notes to the song by Sting, Every Breath You Take, began, Catherine grabbed the rail in front of her to steady herself. Above the crowd's noise, a DJ shouted through a speaker that this was a requested song, and he was assured the person it was for would know it was for them. Catherine's knuckles turned white as she tightened her grip on the iron railing, her stomach somersaulted, and she felt its contents threatening to re-emerge. Swallowing firmly, she turned and scanned the crowd, her eyes coming to rest on a DJ box. Pushing through the people, she waved to get his attention.

'Who requested this?'

'What?'

'Who requested this song?' Catherine was aware she was shrieking.

The DJ laughed, 'Not your taste?'

'I just need to know who requested it.'

'Sorry, love, we don't keep a record! Don't really take requests as a rule, but the lady was quite insistent and gave me £20 for my trouble. Don't tell the boss mind.' He winked. 'Tell you what, I'll play one for you as well, no charge. What do you want to hear?'

'Did she give you a name? Anything to help me find her?'

'Listen, lady, I'm just a DJ. I don't know. Do you want a song or not?' He put his headphones back on as the song came to an end, smoothly transitioning into his next track. Catherine turned away and moved back to the wheel as it slowed to let people off.

'You okay, Mum? You look like you have seen a ghost! Oooh, shall we go on the haunted train next?!'

'You go get the tickets, and we will be right over.' Catherine handed her purse to Josie and hurriedly told Pia what had happened.

'Ah.'

'Ah?'

'Well, it could have been anyone. It's a popular song!'

'But you said, ah. What does that mean?'

'Well, look, I was going to tell you this later, and I'm sure it's nothing, but I did some digging and found out that Ashleigh was released last year.'

'What?!'

'Look, I'm sure it's not her. What would she have to gain from stalking you? Come on, let's go on the ghost train, and we will talk later.'

Pia dragged her friend to the next attraction, and the women silently joined Josie in the little carriage. Catherine's lips were pursed, and she didn't return Josie's smile.

The ghost train was not a ride intended to induce sickness. However, Catherine's stomach churned. Her body felt icy with fear. She strained in the darkness, looking into the faces of the masked characters – *were they real people or mannequins? Could one of them be Ashleigh, waiting for her moment to get to Catherine?* Her breath caught in her throat, and she struggled to get air into her lungs. She jumped as something squeezed her shoulder, realising a moment later it was Pia reaching behind Josie, sensing her friend was not okay. Josie leaned forward in the seat, shrieking with laughter, looking around and ducking as various cobwebs and fake limbs dangled above their carriage. The ride pulled into the station, and Catherine fought to open the safety barrier, running from the ride.

'Mum, what is it? You have been acting weird, and the two of you keep whispering and trying to get rid of me. I'm not a kid, and I'm not stupid.'

'We think we might know who the stalker is.' Catherine glared at Pia. 'Pia didn't think it was important to tell us that Ashleigh has been released from prison.'

'Hang on a minute. I only just found out. It's not as if I have been keeping this from you. I found out a few days ago, and I wanted to tell you in person.'

'Ashleigh married my fa- my da- what do I call him? He wasn't a dad to me. Anyway, she was his wife? She's the one who killed him?'

'Yes.' Pia confirmed. 'Look, if she wanted to hurt you, surely she would have done it already? You were on your own before when the song came on. She could have got you then.'

'Great, thanks. This isn't helping.'

'Look, I'm just saying, she obviously doesn't want to hurt you, or surely she would have done it already. Let's talk about this at home. This isn't the place.'

'She didn't kill Patrick until a few years in. She was just biding her time. Maybe she is doing the same with me.'

'Look. Do you want to go home? We can go back to mine if you want?'

Catherine opened her mouth to answer and then saw her daughter's face. She pulled her in for a hug and reassured her that everything was okay and she was probably just hungry and ready for lunch. 'Fish and chips on the beach?'

Pia and Josie went ahead to find a bench while Catherine enjoyed people-watching as she waited for the food.

'Salt and Vinegar?' The woman behind the counter asked.

'Sorry, what was that? I was in my own world for a minute there.'

'Don't worry, love. I am always doing the same. Drifting off in my own head. Do you want salt and vinegar on these?'

Catherine smiled. 'Is that a Plymouth accent? And yes, please, both on all of them.'

'Sure is. Good spot! You can take the girl out of Plymouth…'

'A good friend of mine was from Plymouth. I owe her everything.' Catherine's eyes misted up as she took the paper wrapped packages. 'Thank you -' she glanced at the older woman's name badge, 'Bernie'.

3
Patrick's House

Catherine opened her eyes and saw the glint of steel in the moonlight. Ashleigh's eyes were wide; the whites emphasised in the darkness, giving her a werewolf-like resemblance. The sound of laughter in the room distracted Catherine from the knife, and she saw Patrick standing at the end of the bed.

'Go on then,' he said to Ashleigh. 'I thought you hated her. You managed to stab the knife into me easily enough, or was that a fluke in your pathetic character?'

Ashleigh licked her lips, looking from Catherine to Patrick and back. She raised the knife higher.

Catherine shot upright in bed, her bedding and pyjamas drenched with sweat. She looked around the shadow-filled room and let out a shaky breath as she remembered where she was. *It was just a dream. It was just a dream.* Glancing at her phone, she saw it was nearly late enough to get up – too late to go back to sleep. She silently rose, pulling on her clothes from the day before and hastily scribbled a note to leave on the bed.

The morning air was chilly, waiting for the sun to rise and warm it up. The streets were shrouded in darkness, and Catherine's heightened senses scanned every shadow, every bush and every corner for danger. The occasional car broke the otherwise silent walk. Pushing her hands into her jacket pockets, Catherine walked steadily in the direction of her old house – Patrick's house. The brisk walk staved off the cold, and Catherine's breath soon stopped making clouds in the air as the sun began its rise. Turning into the street, she hesitated, unsure where Ashleigh now lived. *Will she be in the house?* The last steps toward the house were tentative until she stood opposite the gates. The angle afforded her a glimpse of the front aspect and its darkened windows. The gates had recently been painted, but the exterior was mostly unchanged. Whoever lived there had children. Bikes were lying on the driveway. Patrick would have hated the mess. Catherine smiled briefly, then frowned as she contemplated who the bikes belonged to – *surely Pia would have said if Ashleigh and Patrick had children, unless she didn't know.*

Suddenly feeling exposed in the rising sun, Catherine turned and ran. She ran to the end of the road and turned in the direction of the seafront. She ran down Dyke Road and turned onto West Street, not stopping until she reached the historic railing separating the promenade from the sand. Leaving her socks and shoes on the concrete floor, she strode down the beach, focusing on the sensation of the sand between her toes. The beach and the skyline were bathed in the early morning glow, and she felt a sudden lightness as her toes reached the cool water. Standing and letting the gentle waves lap over her feet, Catherine wept silently. She stepped further into the water until it splashed against her shins and just stood.

She wasn't sure how long had passed when the shrill sound of her ringtone pulled her away from her thoughts, and she saw Pia's name flashing on the screen. After a brief conversation reassuring Pia that she was alive and well and would be returning shortly, Catherine made her way back up the beach. In the time she had stood in the water, the rest of the world had begun to wake up, and people were going about their morning – coffee drinkers were out in force with fresh brews in their reusable flasks, friends gathered, sporty types were running or cycling and dog walkers took advantage of the quiet before the hustle and bustle of the city picked up. Catherine headed back to Pia's to fill them in on her dawn excursion.

4
London

After Catherine had been suitably chastised for disappearing early in the morning, and all three women were full of coffee and croissants, London was on the agenda for the day. Catherine yawned as they took their seats on the train. She faced Pia and Josie and answered Josie's questions as best she could.

'I had no idea you were such a fan of the royal family.'

'I'm not really. It is all just so much more exciting now we are actually going to Buckingham Palace. Can you imagine if they come out on the balcony while we are there? I would be able to tell Mateo that I saw the King!'

Catherine laughed. 'First of all, the chances of them coming out onto the balcony are pretty much zero, and secondly, I think the King is in Balmoral anyway – I saw it on the news. So, sorry, my princess, but I don't think you will get to see the King.'

'But I will get to see his Crown Jewels.'

Catherine choked on her drink, making eye contact with Pia as she coughed and laughed.

'What?' Josie looked at them.

'Do you mean The Tower of London?'

The train arrived at Victoria Station, and the three women were pushed along by the throng of commuters until they found themselves free of the foot traffic and able to stop and get their bearings. Buckingham Palace was a short walk, and Josie huffed that they weren't using the underground. 'I wanted to see what the underground was like!'

'Don't worry, there will be time for all that. It's only a ten-minute walk to the palace, and we can get the underground to London Bridge later. I forgot how much there is for tourists to do in London!'

Catherine instinctively pulled her handbag to the front of her body, looking at Josie's to make sure the zip was closed. She stayed close to Josie, linking her arm through her daughters and guiding their navigation through fellow pedestrians on the busy streets. As they approached the palace, Josie's face lit up as she took in the Queen Victoria Memorial Statue, the gold gleaming in the sunlight, giving the illusion of being freshly polished. She tore her eyes from the statue and its gentle fountain to focus on the royal residence of Buckingham Palace. The flag flew at half mast, indicating HRH King Charles was not in residence, as Catherine had previously suggested.

Josie marched towards the imposing black and gold gates. She turned to smile at them as they strolled with the nonchalance of locals. They caught up to Josie, who now stood with her hands on the wrought iron gates. Catherine glanced at her watch, 'I checked the website for the changing of the guards, and we have an hour until the next change, so shall we grab a quick Starbucks when you have had a look and then come back?'

They took a selection of photos in front of the palace and indulged a few tourists by offering to take their photos before heading for a coffee shop.

'I'll get the drinks – I want to use my English money.'

Not for the first time, Catherine felt a pang in her stomach. 'I should have brought you here before. I feel like I have kept so much from you, and I needn't have. The longer it went on, the harder it was to tell you, and the harder it was to think about coming back.'

'If anything, we have the stalker to thank for pushing you into telling everything and bringing me back here.'

'I wouldn't go that far, but yes, I suppose, in a funny way, she is the one who made me start to face my fears.'

'What's the plan? How are we going to find her?'

'I don't know. Let's have a nice day in London today, and we will think about it later.' Catherine looked around, scanning the faces around them. 'It's times like this I wish I was better at the whole social media thing. Maybe you can find her on there, Pia? See what she looks like now?'

'I'll do my darndest. Right, come on, drink up. We need to get back to the palace if Josie wants to see the changing of the guards. Get ready to see hordes of stereotypical tourists gathered outside – it'll be much busier by now.'

Pia's prediction was accurate, and they wove their way between the people until Josie was able to wiggle into a space at the front. The band took their positions and began to play whilst new guards on both horseback and foot emerged from the palace to-relieve their peers. The traditional red robes and black bearskin hats were striking and left the crowd cheering at the spectacle. Catherine held up her phone to take a photo of Josie with the horses in the background and then panned to record a video for Mateo. It had been so many years that Catherine couldn't help but get swept away by the crowds, excited to watch the new guards take their positions.

The day passed by in a whirlwind of sightseeing until the atmosphere changed and the city nightlife came alive. The same groups of people scurried from place to place – only now the professionals were without ties, the tourists had started to flag, and the dedicated partygoers were mixed amongst the crowds, dressed to the nines and looking for the 'in' place to be.

'What happened to the old club?' Catherine asked Pia, watching a group of girls head to the front of a queue, where the waiting bouncer greeted them like royalty, stepping aside to let them in.

'I forgot to tell you. It shut down. The reputation wasn't great over the last few years – the drug scene kind of took over, and lots of the lawyer types didn't want to be associated with the place anymore. As they were most of its clientele, it ended up closing. I think the building has been converted into flats now.'

'Ironic that they didn't want to be associated with the place – most of them were into coke back in the days I worked there; they just thought they weren't as bad as their clients because they pay taxes and wear suits!'

'Do you want to go take a look?'

'No, I don't think I could face it. It's where it all began.' Catherine noticed Josie stifling a yawn and found herself doing the same. 'Why is yawning so catching? I think it's a sign that it's time to say goodnight to London.'

The underground station was quiet at this time of the evening. Josie looked around at the deserted platform and stood close to her mother and Pia. When they eventually got on the train that would take them back to Pia's, they got seats together and sat in comfortable silence. The station clock showed it was nearly midnight as they disembarked the train and made their way home.

'Cup of tea, anyone?' Pia hung her coat on the coat stand and kicked her shoes in the direction of the shoe rack.

'Go on then.' Catherine answered, dropping her bag on the coffee table.

'What do you reckon then, Mi Vida? Will you be trading in Spanish life for the bright lights of London?'

Josie laughed, squeezing her mum's hand. 'Not quite, but I must bring Javi here. He would LOVE it. I've sent him so many photos. I got him a fridge magnet. Oh, and I must write the postcards I got and send them tomorrow.' Josie rummaged in her bag, pulling out little paper bags with various souvenirs. She slid the postcards out of their bag and frowned at the postcards in her hand. The first showed a picture of Wadhurst Castle, and the second showed the white cliffs of Beachy Head. 'Where are these places? I must have picked up the wrong cards in the shop, but I don't see how.' Josie rummaged in her bag, pulling out another packet containing the postcards she had selected to send. Catherine didn't say a word, just looked at the postcards laid out on the table.

'Mum?'

'It's her again. She must have been following us and put these in your bag.'

'Why would she do that?'

'Wadhurst Castle – that's where Patrick and I got married, and Beachy Head – that's the spot I left my car so he would assume I had thrown myself over the cliff.' Catherine choked back a sob and buried her face in her hands.

Pia came in with a tray of drinks, her expression changing as she picked up on the mood change. She glanced at the postcards and immediately realised what had happened.

'For fucks sake. We need to find this bitch once and for all. We need to find out what she wants.'

Pia pulled out her phone, and Josie saw her open the Facebook app, typing the name Ashleigh Walker into the search box – nothing. She tried Ash Walker and Leigh Walker with multiple results that offered no clues. Pia hesitated and pursed her lips before typing Ashleigh Reklaw. The search results brought up a heavily filtered photo, but it was her. 'Gotcha!'

Catherine looked up. 'That was quick.'

'Well, we still might not be able to find anything. The security settings are pretty tight, but it doesn't look like she uses it much anyway. I can't see anything other than a cover photo of the beach with the old pier in the background. It could have been taken anytime, or might just be a stock photo, it doesn't prove that she is even in Brighton.'

'She clearly is, though. How do we contact her? Can we just send her a message? What if she is listening now?'

The three women stopped and looked around, motionless. Pia let out a breath and declared there was no way she was listening. She glanced at the window lock before pushing the cups of tea towards Josie and Catherine and opening a packet of custard creams.

5
Patrick's House

'Check her Facebook again.'

'Still nothing to see.'

'Can you message her? I could, but what if it's not her? And if it is, then she'll know we are on to her.'

'Does that matter? It's not as if we have anything to gain by her not knowing we suspect her. Maybe give it another day or two and message her if we can't find anything out?'

'Plan.' Pia put her phone down. 'Shall we wake up sleeping beauty?'

'Let's leave her to sleep a little longer. She never gets a lie in. I often offer, but she rarely takes me up on it. I suppose with Mateo in her room, she wakes up whenever he does anyway.'

'Ok. Well, I don't know what else we can do about Ashleigh. We don't have anyone to ring – I'm guessing you don't want to speak to Patrick's family. Unless you have contact details for anyone the two of you used to work with?'

'No. I didn't keep anyone's details.' Catherine grimaced apologetically at her friend as a hurt look flashed across Pia's face.

Josie shuffled in, rubbing her eyes, her hair sticking up. 'Why didn't you wake me? What are you talking about?'

'Nothing for you to worry about, love.'

'Mum. I'm not a baby.'

Catherine held her hands up. 'Fine. We were talking about how to find Ashleigh.'

'Why don't you just go and knock on the door of her old house? They might know, or have a forwarding address. I know it's years since she lived there, but it's gotta be worth a shot, right?'

Catherine and Pia exchanged a look. 'It's unlikely, but she's right. It's gotta be worth a try? Did you see anyone there when you were out the other morning?'

'No. I don't know. I kind of thought at the time she might be there. But that seemed silly afterwards. I don't know if I can go back there.' Catherine gripped her coffee mug. 'I can't – I can't go in.'

'Why don't you guys stay here and have a lazy morning, and I'll go and scout the place out?' Pia offered.

'No way. I'm coming! I want to see where Mum used to live. Sorry Mum, if that's okay?' Her voice dropped. 'I also kind of want to see where *he* lived.'

'Look, honey, if you want to find his family, I suppose there is nothing I can do to stop you. They may still be alive - I'm sure Max, his brother, will be. I can give you their names. I just can't be part of it.'

'No.' Josie shook her head vehemently. 'I don't want to. I don't think I want to. You're the only family I need.'

'Well, I would understand if you wanted to find them. I just can't be involved, and I can't have them knowing where I am.'

'I think I'm just curious about the life you had here and who you were before.'

Catherine sighed. 'Ok, looks like we are all going.'

An hour later, they arrived on foot at Catherine's old house. They lined up on the pavement opposite, the same spot Catherine stood in a few days before and stared at the house.

'It's massive. Did you really live here?!'

'Money can't bring happiness. I loved this house at first, but it just became a cage of misery.'

Josie took her mum's hand and squeezed it. 'I know we didn't have much, but I had you, and we had Maggie, and that's all that matters.'

Pia stepped off the pavement and crossed the road, turning with her hand on the gate. Catherine and Pia followed, and they made their way up the path.

'Wow! A swimming pool!'

The front door looked the same. It was well-maintained, and the windows gave sight of long plush curtains. Some of the shrubs and bushes were familiar, and Catherine couldn't help but admire the longevity of the well-kept garden. This was where the similarities ended – the poolside was scattered with children's inflatables, and the kitchen looked like it had been replaced. Catherine crept closer to the kitchen window to see the aga still in the same spot. As she peered through the window, a woman entered the kitchen and screamed at the sight of Catherine at the window. A man came running from the pool house as the woman emerged from the front door, nearly knocking into Pia and Josie.

'What the hell's going on?' The man asked, looking between all the women.

'I was going to ask them the same question. She was peering in the kitchen window.' The woman pointed at Catherine, then eyed her with suspicion. Her shoulders dropped as she let out a breath. 'Oh, for God's sake, are you some sort of murder enthusiasts? I thought we had finally got over that.'

'Murder enthusiasts?!' Josie blurted out, wide-eyed.

'Well, who are you then?!'

Catherine stepped between Josie and the woman. 'I used to live here. I've been away for some years and just wanted to find out what happened to – to the people who lived here after me.'

The woman narrowed her eyes, looking at Catherine. 'When you say *away*….?'

'No! I'm not the one who killed him. I bloody wish I had.' She glanced at Josie apologetically. 'I've been away, out of the country, not in prison. I look nothing like that trollop.'

The man looked between the women again, scratching his head.

'I'm the first wife, okay. I'm the one who is supposed to be dead – killed herself. Only I'm not. I'm still alive, and I am trying to find Ashleigh.'

'I think I'd better put the kettle on. Do you want to come in?' The woman opened the front door and stepped aside to let Catherine, Pia and Josie past.

Catherine hesitated before stepping over the threshold, grimacing at the woman. She took a deep breath and looked ahead. The wooden newel post loomed ahead of her, marking the sweeping wooden staircase. She winced as she focused on the wooden floor at the bottom of the stairs, squeezing her eyes shut, the pain as raw as if it happened yesterday. She instinctively wrapped her arms around her stomach and let out a sob. 'He – he left me there.' She felt Pia's arms wrap around her, the familiar smell of her perfume enveloping her like a warm blanket.

Pia turned to the woman. 'Do you mind if we take a moment while you put the kettle on? Josie, you go with her.'

The woman smiled kindly. 'Of course, come on through love, let's give your, um, let's give them some space. I'm Sheila.'

Catherine drifted to the stairs and dropped to sit on the bottom step, leaning forward so her fingertips could trail the spot on the floor. 'He or she would be in their 20s now – an older brother for Josie, an aunt or uncle for Mateo.' Her face darkened. 'Although if Patrick had his way, the baby would have been at boarding school and would probably end up groomed into becoming a lawyer, just like Patrick.'

'The baby had your genes as well as his. It would never have been like Patrick. It broke my heart, visiting you in the hospital. I could see him slowly breaking your soul. I don't love that you left, but if you stayed, I know I would have lost you anyway.'

Sheila poked her head into the hallway. 'I thought it might be easier if we sit in the garden; Josie has taken the tray outside. You take your time.'

Catherine rose and thanked Sheila. She looked at the door to what was once Patrick's study.

'Probably not what you expect in there now. Feel free to take a look – but I'm afraid we ripped out all that stuffy panelling and turned it into a playroom.' Sheila pushed the door open, revealing the brightly decorated space.

Catherine took in the toy boxes, the yellow walls and the desk filled with pots of crayons and colourfully scribbled drawings. 'Patrick would hate this.' She whispered, then spoke a little louder, 'He would be turning in his grave.' Her face broke into a smile, and she laughed as they made their way to the garden. Josie's look of concern as she saw them approaching turned to one of relief as Catherine smiled at her. The four women sat around the table, and Catherine told her story for the second time in as many months.

Sheila looked at the three women who, after telling the story, looked at her with hope. 'After hearing what you went through, I wish I could help you. I don't know where she is. There was another owner between us. They bought the house from Patrick's parents, I believe. They stayed a few years, but back then there was a lot of press attention. There were visits from people who tour murder sites, true crime bloggers and all sorts. They sold up because they wanted their privacy. Not sure why they bought it in the first place; mind you, they probably got a good deal on it. Anyway, that's when we bought it. We still get the odd podcaster or journalist here digging for a story or doing a piece on local murders, but they are few and far between. But this Ashleigh, we have never seen her – not that I know of anyway! Though from what you say, it sounds like she did the world a favour. What a different story from the one the papers spun. It just goes to show what these men can get away with, doesn't it? Anyway ladies, not to hurry you, but I need to get off and pick the little ones up from nursery. They are on half days while they settle.'

Catherine, Pia and Josie rose from their seats. 'No, I'm sorry, we have taken up far too much of your time. Can we give you a hand clearing up?'

'It's not much, you get off, and I do hope it all works out for you. If I can be of any help, let me know. Good luck!'

~

Catherine's shoulders sagged as they stepped back out through the gates. 'Another dead end.'

'For now. Let's go back to mine and have a drink and get changed. Maybe we could stay around here today? Do some shopping and walk along the seafront?'

'It makes so much more sense now why Mum and Maggie drank so much tea. It's definitely an English thing!'

6
The Seafront

The three women swung their shopping bags as they walked through the cobbled streets of The Lanes.

'I feel like I am on some kind of weird emotional rollercoaster. One minute we are having a lovely day like any other tourists, and then suddenly, I remember why we are here. I keep getting that feel we are being watched.'

Pia linked her arm through Catherine's, squeezing as she leaned in and spoke softly. 'That's because you are an amazing person and an amazing mum. I can see how much you are freaking out inside, but you are doing the right thing by downplaying it in front of Josie.'

'I know. I know. And we don't even know what she wants from us. I get these goosebumps all over me sometimes, as if she is nearby.'

They stopped as they looked up at the balcony above a kebab shop.

'Do you remember –' Pia began.

'The singing barber!'

'What are you two on about now?'

'Years ago, there was a barber shop where that kebab shop is. The barber who owned it would put on shows singing from his balcony, raising money for charity. People would gather below and put money in his bucket. It was lovely.'

Josie shrugged; the magic of the memory, lost on her.

'What happened to him anyway?'

'I'm sure I read he died a few years back. The shop was sold and turned into a takeaway, and I think it's just a normal flat above now.'

'That's sad. It's a shame no one carried on his legacy.'

'That's Brighton for you. Everything and nothing is the same. It is lovely to have you back, despite the reason.'

They stopped as they reached the edge of The Lanes, stepping from the cobbles back onto the smooth pavement opposite the seafront.

'About time for a drink, ladies?' Pia pointed to a bar a few metres from them. 'We can sit for a minute and re-group.'

'Re-group. Such an old person thing to say.' Josie joked.

'How dare you! We're still young!' She glanced at Catherine, and they exchanged a look before breaking into giggles and launching into a rendition of Love is a Battlefield.

Sitting at a table by the window, they ordered a round of drinks and some tapas to share and began to review their purchases. Josie took photos to send to Javi and sent a selfie of the three of them to Adriana to show Mateo.

A while later, leaning back with empty plates in front of them, the waiter appeared. 'Ladies, it seems you have an admirer. This is with compliments from Patrick.' The waiter set the tray on the table and lined up three champagne glasses before popping the cork on a bottle.

'Who ordered this?!'

'It's from Patrick.'

'Who ordered it? Was it a woman? Is she here?' Catherine looked around, scanning the bar for Ashleigh.

'It was ordered and paid for over the phone. It was a woman, but she didn't give a name. Is everything okay?'

'She must have given you a name on whatever card she used to pay?'

'My colleague spoke to her, but we don't keep that information, and we wouldn't be able to give it out anyway. Sorry ladies. But hey, it's free champagne. Enjoy!' The waiter smiled apologetically, clearing their plates before leaving.

Catherine ran out of the bar onto the street, looking up and down. Pia followed and put her hand on her arm, 'She isn't here. She isn't in the bar. Come on, we may as well enjoy the champagne. Free champagne is free champagne, after all! And it's the good stuff.'

'Yes, but how does she know we are here?'

Pia frowned. 'Well, if she was following us, she isn't here now. And she still hasn't actually done anything. Buying champagne for us is hardly a criminal offence.'

'But what about all the stuff in Spain? Breaking into our flat, the café, putting those wedding photos up everywhere – poking out my eyes in the pictures, that's hardly the actions of a sane person. Hardly the actions of someone who doesn't want to hurt me!'

Pia looked around. No-one else appeared to be listening, but she lowered her voice as she hissed, 'I know. I know. I just don't know what else we can do. It's not as if we can go to the police! You're supposed to be dead!'

Josie stood in the doorway, watching the exchange. Catherine looked in her direction, and her shoulders dropped, 'I know. You're right. Come on, let's go back in. People are starting to look, and more attention is the last thing we need right now.'

Pia ushered them back inside and indicated for them to sit down. 'I'm nipping to the loo. Cat, why don't you guys order something else to drink and then we need to figure out what we are going to do.'

Catherine nodded as her friend took charge – I'll go to the bar. Josie, are you okay here for a minute?'

Josie pulled out a chair and waved them away. 'I'm fine. Go order what you want, and I am happy to drink the free champagne.' Catherine disappeared from view to order drinks, and Josie pulled out her phone to check for messages.

'Miss, I need you to come with me.'

Josie looked up. The woman flashed an ID card at her and indicated for Josie to step out from behind the table. Josie glanced in the direction of the bar, unable to see Catherine.

'Your mum and Pia will be escorted out by my colleague. Right now, your safety is my priority. We have just been made aware of a plot to harm you and your family, and until we have the suspect in custody, we need to get you to safety. We have alerted officers in Spain, who will send security for your son.'

At the mention of Mateo, Josie's eyes widened, and she stood, looking in the direction of the bar.

'Miss. Come on. Your safety is paramount, and I have instructions to get you back to the station as a matter of urgency. Once we get there, we can fill you in on everything.'

Josie nodded, expressionless and moved ahead of the woman to the door, not noticing the woman whisper to a passing waiter. 'Please can you let the table know Ashleigh and Josie will meet them at Beachy Head.'

Ashleigh closed the gap between her and Josie, who allowed herself to be ushered into a parked car.

7
Beachy Head

The wind whipped through them as they got out of the car. Ashleigh smiled as she surveyed the empty car park. The turn in the weather, together with the late hour, meant they were unlikely to be disturbed. The crashing of the waves against the rocks gave the illusion of the cliffs being further away than they were – the sound buffered by the rock face.

'What are we doing here?' Josie looked around, taking in the wide empty expanse, pulling her coat tighter around her body.

'Let's go for a walk.'

'I thought we were going to the police station.'

'Yes. About that.' Ashleigh licked her lips. 'I'm not really a Police Officer. I'm an old friend of your mum's. Well, friend might be pushing it, but anyway, I thought we could have a bit of a chat before she gets here. You'd like to know more about your parents, wouldn't you?'

'Mum's already told me what sort of man my father was.'

'She hasn't told you everything. She hasn't told you what she did to me. Catherine and I worked together before she married your father. I married him after she left.' Ashleigh held out her arm. 'Come on, Josie. I just want to talk.'

Josie took a step back, shaking her head. 'I want to go back. Take me back to my mum.'

'All in good time. Now. Hand me your phone, and we're going for a walk.'

Josie looked around.

'There is no point looking around; where will you run? There is no-one here to go running to, and you don't know the way back, so don't bother trying.'

Josie's shoulders sank as the reality of her situation hit. She nodded and stepped towards Ashleigh. They walked side-by-side in silence, Ashleigh leading Josie to a bench overlooking the sea. The wind whipped around them, blowing the salty air in their faces. She gestured for Josie to take a seat, remaining standing herself. She stood between the bench and the flimsy safety barrier, warning people not to get too close to the edge, looking out at the waves smashing into the rocks below. Josie watched as the wind got underneath Ashleigh's coat, pulling at the fabric and causing Ashleigh to sway as she fought against the elements.

'This is a well-known suicide spot, you know,' she said, gesturing to a placard cable-tied to the barrier. Many people are scraped off the rocks down there every year.' As she spoke, the waves crashed violently against the cliffs; the resulting spray slapping the water as it landed, daring her to step closer to the edge. 'Those people leave the ones they left behind suffering. Once they've jumped, they can't undo it. Your mum is a fake, a phoney. She had a choice. She only faked her death. She could have come back; she could have stopped him - stopped my suffering. But no, she left. She left and didn't come back. She must have heard about his death, but she still didn't come back.' Josie jumped as the waves gave a ferocious roar. 'I spent 15 years in prison because of HER. Because she didn't come forward and tell the courts what kind of monster your father really was.'

Ashleigh stopped, turning her gaze from the sea back to Josie. 'That's right. He was a monster. I bet she didn't tell you what kind of blood you have running through you, did she?'

Josie's eyes widened as Ashleigh paced precariously near the flimsy barrier. 'Please, just come away from the edge. I want to hear your story.'

Ashleigh laughed. 'Oh, you want to hear my story, do you? Only it's not a story. It's my life. My shitty life because your darling mother left me to rot in prison instead of doing the right thing. Do you know what I went to prison for?' Ashleigh stepped towards Josie. 'Do you?' she raised her voice.

'Yes, but I don't mind. It doesn't matter that you were in prison.' Josie shook her head, looking down.

'You don't mind?' Ashleigh's voice rose to a shriek. 'You don't mind that I stabbed your father. That I killed your only other flesh and blood? I watched the life leave his body. There was blood. So much blood.'

'STOP IT. I don't want to know the details. I don't need to know.'

'But I want you to. I want you to know what sort of monster he was. I want you to know that he deserved it. How much did she tell you?'

'Just that he wasn't very nice to her.' Josie mumbled. 'She said he used to hit her and control everything she did and that when she found out she was pregnant with me, she knew she had to leave.'

'Wasn't very nice to her? Wasn't very nice to her? Oh, poor Catherine. Well, in my marriage to him, he beat me. He controlled what I wore, who I spoke to, where I went. He beat me. He raped me -.' Ashleigh paused, looking at Josie for a reaction.

Tears flowed down Josie's cheeks as she leapt from the bench. 'STOP IT. JUST STOP IT. I'm not him. I don't need to hear it.'

'Oh, I'm sorry. Is my life making you uncomfortable? You had better hope you never have to be in an abusive relationship and then spend nearly 15 years in prison just to escape. It could all have been avoided if your precious mother had spoken up. She's a coward. Nothing but a coward. And you – you look just like him. Oh, his legacy lives on alright. Catherine saw to that. She should have flushed you down the toilet. Your D NA is POISON.' Ashleigh face was inches from Josie's now as she spat her words out.

Josie choked back a sob, wringing her hands. 'I'm sorry'. Her voice was so low it was barely audible over the wind. She sank down onto the bench, dropping her head into her hands, her shoulders shaking as she sobbed.

The two women were interrupted as the beeping of a car horn pierced the crashing of the waves. The car advancing towards them had left the car park and was bumping over the grass in their direction. Josie leapt to her feet beside Ashleigh, and they stared as the car continued in their direction, showing no sign of slowing. Josie fell as Ashleigh shoved her out of the path of the car. As she looked up from where she landed, the car skidded to a halt inches from the bench they were standing in front of. Her mother leapt out, eyes wild in the dusk.

'Get away from her.' Catherine screamed at Ashleigh. A car door slammed as Pia exited the driver's side and edged toward the trio. 'Get away from my daughter.' Catherine repeated.

Ashleigh laughed. The wind swirled the sound all around them. 'Me? I'm not the one who just drove a car at her on the edge of a cliff. I'm the one who pushed her to safety. It's not her I wanted anyway. She was just a means to an end – I knew you'd come. Getting a chance to fill her in a on a few home truths was just a bonus; bonding time with my step-daughter.'

Josie scrambled to her feet, rushing toward Catherine.

'Go with Pia, please.'

'But Mum.'

'NOW.'

Josie rushed into Pia's arms, a high-pitched sob escaping as Pia's arms enveloped her.

'It was you all along, wasn't it? In Spain?'

'I don't know what you mean.' Ashleigh smiled smugly.

'You were always jealous. Jealous that Patrick chose me. You always wanted him. Well, you got what you wanted. Surely you can't blame me for that? What do you expect to happen when you sleep with other people's husbands? Did you think he would never do it to you, that it was all my fault for being a bad wife, and you would live happily ever after?' Catherine forced a laugh. 'Why? Why have you been following me? Tormenting me?'

'Don't you get it?' Ashleigh snarled.

'Get what?'

'My life. My shitty life is all your fault. You got away and left me stuck with him. I thought I had everything I wanted. I thought it was my happy ever after; I really did. It was actually a living nightmare. I couldn't take it anymore. And you didn't come back. You didn't come back even when you must have known I was on trial for murder.'

Catherine looked back at Pia and Josie, who were standing beside the car. Her voice dropped. 'I couldn't.'

'You couldn't? More like you wouldn't. You left me to rot.' Ashleigh took a step back. 'And what have I got to show for my life now? Nothing. I have nothing. Nothing and no-one. I'm just a murderer who killed an *innocent* man. Without your testimony, no-one believed me. Maybe if you weren't such a coward, I wouldn't have gone to prison. Maybe if you spoke up before running away, he would have been exposed for the monster he was.'

Catherine's eyes focused on Ashleigh's feet as she moved; the dark clouds appearing overhead caused the cliff edge to blur with the landscape.

'If I stayed, they wouldn't have believed me any more than they believed you - you know that. It would have been my word against his.' Catherine spoke softly. 'Maybe I should have come back and spoken up when you – when it all happened. But I couldn't. I couldn't risk his family reporting me or finding out about Josie. I couldn't risk losing her when there wasn't any guarantee they would have believed me.' Her arms dropped by her side, the fight leaving her body.

Ashleigh looked behind her. 'I have nothing left to live for. I don't have a life. At least you have her.' She gestured to Josie. 'Even if she is a part of him, you aren't alone. I don't see any point in being here anymore. He's won. Patrick has won.' She stepped over the swaying barrier, turning to face the wind. 'FUCK YOU PATRICK.' The waves thundered in response.

'Ashleigh, wait.'

'Don't come any closer.'

'Ashleigh. Look, I know we haven't ever really seen eye to eye. But you can't let him win. You can't. You can get your life back on track. I'll help you. *We* will help you.' She looked back at Pia. 'Come on. Step back over the barrier. If you jump, he will have managed to destroy all of our lives. I couldn't live with it. I couldn't help you before, but I can help you now. I'm sorry. I'm so sorry.' Tears rolled down her cheeks as she looked at the other woman. 'I'm sorry.' She stepped toward Ashleigh and held her hand out. 'Please.'

Ashleigh looked at the waves, breathing in the salty air, tasting it on her lips. Her nails dug into her hands as she threw her head back and let out an animalistic roar. As the sound left her body, her shoulders sagged and she took a deep breath.

'Ashleigh?'

EPILOGUE:
One Year Later

Josie

'Are you sure you have everything you need? Passports? Money? I'm going to miss you so much!'

'Yes, Mum.' Josie rolled her eyes and looked at Javier. 'Besides Pia's flight over isn't until tomorrow, don't forget. So you don't have to worry.'

'I'm your mother. I'll always worry!'

'I know, I know, and I love you for it.' Josie hugged her mum and bent down to give Mateo a kiss. He wrapped his arms around her neck, and she blinked rapidly to stop the tear from falling. 'Right, come on, Javi, London is waiting for us. You're going to love it! Mateo, churri, I'll see you in a few weeks.'

'I'm so proud of you.' Catherine called as Josie and Javi left the café.

Javi's father was waiting at the B&B to take Josie and Javi to the airport, along with some guests who had finished their stay. The flight was uneventful, and in a few hours, they landed at Gatwick airport, where Pia awaited. Pia was flying to Oliva the next morning while Josie and Javi stayed at her house.

Pia

The plane began its descent, and Pia looked out of the window at the familiar country below. The morning heat created wavy lines in the air, and Pia felt the familiar tug of her second home welcoming her back. Catherine would be waiting in arrivals, and Pia planned to start looking for a holiday apartment to buy so she could spend longer in the sunny paradise.

Catherine

A whole year had passed since the day at Beachy Head. Catherine thought back to it as she bustled around the café, baking and getting everything ready for opening. A couple of months after returning to Spain, she received a postcard from Brighton with the simple message, 'I forgive you.' Catherine hadn't heard from Ashleigh again, and there had been no contact from the police, so she assumed Ashleigh hadn't handed her confession in. The bell on the door tinkled, announcing the arrival of the first customer of the day – Maria.

'Hola!'

'Buenos días, Maria.' Catherine smiled warmly at the older woman.

'Why are you so happy today?'

'I was just thinking how life has come together everything feels exactly as it should be.'

'I'm happy for you. Maria's eyes crinkled at the corners as she patted Catherine's hand.

Ashleigh

Ashleigh took a break from her shift in the arcade and made her way to the beach, sitting on the edge of the promenade, her legs dangling above the sand. She opened her bag and pulled out the well-read confession Catherine had given her before they parted a year ago. The women had reached an impasse of sorts, with Catherine giving Ashleigh a written confession about her faked suicide and an account of her marriage with Patrick. It was too late, but Catherine told her to do what she needed to do with it. Ashleigh never handed it in to the police; it wouldn't change anything, but reading it helped on the days she struggled – reminded her she didn't imagine it all.

Pia had introduced her to a contact in a Women's Refuge, and Ashleigh found this gave her some comfort and a place to direct her anger – other people's abusers. The refuge put her in touch with a counsellor who helped her to revisit memories she had forced herself to forget. She looked out to sea and finally felt ready to look up the child she gave up for adoption after giving birth in prison all those years ago.

Acknowledgements

Gosh. Well, everyone, it looks like I have made it to the end of another book. I can probably do without writing War and Peace in the acknowledgements this time! But please do know that I love you all, and I really do appreciate EVERYONE'S ongoing support.

A few people that can't go without a mention…

My lovely Editor, Tracey, who makes sure I make sense.
Tony of Citrus Headspace, who makes sure everything lines up and looks pretty.
The wonderfully supportive writing community at Write Magic – regardless of if I am kicking and screaming through a chapter or sprinting my way to the end, the Write Magic squad have been by my side.
Victoria – without your help, this book would be full of Mexican words and goodness knows where in Spain Catherine would have ended up! Thank you!

My readers and reviewers, dare I say, Fans?

If you got this far, it means you showed up for me! Thank you for being here, it means the world!

To the people who have faced situations similar to those raised in this book…

If you are still going through it, or have come out of the other end – please know that you are not alone. Seek help. Speak to someone. Stay safe.

To my friends and family…

Thanks for sticking with me on the rollercoaster… buckle up… this is just the beginning!

Caroline xx

Also by C.M. Serpell…

HER

If one of the good guys is killing the bad guys, is she a hero or a villain?

She works for the local authorities and is on a killing spree in Plymouth. She only kids bad guys. That makes it okay, right?

She said she will help you get your life back on track.
She told you, you are worth more than this.
She said she wants to help.
It's her job.

She said you should have done more.
She told you, you had your chance to change
She said she can't stand by and watch you destroy others.
It's you next.

Printed in Great Britain
by Amazon

27649674R00169